UNDER THE BRIDGE

A novel by hwneild

Published by HNL

First published in 2017.
This paperback published 2017.

ISBN: 978-0-9935318-3-5

Contents

Dedicated to:

My father, Roger OBE (deceased) and
my sister Frances.

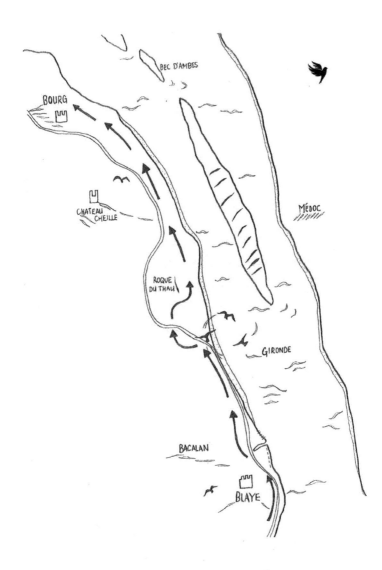

BEC D'AMBES

BOURG

CHATEAU
CHEILLE

MÉDOC

ROQUE
DU THAU

GIRONDE

BACALAN

BLAYE

CHAPTER 1
BACKLOG

It had taken six long weeks for the cardboard boxes to arrive - a full two months after the old man had died.

The not-so-old man in question's son, Will, had stashed the two paper crates in an upstairs cupboard unopened until today, forty days later, when he felt he could deal with uncovering the family possessions he'd inherited. Memories: that's what the problem was. That's what Will had been avoiding. Memories stirred up by trauma.

Coping with his estranged father's sudden death and coming to terms with the fact that they'd never be reconciled had been quite enough to deal with for the time being. His father had been only seventy-two, and Will twenty-eight, so he'd always thought there'd be bags of time to heal the festered wounds. His father's death couldn't have come at a better time - or worse one, Will wasn't sure; he was at a crisis point in his life generally: a dead-end job, his girlfriend getting broody and recently he'd received distressing news about his father's will, which had only added to his grief and confusion, and had delayed the opening up to potentially further heartache.

Today, though, Will galvanised himself; he tidied up his sitting-room, lit the wood-burner, made a pot of tea, and sat himself on the floor in front of the boxes. He'd even plumped the cushions. The room was immaculate. *It's going to be a ritual this*, he said to himself as he crossed his legs. *Let the rummage commence.*

He leant forward and tore open box numero uno. It was fun, and exciting, for a minute or two, opening that first parcel. Even Nelson, Will's fox-terrier, thought Christmas had come early and started tearing at the brown paper.

'Get off, you,' Will said playfully as he tug-of-warred with his dog.

But, in under five minutes, a shocked Will had stretched back on the carpet. With his neck craned, he stared agog at the ceiling. He'd discovered only bits and pieces inside the box. That's all it was, it seemed: stuff, junk really, just rubbish. He sat up slowly and stared again at the few items he'd unpacked, utterly gobsmacked. All it had contained, this big box, were two silly cheap model soldiers, a set of broken decanters with no lids and a whopping pile of funny old maps. Will glanced beyond the one opened box, with its paltry contents spread in front of him, to the contained flames flickering within the wood-burner, radiating warmth, seeking solace. And then, throwing his head back again, he emitted a giddy laugh.

Will had somehow trusted he'd unwrap a family treasure or two, some family heirlooms or anything precious, with an emotional connection. Something to cherish. Anything. He was dumbfounded to realise that he'd been sent his father's junk. He rummaged in the box again, fumbling in all the soft corners on the off-chance that there was something he'd missed. Nada, not a sausage. He shook his sunken head remembering that it had cost him and his sister just under £1000 to have the packages sent over to the UK from South Africa where his father, James, had ended his days. Now it was looking as if Will and his sister had been sent what should have been his father's garbage! Nothing decent of either sentimental or financial worth that he remembered seeing all over his father's house had arrived in that box: no silver photo frames, or small exquisite sculptures, or ornate boxes, or Persian or Afghan rugs; nothing of any value had been sent to James's only children. As Will stared glumly at the items on the floor he did a quick tote-up and valued the contents received in box number 1 at no more than £30 making the true worth of the bits and pieces, so far, total well over minus £900! The heirlooms bequeathed were in negative equity. *Nice one, Dad.*

Will stuffed the wrapping paper deep into the burner. And then, as he pushed the items together into a heap, and felt the immediate surge of released heat burning his back, his feelings of incredulity turned to anger. He picked up one of the toy soldiers and stood poised, ready to throw it against the wall. The realisation that the broken bric-a-brac that had been delivered was not only baffling, it was insulting. He put down the soldier, hesitated before opening the second box and braced himself. *More shit?*

It wasn't just an isolated insult from his father - it was beginning to feel like the final insult. Will was reading it, at that moment, as being a coup de grace: an 'up yours' gesture. A kick in the teeth. His mind recoiled. It couldn't have been done on purpose, as some sort of cruel joke, could it? He stood up quickly, turned away and paced the two strides to the window where he stared unblinkingly through glass at the green fields of England outside. British countryside had always soothed him and immediately he felt able to breathe again.

The scene outside was far from picture-perfect; it was winter, the land was barren, pared, stripped-down, and it was upcasting on the horizon. The scene summed up his life perfectly. Dark clouds had massed and were gathering to sweep in. Imminently there was going to be a land lash. Wind and heavy rain were on the charge.

For a moment Will fought hard to hold back tears. He swallowed. He was on the cusp of cracking. He just felt there had been endless insults and disappointments from his father ever since he could remember. And now he had to absorb this final act. He'd received knock after knock of shabby behaviour, which had beaten him about for the whole of his life; now he was battered, bruised and reeling from this knock-out upper-cut. With time-out called, he was utterly dazed, confused, cornered and – well, punch drunk.

He rested a hand on the arm of a chair to steady himself and continued to stare with misty eyes through the window at the desolate, darkening late November countryside. No tear ran down his cheek. A car whooshed past on the lane outside and splashed through a deep puddle, which shook Will awake from reflecting that it wasn't just a matter of being sent physical rubbish, like now, but that during the living years it had, more often than not, been thrown nothing - not a scrap, nothing whatsoever, for years on end. He remembered that ever since he was about fourteen or fifteen, birthdays and Christmases came and went without a card or even a phone call. He pictured an image of himself flipping through his cards only to realise there wasn't one from his father. And then what should have been happiness had become immediate sadness. His father had spoilt those days.

As a result of that adolescent neglect, the only messages received, generally through third parties, were in fact eye-watering slices of added pain.

'How's your dad?' old family friends would ask, innocently enough; standard drinks-party small talk when Will bumped into someone he hadn't seen in a decade.

'He's fine,' he'd lie. 'Very busy…'

The truth would be not only socially unacceptable but shamefully embarrassing: 'I have absolutely no idea. I haven't seen or heard from my father for nearly four years,' would have been the truth.

Or, even worse, a family friend would say, 'Hey, Will, I bumped into your dad the other day. He was on great form.'

Gulp. 'Yeah, I know, he is, isn't he? The ol' bugger,' Will would lie, laughing.

Will wasn't winging to himself, or playing a 'poor me' card now. This wasn't a blub of self-pity. It was simply acknowledging the pain of the truth. That was the reality of the situation. The bare, sad facts of the matter. No avoiding the truth in life or glossing it over. He could do that to others but he knew lying to himself would be fatal. His father had neglected him. Plain and simple. He stared forward, resolutely now. The chance of tears erupting was pushed firmly back, into the past.

Will hadn't assimilated his current feelings into thoughts quite yet but somewhere deep in his entity, something different *was* starting to bud and come to life. That soon-to-flower truth, deep within him, was the seed of realisation that there was a definite peace in his father's death. Will's deep consciousness sighed. An inner echo let him know that the torment was finally over. The layers of pain and anger that Will had subconsciously built up around himself, like a defensive callus since childhood, had started to peel off and fall away at last, to allow fresh growth to flourish. A voice was whispering to him, 'It's going to be alright.'

For Will these reminders of the hurt he'd experienced for so long from his father had been like a broken bone that tries to heal itself too fast. Calcium, in a desperate rush to mend the fracture, absorbs and locks in air like a honeycomb. Then, whenever it is hot or cold, the bubbles within the callus expand or contract and cause soreness. Reminders. Will's painful memories were like those trapped air bubbles unable to escape. The calcified knot desperately needed to be filed down, layer by layer, to release the ensnared air.

It was as if the core, the essence of William's soul, had been so badly bruised by the ongoing hurt of his father's fifteen years of casual absence that his psyche had never been able to fully mature. Underneath, it'd made him a bit of a man-child, emotionally. Ever since he was a young teenager he had shrouded his injured heart in a blanket, attempting to cocoon himself from further damage. But, of course, it couldn't really work. He'd shoved his organ of light, his heart, into the dark so long ago and locked it up so securely that it was in danger of becoming a festering, shrivelled, cancerous prune. He could chat away with the best of them but emotionally that was another story. He'd tried to mothball his inner fear but it was always there, his love, waiting, pulsing to burst out again, to rear its beautiful head. And now that the original source of his troubles had vanished from the planet he was being given an opportunity to begin, at last, to discard the buried detritus and get back to a place where he once belonged. He had to start over.

Strangely, in all those raging adolescent years, Will had never once wished his father dead, however dreadful the rejection felt. He'd always thought they'd make it up. It is undeniably hate-worthy to be dumped by your father - or indeed either parent - particularly as a youngster, as a teenager in need of guidance and not simply be left tossed about by life. He'd always hoped for reconciliation where forgiveness and apologies could be dealt with during the living years but this was never going to happen now. Will had always held out a mental olive branch for his father, willing him to love him. But now, seeing the wind gusting the boughs of the grand old oak in the field opposite and rain start to splatter the lintel in earnest, he became reconciled to the fact that he'd simply inherited sadness. He acknowledged, there and then, standing proud, facing the storm, that he could live with that; it was the raging madness with which he'd existed before that he couldn't take any longer. Will's suppressed anger, the shame he'd felt, the sorrow and embarrassment, were finally beginning to dissipate. He *could* feel it. A change *was* going to come. Definite resolve had been born in the past month. And week by week, ever since getting the call from his uncle informing him of his father's death, he had felt the stirrings of something lighter. Through all this grief and confusion, somewhat bizarrely, Will began to feel slightly better about himself. More at ease. And that was what was making him want to make a decision to move on, upwards in life, and take it by the…

Swerving any guilt sensation about the possibility of being happy that his father had died, Will turned back to the warm room to tackle the second box. Here, amongst other things, he found a loose pile of old photographs. He pushed them together, stood up, and placed them beside the pile of old maps. '*What the hell are these*?' Will said to himself, shaking his head and brushed the maps aside with his foot. His eyes shifted back to the photos. He determined to be able to cope with the memories that looking at them closely would inevitably evoke. He realised that this *was* the ritual he'd prepared his room for, and sat down again for the therapy he needed. Squatting, Will galvanised himself, determined to try and put the sorry business to bed once and for all. There and then he decided he'd put his father's life into some sort of order, for his own sake. He would rinse out his dirty laundry, hang it on a metaphorical line and then let the Marshall genes move forward. Forward to a place greater than the sum of their sorry past.

The contents of this box weren't much better than the other, larger one. Out came another brass soldier and a flimsy balsa- wood box with horses etched in the top, which his father's ashes had been contained after cremation.

Will hadn't been present for the funeral. He'd cancelled his airline ticket to the Cape as soon as he'd heard the second shattering piece of news about the will, which had arrived hot on the heels of hearing that his father had expired.

There were also ridiculous, cheap bookends. Laughable, really. '*Oh, at last*,' Will thought as he unwrapped two small old watercolours: Devon seascapes he could remember well hanging in his grandparents' house. These were the only two items that had any value. At last something familial, something of sentimental value that should have recalled happy days of childhood. Instead another 'oh-no' moment swept in and overwhelmed him: the shocking memory of his grandfather grabbing him by the throat. This shuddered back and clouded any happy recollection. His grandfather, James's father, had put his contorted face and clenched fist up to the eleven-year- old Will's face, as if to punch him - and the raw memory of that seminal incident barged right in, engulfing him. He winced and craned his head back. *That was a shock.* Back then Will had casually said that he hated someone on the TV, flippantly, as kids do, and the next thing he knew the old man had pounced, held Will up and roared in the poor child's face: 'You don't hate anyone.'

With hindsight, although it was a tough lesson, and perversely delivered, it *was* poignant. William had never hated anyone in his life since – he was too scared to!

These small paintings, in very ornate gold frames, he could picture in-situ, not in the full-of-people sitting-room in which they hung overlooking the silty creek outside, but in the empty sitting-room, still and peaceful, where his childlike imagination had been left alone to lose itself. It was these memories of comfort he held dear. They meant so much to a child coming home every two years from war-ravaged, famine-struck countries. England's green and pleasant and peaceful land was like a paradise. These paintings; watercolours in mellow yellows and soft gold's, were of unspoilt West Country beach scenes on beautiful days, devoid of people, gentle and serene, with waves rolling gently onto sand. The painted landscapes looked so invitingly uncluttered that he could actually immerse himself into them with ease; he'd imagined walking the painted Cornish beaches as a child. He began to sniff; these simple paintings evoked the musty smell of the room he remembered them hanging in, which, as he stared at them for the first time in fifteen years, he thought peculiar and interesting, and amusing. He'd never before appreciated that paintings could awaken the nose as well as the eyes.

He propped the small paintings up on the couch and turned back to sort through the random photographs and put them into new piles: his father's childhood, his military service days, his marriage and child-rearing phase, then a pile for his diplomatic days, and finally a pile for his retirement. Will wasn't simply curious - he wanted to gather a chronology of his father's life. And as he tried to do this in a professional manner the memories kept interrupting. There were quite a few photographs of Will as a baby, held in his proud father's arms, or grinning happily in his cot, or sitting in a car in some unknown country or another, long before his conscious memory began. Photos of his father looking young and athletic, at military balls, on exercises, or on parade with Will's grandparents at some academy somewhere – Sandhurst, probably. Others were of his father and mother posing closely together on a tropical beach before Will and his sister, Louise, had been born. Some of the later photographs made Will choke as he, tide-tugged, struggled to hold back tears, again. There were photos of his sister as a teenager that she had obviously sent her father; the messages on the backs were veiled pleas for love and attention that Will knew had gone unheeded. Their father just hadn't been there for them at all, either physically or emotionally, since he and his wife had split up in Geneva over fifteen years ago, when Will was thirteen and his older sister sixteen. It was all too much. Will piled the photographs back together and returned them to the shabby brown envelope in which they'd come.

CHAPTER 2
THE SEED

The following morning Will picked up the phone.

'Hey, Lou, how's it going?' he asked his elder sister. 'Look, I finally unpacked and went through those things of Dad's that arrived. I'm sorry to report, it's pathetic. We've been sent a load of junk.'

'Humm, surprise, surprise.'

'Don't,' he said, stifling a giggle. 'Seriously, though, there are some interesting old photos and I've decided I'm going put a couple of albums together of his life. D'you want any of the ones I don't use? Otherwise I'm going to throw them away. I don't want his clutter around anymore.' The briefest of silences from the other end. 'So, do you want any?'

'Nah, not really,' Louise replied. 'Bin 'em. Thanks for asking though. What else was there?'

Will went through the list of odd objects he'd unpacked the previous day, now laid out on the dining table; his eyes finally settled on the pile of maps. 'Oh, and a pile of maps,' he concluded.

'Maps?'

He sighed loudly. 'Yip, that's right, a great big pile of maps.'

'Are you kidding?'

'Nope, I'm not. There are dozens of the damn things and they weigh a ton. God only knows what they cost us to be shipped over.' They both broke into a laugh.

Will replaced the receiver and went straight to the kitchen. What the hell, he'd treat himself; he opened a decent bottle of Sauvignon from Touraine, a white, Dom Jacky. He stood for a moment in the doorway, musing, soaking up the soft elegance of the chilled vintage before moving in to untie the bundle for the first time.

The pile of maps was tied crossways with a red ribbon, like Little Red Riding Hood's picnic, loosely protected by a layer of bubble wrap. As Will approached the maps a little too casually an odd, supra silence descended like a strange tremble, as if something very heavy had thumped onto the table - as if the dense silence was on a collision course with meaning. He heard a ringing in his ears. He looked around furtively as if there was something behind him. His wine spilt. Then he took stock by standing still and looking straight out of the window. *What the heck had gone on there?*

He could see it had been wet overnight and the sun, coming out for the first time that day, created a hazy golden light over the sodden, slightly steaming land. Will's focus came back to inside the room and he sat down on one of the dining chairs. He shook his head. He didn't know what had brought that on. '*Just one of those funny moments,*' he concluded. '*Oh well, on, on.*' The leaden feeling came straight back, though, and he hesitated before beginning to untie the bundle with an awkward caution, and a bit of reverence, as if in slow motion; then he opened them up, laying them out on the long table one at a time, deliberately. He couldn't understand why he was behaving like this. He was sort of mesmerised. A musty, exotic scent filled the air around him as he laid them out. He took a sip of his wine. There were floral notes on his tongue, and the smell of mildew in his nostrils.

As Will flipped through the pile with care his thoughts were the opposite. '*How mad is this? Why on earth have I been sent a pile of shitty old maps of sub-regions of France?*' He sort of hissed a laugh between his teeth with his tongue. '*I just don't believe it; what an absolute waste of money, sending these valueless old maps halfway across the world. What's it all about? Why?*' Will shook his head in incredulity. He desperately wanted sensible answers. And the posing of some basic questions to himself got him thinking a bit more objectively about why on earth his father would have requested these maps to be passed on to him, and why his father had even taken them to South Africa in the first place. Or was it some sort of perverse joke?

Will quite - and only quite - liked cartography, and he liked France, okay, and…? He was trying to rationalise. His father had known that Will loved researching things; he was a journalist, after all. Will would often refer to Ordinance Survey maps of his locality to search out new walks nearby that he, his partner and their terrier could discover. And he generally preferred to look at a map as opposed to using a sat-nav when he was doing a road journey, but he was by no means a map-reading aficionado: never had been. He'd studied maps and globes as a child and had always wanted to know where he was, where he was going and what was around him. He'd collected stamps as a way of getting to know the planet's countries and to try and understand Earth's divisions, but a cartographer he certainly wasn't. There was no way his father could have thought Will would want these maps. And random sub-regions of France didn't have a single relevance to his family, either - or did they?

He went through them again, this time opening up each in turn. All the maps were in black and white, hand-drawn in permanent ink, and on wonderful old parchment, each covering fifty square kilometres or so of land surface. They were quite old: probably fifty or even up to 100 years of age, but no more than this. Beautifully crafted, without doubt. Perhaps they had a value: a financial one? It couldn't be massive, though; the set was incomplete by a long shot. Will scratched his head, desperately scrabbling for answers.

The forty maps were of small pockets of land randomly spread around France in no particular order, like a jigsaw puzzle with seventy percent of the pieces missing. His attention moved to focus on one map in particular where the map's surface was graffiti'd with lots of fine markings following roadways. Routes marked in black graphite arrows, fine green dashes and red crayon crosses, all of which gave the impression an ancient battle plan. Or the route an army took on a march. Also, strangely, written clearly in his father's definite handwriting was word 'START', underlined in blue biro at a certain point on the map's face.

Will sipped his wine, put down the glass and went through all the maps again carefully, establishing that there was only one out of the forty with any markings. All the rest were simply bare with no added dots or dashes. He gulped the remaining wine in the glass and opened the map in question again. It covered a small area just outside Bordeaux, that ran along the river Gironde on the north side, from Blaye to Bourg. It was a pocket of France he didn't know well. He'd driven up the other side of the wide Gironde three years ago as far as Pauillac, exploring the great wine chateaus of Bordeaux's Medoc region for a piece he'd written for an in-flight magazine. He'd visited the main Graves chateaus such as Margaux, Beychevalles, Lafitte and Latour which all sat on the wide salt flats that produce the finest clarets in the world, but he'd never crossed over and done the other side of one of France's greatest rivers, the Gironde, and on to the Cotes de Bourg. It was that trip which had first fired his interest in wine. Perhaps he'd mentioned it to his father? He couldn't remember.

Will folded the maps up, placed the intriguing one on top of the pile and went to refill his glass. He paced around the house in a dreamy haze, head bowed like Darwin on his gravel path, determined to establish if there could be any reason - any reason at all - that these maps, and the one in particular, had any resonance for him. What on earth was the relevance? He scratched his head hard, wondering why on earth he had inherited them. Where did the answer lie? If there even was one! He was on the verge of deciding that the only answer was to create a ritual pile of all his father's stuff in the garden and burn it. Finito.

But having paced about for a further five minutes Will flopped down on a carver at the end of the long dining table in the sitting-room; as he took another sip of wine, his daydreaming eyes turned away from the rain spitting on the windowpane to a cheap French painting that he had recently bought on the internet and that now hung low on the wall beside him. It was a river scene with a tall old building, like a mill, nestled on the bank and two men walking along a towpath, their backs to the viewer and their heads bowed.

Woah! Will thought as he absorbed the image as if for the first time. His imagination began to fan. Was this a coincidence or what? He put down his glass and leant in closer to the painting. It was if the picture suddenly had a definite importance and was coming to life. The painted scene before him could very easily be the banks of the wide Gironde, where the marked map he had just studied was of. He imagined that the two men walking the towpath were him and his father deep in conversation. The only reason he'd bought the painting was that it was a similar scene to Monet's The Petit Bras, which he loved.

Will's thoughts momentarily zipped back to his childhood. He pictured his father appearing at his seat as soon as his plane landed in Geneva, when he was ten, eleven and twelve, and had come over on his own from school for holidays. His father would enter the actual aircraft cabin and escort him off the aircraft before any of the other passengers had even got up from their seats. James, as Chief of Security to *the* United Nations, seemed to have an access-all-areas pass in Geneva. They'd waltz through security like VIPs.

This memory prompted Will to take the maps seriously again. And the wine, of course, the wine he'd drunk had made his imagination race. The maps couldn't be junk, surely? How had they come to be in his father's possession? And why had he held onto them? Whose were they originally? Why were they in Will's possession now? Why had James written 'start' on the marked map? And the important, lasting question that he kept coming back to was: *what am I going to do about it... and? And... what?*

'Sophie, honey, I know you're going to think I'm completely bonkers,' Will said to his girlfriend after supper that evening, 'but I've got this really strange feeling about those wretched maps that were sent over with my father's nonsense from South Africa last month. I just can't believe they were sent for no reason. I reckon it's not just random that they were put in the boxes.'

'Mmm, okay, Will, and why do you think that?' she asked with a wry smile.

He was off. 'Well, to start with there are forty of the damn things, which cost a lot to be couriered over here, and God knows why James took them to South Africa in the first place. And strangely one of them - I've been through them all closely - has these markings on it,' Will gabbled. 'And the markings on it are really odd. Black crosses, green and red lines, that sort of thing. They're like a very carefully, precisely marked military movement order, and I can see that James even wrote 'START' at a particular place on it, as if he went there. I just can't work it out.' He was wide-eyed now, finally relieved to be unloading his confusion.

Since he was a teenager he'd mostly called his father by his Christian name. Psychologically, emotionally, it felt safer to regard his absent father as more of a distant acquaintance than a parent.

'Okay,' Sophie said, after the empty moment. 'Let's have a look at them then, Sherlock.'

Will and Sophie had been together for five years and living together for three. They'd got together in their last year at university where they'd both studied English Literature. She'd got a job in a school in Salisbury and, not wanting to be apart from her, Will had found an internship with a local but reasonably well-regarded regional newspaper, and had worked his way up to being a features reporter. As he'd been rootless as a child, moving from country to country and then boarding school, living in a solid community in the English countryside was just what he'd needed. But now, he was at one of those frustrated crux points in life where he either needed to step up a career-gear, alter his direction altogether or simply make that change.

They rented a very ordinary two-bedroom workman's cottage in a small characterless village six miles south of the cathedral city. Will was employed freelance for the paper and had begun to spread his wings a bit and write for various magazines; occasionally, he'd also had articles placed in a few American periodicals. He dreamt of being a proper travel writer rather than a journalist. That's what he really wanted to be.

He brought in a little under fifteen hundred pounds a month, on average. Sophie earned about the same as a teacher at the secondary school twenty miles away. As a result they had a comfortable life, running two cars, eating out once or twice a week and having a good bottle of wine at weekends but there were no great frills to their life and, like everyone else, they were mainly slaves to their bills. But they were happy and had the long summer months to enjoy one another, and their two-year-old dog, Nelson, a Lakeland fox terrier whom they adored like a child.

Will fetched the pile of maps and, having cleared the table, unfolded the map in question and laid it out carefully in front of Sophie. He ran his fingers lovingly over the parchment to de-crease it for her. His caresses released the scented must.

'What do you reckon?' he enquired proudly, stepping back.

'Mmm, I don't know,' she replied. There was a brief silence as Sophie scrutinised the map. 'But I see what you mean, it is a bit peculiar: beautifully made, wonderful paper, and yes, it does have… I don't know… the vibe that it sort of… suggests something. It does look professional, not amateurish.' She looked up at Will and flicked an eyebrow. 'Potentially even… intriguing, Mr Holmes.'

Will felt vindicated. A waft of smugness washed over him as if he'd discovered something important and then a moment later the emotional backdraft came up from behind and he felt incredibly awkward so he stepped forward and hastily began to fold the map back up.

'Thanks, Soph, I agree. It's been hand-drawn and it's very precise. The more I look at it the more significant it seems… odd, very odd… ' His voice trailed off as he went to replace the map. 'There's a story here, I'm sure of it.'

Again, the lasting question that was in both their minds when he returned to the table but that went un-uttered in the awkward silence that followed was, 'And? What now? What are we going to do about it then?'

Sophie broke the silence and said abruptly, 'Let's watch the news, hon, I want to see what the weather's doing tomorrow. I'm taking some of the kids out on a field trip.'

Will couldn't quite articulate it yet but as he flipped on the TV, he knew that he was going to get to the bottom of this riddle. There was no way this conundrum was just going to go away or fizzle out. The image of the two men on the towpath phished across his mind. He mentally picked up a pebble and sent it skimming across the water to rid his mind of the implications.

He woke up the next morning more excited than ever, and more convinced that the maps, or the one map, had a deep significance for him. Somehow the wretched map had energised him; it had fired his imagination. He was trying to keep rational about it, torn between genuine excitement and a nagging feeling that he might be feebly grasping at straws. Trying to wish a legacy to life and give his fast becoming humdrum rural existence a bit of a lift. His heart and mind were scrapping for dominance.

CHAPTER 3
ROOTSTOCK

Having received an email response from his uncle in South Africa a few days later Will was confirmed in his hunch that James *had* made a definite point in his will that his son must get the maps. No other explanation: just that. Apparently the maps were even on James's bedside table when he died.

The actual content of James's will was the further upsetting news Will had received a week after hearing about his father's death. That news made him and his sister cancel their flights out to the funeral. His father, by the sound of things, knew he was dying and had hand-written a will, which was notarised by his lawyer a few days before his death. He'd left everything - his house, cars, bits of property, money in bank accounts, carpets, paintings, possessions - to his girlfriend whom he had only been seeing for eighteen months. She had copped the lot. However, he was insistent the maps should go to 'the boy'.

That depressing bombshell was the punch to the solar plexus insult that Will and his sister had been thrown by their father in death. It had and still felt like a final, absolute rejection of them. It was the reason why Will and Louise didn't attend their father's funeral on the other side of the world. To have seen James's girlfriend, a blousy white Afrikaans girl thirty-five years his junior, take centre stage, parading as the grieving widow whilst no doubt wringing her praying hands with glee, would have been just too awkward and too painful to witness. And the cost of them going down to the Cape? Four or five grand between them. Neither of them really had that sort of money. And did the man deserve it anyway? This was how they'd reassured each other.

Will was desperate to have a positive memory of his father and the maps seemed to offer the only glimmer of light in that tunnel. And so, over subsequent days, he put his investigative journalist's hat on and got down to some serious research, starting by ordering an up-to-date Ordinance Survey type map of the Bordeaux area in question. In France they are called IGN Series Blue. That was easy enough; the internet's made for that sort of thing. He then superimposed on this new map the same marks that were on the original. He Googled and searched and cross-referenced and trawled through the internet but couldn't grasp anything or anyone that sounded relevant to the area. Nothing had any noticeable or immediate significance and soon Will was pacing around, scratching his head again as to where to go next. Up and down the route he went on Google Earth, jumping on and off his chair, pacing around and then dashing back to the computer or just sitting with his head slunk over the map. He researched wine chateaus the route passed. Nothing.

Finally, two weeks after opening the boxes and having come back from a long walk, Will admitted defeat; he'd reached an impasse. He didn't know what to do next. His work with the Salisbury Chronicle had become mundane and was fast taking a back seat in his life.

He kept reiterating the facts to himself; the signs on the map were a definite plotted route, marked out clearly and precisely. There was no doubt about that. The markings led a course down some very much B-type minor roads. There were various green crosses, the red crosses, and then, marked in black, arrows above at specific points on the main road that ran parallel to the B roads. The marked route ran along and followed the banks of the Gironde from the town of Blaye to Bourg, another small town on the mighty river fifteen miles upstream, and at various times the plotted route had to cut inland but always came back down to the lesser, minor roads which seemed to indicate the course could well be to avoid the main road at all times. All this he did deduce.

The new map Will ordered pretty well corresponded identically with his father's older one. The route of the old roads was just the same as they were today; nothing seemed to have changed since the maps were produced. *Roads are roads*, Will said to himself. Even most major roads were once animal migration routes, like the nearby A303 here in England.

Will was well aware that part of him was desperate to find something, anything, of substance that his father had left him. Some decent legacy. Something to let him know his father had loved him. Or even to produce some excitement in his life. Maybe that was it. If his father could offer him a bit of an adventure, that would be enough. A thrilling memory or two. He was clutching air, okay, he knew that, but over the next week he just couldn't shake the map out of his mind. He tried. Hard. One day he even managed to keep it locked up for a whole twenty-four hours, but he seemed to get withdrawal symptoms and he just had to open up the original map and gaze at it. He'd unfold it, generally on the dining table, and crouching over it he'd breathe in its unique aroma that sent his imagination into a spin. He even thought perhaps it was the smell he was becoming addicted to. His hands would always caress its creases. Like something precious. Very precious.

Day by day, and without any progress on understanding the meaning of the map, Will had convinced himself that the only way of making any headway whatsoever with understanding the riddle of the map was that he'd simply have to go down and walk the route himself. It was going to be the only way to discover if there was any definite significance. He would then see the route for real and uncover any anomalies or features that had any resonance or answers. See for sure what the crosses meant. He could do further research from there. And he convinced himself that he could write a decent travel piece on the area. Driving or even cycling would be just too fast for this sort of activity. He went back through the marked route on Google Earth time and time again, crossing back and forth over endless fields of vines, villages, chateaus and gorgeous riverbank footpaths, trying to find some reason for the markings. He dreamt about the route. It began to plague him. He couldn't get away from it. Interspersed with him popping out to write about a car-crash or a local Christmas market, this little pocket of France had become an obsession.

He scoured the areas where the crosses were marked and found only piles of old broken-up concrete. He gradually became so familiar with the route he felt he could walk it blindfolded. The images of the mapped course became so familiar that eventually he convinced himself there was no other course of action left; he positively had to go and see the landscape in the flesh, see it for real. Walk the walk. There was no way this was just going to disappear now. He had embarked on a journey which he must see to the end. It was one of those small steps taken, we all make in life, which have to be followed to their conclusion, wherever or whenever that end may be.

I'm going to be practical about this, he said to himself. He found online antique shops in Bordeaux. He phoned them up and, in his hesitant French, explained what he had to sell. Thirty-nine very old maps of regions of France. Were they interested?

That evening Will broached the subject again. He knew he had to be positive. 'Sophie, honey, I'm thinking about going down to France and walking the route on that damn map to see if I can find out what it's all about.' He sighed. 'You know I told you they were by James's bed when he died. They must have been important to him and I just can't believe that he would have left me nothing in his will. Do you mind? I think I can do it over a long weekend.' Sophie's eyes came up from her plate of food like a pair of powerful search lights. Caught in their beam Will had to qualify himself. 'I'm going to write a travel- based piece that I'll sell when I get back, which'll pay for the trip.'

'Do you have to?' she said quietly.

'Look, hon, I can get the overnight ferry from Portsmouth one Thursday night and then get down to Bordeaux in the afternoon on the Friday. Saturday and Sunday I'll walk the route, hack back to St Malo Sunday evening and get the ferry on Monday morning, so I'll only miss two days of work. Also I've been in touch with a couple of antiquarian book dealers in Bordeaux who said they'd be interested in perhaps buying the maps, so hopefully the trip won't be that expensive.' He looked at her wide-eyed and took a breath. 'Are you busy any weekends soon which would be good for me to get away on?'

After a tut-tut and a scrape of fork on china Sophie reluctantly got up, went to her handbag, returned to the table and opened her diary. 'Well, actually Will, yes I do. I've got end-of-term pre-Christmas exams to mark over the weekend after next, the fourth, so I'll just be sitting here at the table all weekend. It really would be good if you could get away that weekend anyway. Anywhere. And Will, if Nelly's passport is up-to-date take him down too, would you? It'll be company for you and I can just get on with the marking here alone without any distractions.'

She'd conceded. Sophie could see her partner struggling, obviously, not just to understand the enigma of the one map in particular over the past weeks and why his father had sent it to him - that was really incidental to her - but importantly she could see that Will was wrestling to come to terms with his father's death and to conquer the long-term effect that James's behaviour had had on his development as a person. She really wanted a child with Will but she knew he wasn't quite ready to settle down. Her feelings on the matter were that this map and Will coming to peace with himself were intrinsically linked. That was all that was important to her.

Two years after Sophie and Will had started going out there was a period of a year or so, when Will's father had reappeared in his and his sister's life and there was starting to be regular contact but this had ended abruptly eighteen months before James died, when he'd met and started going out with the Afrikaans girl. It was all a bit ridiculous, a seventy-year-old man going out with a thirty-five-year-old woman. To begin with, on one hand, they'd all found it amusing and thought 'Good on you, James!' but on the other hand, it was a total embarrassment. They had so little in common and looked so daft together. Soon Sophie could see that James's way, his behavioural pattern, was starting to repeat itself. She realised that whenever James met a woman he quickly became involved in their world, their life and their family to the exclusion of everyone else. The result was he'd elbow his own family out of his life quite readily. He was that sort of a man; that was the cycle, and she wanted to be sure Will wasn't like that.

James, she felt, who had split up with his previous girlfriend when he was in his late sixties, and had finally got back in touch with his children, may well have felt his life was nearing its end and that he must make good his wrongs and clean his slate in preparation for the great unknown. She wasn't sure. Added to that Sophie knew older people generally felt more vulnerable so perhaps he'd selfishly wanted support and help from his children in his dotage? Although he'd owned a property in the Cape for quite a few years, he was probably lonely, too, having only just moved to live permanently in South Africa. So getting back in touch with his children, making amends and enjoying their company was a perfectly natural desire, an understandable thing to do. Both Louise and Will had been completely forgiving and had taken him back into their hearts and lives freely, without rancour. She had urged Will to err on the side of caution but he hadn't listened to her and forgave too freely.

As a result Will's still raw, vulnerable wounds had reopened in a very childlike fashion as soon as his father had begun to oust his children from his life again when he met and started going out with Angie, the Afrikaans girl. Will had naturally felt betrayed. He'd forgiven his father only to be shat on once more. James had stopped phoning his children completely; he hadn't even phoned them once in the eighteen months before he died. There were no invitations to go out to South Africa any more and he wouldn't even call when he came to the UK, which they'd heard he had done through the grapevine on a couple of occasions during that time. Sophie had had some tough times with Will then, as his anger, particularly when he'd had a few drinks, had nearly made them split up. He was really tortured up until his father had died. And then, almost immediately, over the last two months, he'd begun to recover. She could see it clearly. Much more clearly than he could. She thought of him a bit like a prisoner kept in solitary confinement for fifteen years who had emerged, blinking at his new reality. Liberated from a darkened dungeon.

Sophie clearly recalled one night in late autumn, two months previously, just after they'd got the news of James's death, when she and Will had come back from a party at 4 o'clock in the morning and they'd walked up to a vantage point nearby with Nelson to watch the sun rise. As they sat on a blanket, sipping Prosecco from the bottle and smoking, feeling small in front of creation, she'd brought up the subject of his father. She remembered how he'd managed to articulate so beautifully that even now that his father was dead he could still never really forgive him, out of sympathy for the hurt child he once was and how his father's lack of compassion for that child, the one he'd emotionally torn apart, was a cruel and wicked thing and made forgiving an adult impossible. It was that plain and that simple. She knew then that he should never have let his father back into his life. Even Will himself had felt weak for having done so.

So the idea of Will going down and doing the walk was not such a surprise to Sophie having seen her loving, sweet partner wrestling with these big issues for so long. She commended him for striving, she did, to truly desire coming to terms with his pain rather than forget it even existed. The trip, she thought, could only benefit their relationship and might even lead to a lasting peace and, in turn, to Will becoming a great father to her child. She had noticed a gradual improvement in his wellbeing since his father had died and concluded it could only be a good thing for him to do the walk, not to try and solve not the puzzle of the treasure map, or whatever nonsense it might be, but to help reconcile something deep in his psyche, in his personal life - to finally resolve the issues with his father. The result being, hopefully, to enable him to finally grow up and become a complete being. There was always something impenetrable about Will. She could never ever quite get to his core. There was always a point, a sore spot she'd hit and could go no further. He'd clam up and close doors to her. The walk might help open them up.

'Oh thanks sweetie, let the fun begin - or should I say *commençe*,' Will said, ending with a French accent and giving his partner a kiss on the cheek. 'Better give you two, froggy style, hungh, hun.'

'Okay, monsieur, you can have your pink passport for that weekend, but darling, seriously, prepare yourself that this is going to lead nowhere. I mean it. Treat it like a walk, a sort of pilgrimage if you want. But, please, do not allow your father to let you down again. Keep your expectations to an absolute minimum. I mean it, Will,' she said emphatically.

'Yeah, you're right. I know. I will. Thanks, hon. I promise.' Will had replied sincerely enough to Sophie's words of wisdom for her to add lightly: 'Just enjoy it.'

CHAPTER 4
A WALK

Will's trip to France loomed large on the horizon and being only ten days away he galvanised himself to take the hike seriously. He knew two long days of tramping twenty-five kilometres each day wasn't going to be any old stroll in the park. If he was going to complete the challenge he'd have to walk five or six hours each day, minimum. It was now late November and was bitterly cold in the Aquitaine region of southwest France, sometimes down to minus 10 degrees and, with a wind chill factor, well, it might be glacial. Sensibly, he braced himself for what might turn out to be quite an ordeal.

The practicalities of what he was in for were the only thing Will had considered rationally; the emotional ride, well, that was something else. He knew that particular region of France's flat terrain should make walking a little easier but if the wind was up, and with a bit of biting rain, then, ouch! What might, on first impressions, very much look like a mere stroll could easily transform into one hell of a trial. More like a polar expedition. Will was under no illusions on that front.

As he was toying with being a travel writer he really wanted the walk to be a further step in that direction. He needed to get fitter, too, so he resolved to get some serious practice in. To do this he decided he'd complete a long walk near home, not just for him but for his dog too. His terrier was bred to run all day and then kill a fox at the end of it, singlehandedly, but Nelson was used to a very different lifestyle to what he'd been bred for and was definitely a sedentary, overweight, pampered pet, sleeping for eighteen to twenty hours a day. No fox killing no more. Basic yet vigorous training was definitely on the agenda for both males in the Marshall household.

Will approached this practice walk professionally and, to sharpen his sense of observation, he decided to take some notes and photographs en route to help him search-out and read the signals hinted at on the map.

He got all his kit laid out; his Ranger walking boots got a polish, much to the excitement of Nelson who could read these sort of signs blindfolded. He could sniff out a walk at a hundred paces. Will charged the batteries for his camera, bought spares and ordered some Kendal mint cake and a new pair of alpaca socks online.

He and Soph had walked small sections of the ancient Ox Drove, now called The Wayfarers Way, which ran near their home, on many occasions. But Will decided he'd do eighteen miles of that magical old green lane that very Saturday, for starters. He'd drive to Alresford, the old market town at its end, and then walk the drove back out and across the countryside from there.

The green lanes of the United Kingdom were becoming a hobby of Will's and his research had uncovered that these routes were the ancient highways drovers would have taken, driving their livestock from farm to market. These arterial routes criss-cross the length and breadth of inland Britain. They are everywhere and were the lifeblood of the nation's economy for millennia, before motorisation.

Will had come to appreciate that drovers were the national news carriers of the day, relaying stories of events to interior communities up and down the country. He understood they weren't just the lifeblood of the economy, they were the lifeblood of the nation itself. And he realised that, sadly, the immense national historical importance of these routes, the droves, mostly went unnoticed these days and that they lay redundant, unappreciated. They were still there, though, everywhere, lying silent like bloodless veins. And he wanted to discover as much about them as he could, to write about them and to inject some life back into them.

Will pulled up in the old T-shaped market town of Alresford on the following Saturday, fully kitted for his heavy duty ramble with Nelson. He was The Rambling Man in his shiny boots, new socks and a camera slung around his neck.

A huge livestock market used to be held on the main and broadest street in the town centre that Will dawdled down. In the thirteenth century it used to be one of the largest in the country but that was long gone now, it now simply housed some fabulous homes. At the bottom of the old market street the lane narrowed to become a path for a short distance - or actually more of a dog-shit alley that led him out onto the banks of the river Arle. Alresford in ancient Saxon means 'the river crossing where the Alders are'. And there, where the ancient drove enters the town, Will could see tall clumps of alders clasping the river bank, their branches like distorted human limbs fishing out over the fast-flowing river, their red wine- coloured winter catkins dancing on the rushing current like bobbing lures. Will wondered if these very trees or their relatives had been here since time immemorial. When Stone Age man had first named the town.

As Will stood, lost in thought, gazing at the river beside an old whitewashed thatched fulling mill a tall, lanky local brushed past, walking his aged greyhound.

'Excuse me,' Will asked, turning, 'is this where the Ox Drove comes into Alresford?'

'Arrh, that's right,' Jim replied. 'The ol' drove used to come into town from the other bank, just over there, through the actual river and it comes out about two hundred yards down there.' He pointed to the opposite bank, and then downstream. 'You be lookin' at one of the only river roads in England - legal ones I mean.'

'Oh!'

'That's right. I remember when I was a nipper, off-roaders, you know, Land Rovers and the like, using it all the time as a road, for a bit of a laugh. Then the council decided to build up the banks to stop all that but horses and carts can still go through it, legal like. It ends up here - come, have a look.'

They strolled the towpath together. The river resembled a wide, even carriageway with straight high banks but in place of tarmac was flowing water. This led directly into a proper road which now had a high ledge, the drop deterring vehicles from entering the river this end too. The bulk of the river was channelled to flow away at a bend.

'Crikey, you wouldn't know it if you weren't shown it,' said Will.

'Clever bit of engineering,' said Jim. 'The livestock had their own route into town, see, with a wash and freshen up to boot,' he joked. 'The water cleaned 'em up like, and stopped all their muck going on the roads in town. Tidy, no?' he said.

'Very smart idea,' Will replied. 'Like an ancient cattle car wash.'

He stood for a moment and pictured great herds and flocks massing up through the river, mooing and bleating. Thousands of hoofs churning up the river bed, men shouting, dogs barking and now... the only sound to be heard came from a few ducks aimlessly quacking and squabbling in the shallows.

He bid farewell to Jim and continued along the path which dog-legged through a small wood and soon swept back down to re-join the river. In those few moments the river had swelled and quietened considerably and changed character dramatically. The body of water had now broadened and thickened to become a slow-moving, viscous mass with a shiny, mercury-smooth surface whose glisten was only occasionally disturbed by clumps of florescent green weeds gyrating gracefully in the undertow.

Although it was late November, the weather had been mild with very few frosts, so most trees were not yet bare. The majority were still heavily draped in cloaks of sage leaves. The only tree species turning their attire to an amber cloth were the sycamores, Acers of the maple family, and the Horse Chestnuts. It was a bit disappointing as Will knew that it's often better to study a landscape in winter, when the scenery becomes skeletal, the basic framework is revealed and the structures of the countryside lie naked. It's only when nature is stripped to its bones that all imperfections become obvious. It's when the countryside is exposed without foliage that the landscaping can be fully appreciated.

As Will walked along the towpath he came to an impressive, solitary grave stone tucked into the bank dedicated to Hambone Jr – Faithful Friend of 9th Division of US Army May 1944. Will assumed it was the regiment's dog, their mascot, who was interred below the memorial a year before the Second World War's end. He had read a plaque on his way down, attached to one of the houses on Alresford's main street, saying American airmen had been based in the town during that war. On their return journey from one failed bombing raid, where the fuselage refused to open, the badly damaged American bomber, still fully laden with bombs, unable to land and about to crash into the actual town of Alresford, was steered to safety. All the crew were ordered to bail out apart from the pilot, a Captain Cogswell, who flew the stricken plane solo, risking his life to avoid the town. He just managed to bail out himself at the last moment once the townsfolk were safe. The aircraft then crashed near the river where Will now stood. It had been a mighty explosion and had sent metal fragments into all the trees in Will's vicinity nearly seventy years before. Fortunately there was no loss of life. It was a strange thought for Will that the majority of the trees around him today still held, blasted within them, fragments of this heroic event.

He looked around and could see the countryside beyond the river was expansive. The vista he looked out at was peppered with strange autumnal pockets of light, illuminated by shafts of sunlight puncturing the cloud cover above. Spot-lit pools of light, randomly dotted across the landscape, exposed certain features with intense brilliance. On the horizon a black mass of woodland had a small square patch of sunlight blazing in front of it. Another ecclesiastic shaft of light burst through a break in the dense purple and brown clouds to expose a slate rooftop to Will's right. Autumn's subtle fingertips of light were at play on the keyboard of life.

Now looking directly down, his head bowed in contented silence, Will could peer through the inaudible river's clear water and pick out small quivering grayling and brown or silver trout eddying in the current, each perfectly camouflaged against the flinty, silted or chalk stream bed.

Then Will craned back and stared overhead at tall ash trees laden with a billion leaves phishing gently in the breeze; it sounded like a huge parade of silk ball-gowns rustling towards an extravaganza. And then the solitary crack of a shotgun echoed out across this pastoral scene, shaking him off balance. It was only a scarer deterring congregations of crows and pigeons from stealing the recently sown winter crops; the birds then showered up from the adjoining fields in one big wave of applause.

Will crossed the river around an old eel house which, like the fulling mill upstream, straddled the river passing beneath. He paused to read another plaque about the life cycle of eels (Anguilla Anguilla) on the river. He discovered that they started life in the Sargasso Sea, between Bermuda and the Bahamas, and then migrate across the Atlantic and enter freshwater rivers as thin, small one-year-old silver worms called elvers. These centimetre-long squiggles then work their way up the rivers to spend their adult life in reed beds or ponds, growing into up to a metre long, fat, black, snake-like creatures with fins on their backs. Then sometimes, after up to twenty years, on full moons when the water is highest, they depart the river and mass back, beneath the Atlantic waves, to where they'd been born to mate, breed and die. The cycle then starts again.

Will left the river and continued along the path where it re-joined the drove by crossing the aptly named Drove Lane, now blocked to four-wheeled vehicles by a huge old rusty ploughing machine and a council-erected height restriction barrier: an outdated, left-over deterrent to rogue caravaners from the New Age traveller problem that had existed twenty years previously.

The drove soon narrowed to become simply a path through dense overgrowth. Will could see that the original drove had been very much wider by the hedges set back to either side. He walked beneath a massive chestnut tree overhanging the path that had littered the hardened lane with spit'n'polish bronzed conkers, which he unavoidably had to crush as he walked awkwardly through the shiny covering of massive seeds. Feeling guilty about the waste of potential life, he picked up two and put them in his pocket.

The solid path, hardened by a hundred generations of plodding herds, was open in patches. Will could see that the drove surface here had actually been paved with flints set closely together into the chalk bed. It was if the ancients had actually cobbled a roadway here, perhaps to stop the route becoming a quagmire, to again minimise the herds bringing mud and mess into Alresford town.

The path then dropped down into a silent gully. This is what chalk hills do; they take you on a whale's back ride. They slide you down and concertina you up and then funnel you through a series of gentle creases. Will's path, for a moment, had been squeezed shut by the skin-folds of the hills. He pushed through until the way levelled again in the gulch. The green lane he was on had been joined by another drove coming from a groove to the east at the exact point where two small, yet feisty, feeder streams met. Will could see that it was here the two babbles of silver water embraced, entwined and then ran off together to join the main Arle River, a mile behind. The Arle then united with another similar-sized body of water coming from the south to become one new entity: the River Itchen. But these were all small-fry, elver proportioned rivers compared to the monster that was the Gironde, which Will was preparing to encounter.

It was here where the two busy feeder streams met, under a yew tree, with the dashing sound of water scrambling over flints, that Will tossed the two conkers he'd just picked up into the water. They'd be talismans for good luck on the journey he'd embarked on. He threw one for his journey and the other for his deceased father's voyage, into the great unknown. One conker sank and the other skipped off on the current, dancing merrily away. He wondered whose was whose. Like scattered conkers we do not go at will through life; we are carried away with it, like floating objects, one minute gently, the next violently. Even these seemingly inconsequential feeder streams had the power to lead to greatness. God willing, Will thought, that one chestnut seed at least would spawn a tree, just as his father's seed had created him.

Will steadied himself on the yew's trunk as a deep old voice came to him: 'The real secrets in life, my boy, lie in the small things. The devil's always in the detail. Simplicity is the key that unlocks the truth each and every time. The answers will always be there right under your nose. Remember that, my lad, success lies in the obvious.' Will's head darted around furtively, spooked, as the canopy above caught a gust, and the creaking branches shook away the ethereal voice in his mind.

Will was soon out in open ground which then elevated him out of a thicket and up onto a flat ridge which ran for two miles along the crest of a hill. This section of the drove wove them through a canopy of unmanaged hazel coppice, which had enjoined from either side and met high overhead, entwining to create a natural hilltop, bow-top tunnel which gave travellers protection from the horizontal wind and rain which inevitably lashed the brow of this peak. In the hedgerows an abundance of blackberries, elderberries, hawthorn, rosehips and sloes burst out. And from this high point, through gaps in the hedges, Will saw pockets of woodland etched onto other hilltops in various shades of soft blues, rippling into the distance. Rounded, wooded peaks rose out of the misty downland valleys like faraway archipelagos appearing out of the Baltic Sea. Some hilltops were clear, others dreamy and opaque.

At the crest, before the route dropped away, Will and Nelson reached a point where five paths and droves met. An incredibly rare five-ways junction of green lanes where he could see tumuli marked on his map. Tumuli or long barrows are burial mounds for individuals or families that lived in and farmed this area up to five thousand years ago. So the path here had been trodden by man for that amount of time at least, Will thought, and probably a lot longer. Perhaps he was even walking an ancient animal migration path going back to the dawn of time. At this five-way point Will guessed must be a perfect place to plot a ley line.

He'd recently read that ley lines had been suggested by a certain Mr Alfred Watkins, who had devised the concept in 1921. The idea is to pick out topographical features; say tumuli, wells, fords, or standing stones and then ring them on your map. These are called Mark Points. Now choose a Terminal Point, a nearby mountain top, and stick a pin in its summit with a long line of thread attached to it. Hold the thread tight and rotate it across and around your map. When you have lined up two or more of your circled features, your Mark Points, you have discovered a ley line - believe it or not!

Will knew that you can take as many journeys as you want, or travel as far as you want to go in life, and the routes trodden or rough tracks tramped will never compete in meaning with your ongoing exploration of the more obscure places in your imagination. Your longest journeys in life, without maps or guides, will be voyages of self-discovery. And the only path that can lead to any sort of palace of wisdom will be a rocky one, that is for certain. Rarely, Will knew, is anything worthwhile or cherished in life easily won.

He decided to sit and have his sandwich here, right in the centre of the five-ways junction. When he'd finished chewing and had thrown a crust into the nearby bushes he poured a sweet, sticky cup of coffee from his flask and handed three biscuits to Nelson. He scrabbled for his notebook and wrote:

> As this route in life I am walking takes me forward
> So it takes me backwards too,
> Backwards in time
> To walk with my forebears.
>
> And this journey will take me upwards also
> Like a star to obey its course
> To commune with the heavens with every footstep
>
> And sideways too I am stumbling
> Into poetry and funny words and thoughts.
>
> Whichever way I go, whether it be left, right, up,
> down or sideways, unavoidably, I will be carving
> a deeper path, towards my own world.

Will suddenly sprung to his feet, startled by a frantic whirring noise around him. He laughed when he saw Nelson burst out of the hedgerow with the crust in his mouth having thrown up a covey of partridge who took flight in a mad dash across the stubble. Their little wings flap, flap and flapped low across the land.

Will packed up and moved fast now, leaving the convergent point, eager to reach his target for the day and have a beer. When he was about an hour from finishing he called Sophie on his mobile and she was duly there, in a public car-park, to meet him at the appointed place.

'How you feeling?' she said, stroking a panting Nelson, as

Will jumped into the car.

'Absolutely cream-crackered, but exhilarated! I absolutely loved it. It was fabulous just being out there, alone with nature. There was so much to see and appreciate.' He strapped on his seatbelt. 'Come on, let's get into Alresford pronto, I'll buy you a drink at The Bell.'

CHAPTER 5

MR FOX AND THE EAGLE

As the young couple supped pints, enjoying the convivial ambience of The Bell inn, over in Bordeaux one of the antique dealers that Will had been in touch with was doing a little research, going about the business of trying to find a buyer for the thirty-nine remaining maps. It had been such a quiet day that the bored and thirsty proprietor had time on his hands and was really just waiting to close up for the day and get across to Chez Nico for a drink himself.

Will had pitched his wares professionally. He'd scanned one of the unmarked maps and sent that image as an email attachment to three antique dealers in Bordeaux with a few digital photos of the maps and a rough description of their quality, and had also listed the small regions the collection covered.

This one dealer was now forwarding Will's email as alerts to the wider trade across France in a bid to establish interest and their worth and therefore arrive at a price he would be willing to pay for them the following Friday, when Will said he'd be arriving in person.

By Wednesday the following week he had received interest from a very strange quarter:

Monsieur Degas, the Bordelaise antique dealer in question, was sitting behind his roll-top desk in Bordeaux's ancient Chartrons district. It was late morning; he was beginning his clockwork tic. He began to twitch. It was nearing opening time. He was counting down the minutes to his pre-prandial lunchtime drink and lunch. Not a soul had come into his shop all morning and the phone hadn't even rung once. The only sound and movement he'd seen for hours was rain; it hadn't stopped hammering down all morning, wave after wave of wet sheets had swept in relentlessly, pounded the window and then splattered onto the cobbles outside, until a hard ping of his door, rudely opening, echoed around the objects in his shop, waking the old man up from his meditations.

Monsieur Degas was in his late fifties. He'd aged badly. His hair used to be bushy and carroty but recently he'd lost pretty much all of it. He was now virtually as bald as an egg, apart from a ring of golden curls massed around his ears and the back of his neck. Due to his determined drinking habits, and being short and fat with a red face, he looked as if he was always on the point of bursting or, at the very least, breaking out into an all-over violent sweat.

A tall man in a rain-stained grey and white Burberry mackintosh brushed into the shop and approached Degas's desk. He kept his head bowed below his brown trilby. Degas immediately began to perspire. This wasn't a customer, he divined.

'Bonjour. Monsieur Degas?' the deep voice enquired. Degas nodded obediently. No handshake. Obviously the non-existent courtesy was over. 'My name is Reynard, Alain Reynard. I believe you have some maps to sell, am I correct?' he continued, looking up. Only now did he take off his hat. His rough Marseillaise accent made Degas's forehead release a ripple of moisture. Most likely of Corsican descent, Degas surmised, sneaking a one-eyed beady look.

Alain Reynard was in his fifties too, the same age bracket as Degas, with a dark complexion, a big hooked Roman nose, a short clipped beard and piercing black eyes that seemed to look inwards as opposed to outwards, making him menacing and disconcerting to look at. Old Degas instinctively knew to play it straight with Reynard's type.

'No, not exactly, monsieur. You are interested in the maps, yes?'

'I may well be, Degas, I may very well be. Show them to me.'

'I am afraid I cannot do that, no sir,' said Degas, and continued quickly. 'I only received a phone call and email from the vendor, an Englishman. This was last week. He said he would visit my shop here on Friday. That is all. I do not have the actual maps here yet.' He glanced up at Reynard feebly. 'How did you hear about them, monsieur, if you don't mind me asking?'

'My employer, is a… a… an avid map collector. He heard about them and wants to buy them. I am interested in who this man is, the Englishman, have you got his name?'

'Only his Christian name, monsieur.'

'And what is that?'

'Will-iam, monsieur.'

'A phone number, address?'

'Non, monsieur. He just said he'd be in on Friday afternoon with the maps.'

'What about his email address, have you got that?'

'Yes, monsieur, I do. Are you from the police?'

'Give me his email address, Degas,' Reynard said slowly, dropping down and looming over the quivering antiquarian.

'Oui, oui, yes, but of course, monsieur,' stammered Degas, fumbling on his old keyboard.

Reynard's feet didn't budge but craned even further forward, his eyes grilling the sizzling antique dealer. His big brown hands, like gnarled root vegetables freshly pulled from the soil, splayed out across the desk's green leather inlay.

'Ah, here it is,' Degas announced proudly, scrolling down his in-box, 'lovenelson@gmail.com.'

'*Quoi*?' Reynard said.

'lovenelson@gmail.com, monsieur,' Degas repeated.

'Write it down for me, Degas,' Reynard ordered.

'Thirty-nine of them, you say?'

'Yes, that is correct, I am told,' said Degas, handing over the scrap of paper.

'And he said hand-printed and of small areas, fifty kilometres square, and about seventy to eighty years old?'

'Yes, monsieur, that is correct. He said they were about fifty kilometres square and randomly spread around the country. Some in Burgundy, Loire and Gascony. I have a list. I can print it out for you, if you wish?'

'I have the list. So… there is nothing we can do but wait until then - this Friday, you say?'

'That is correct, monsieur. Or I can email him, if you wish?'

Reynard resurrected himself and looked around. 'Yes, Degas, do that, do that,' he said slowly. 'Email him back and say you are not only very keen to see the maps, but you think you have found a buyer, a private collector, who will pay an excellent price for them.' And then he snapped back at Degas. 'Do it now.'

'Yes, of course monsieur, I surely will.'

Degas fumbled, his pudgy fingers making a slow and messy reply to Will's email as best he could in broken English.

Occasional drops of sweat fell as his fingers worked the white ebony inlaid ivories of the plastic console.

'Have you got a back room here, Degas?'

'Yes, there is a storage and cloak room behind that curtain over there,' Degas said, flicking his head back as he typed.

'Well, Degas, that is good, very good.' Reynard put his hat back on. 'I will see you again on Friday. If you hear from this man, Will-i-am, before then I want you to call me immediately, do you understand?

'Oui, oui, monsieur, immediately,' Degas repeated.

'You will be well rewarded, Degas, be assured of that. Very well rewarded. *Au revoir.*' He slapped a business card purposefully down on Degas's desk.

Reynard then offered his heavily tanned bulbous hand to Degas. His little finger, as fat as Degas's index one, housed a gold signet ring with a red emerald in its centre that sparkled ominously. Degas's small fat, sweaty offering took hold and they shook hands, with the nervous antique dealer looking up yet avoiding all eye contact. As they clasped the stranger repeated his last utterance. 'You will call me if you hear anything more. Am I assured of this?'

'Yes, monsieur, if I hear anything, anything at all I will be in touch straightaway.'

'*Très bien.* Until Friday then, my friend. Tell nobody else about this. I will be here at nine am sharp – be open.'

And with that he vanished. In a blink of Degas's bulging eyes, Reynard had gone. He'd moved like a snake. The door, pinging shut after him, was the only proof of his presence, apart from his card sitting on the desk. Degas's shaking hand picked up the white card and saw an embossed golden scallop shell logo. It simply read: Perle Fruits, Marseille, France, with a PO box address, and a phone number.

The other lingering reminder of Reynard's visit was the scent of his aftershave, which left a certain pungent acidity that Degas wanted rid of so quickly he put on his coat and beret, flipped the closed sign, locked the door and headed across the wet cobbles through the rain to his favourite bar, the Brasserie l'Orléans.

'Vin rouge, Monsieur Degas?' the waiter said, as he shook Degas's hand.

'Non, cognac today, Alfonse.'

*

Ten years earlier, before his death, James Marshall was sitting on a high, plush, red velvet upholstered chair at the bar in an upmarket steak-house restaurant near his apartment in Grand Saconnex, Geneva, Switzerland.

He liked the low lighting and the heavy use of burgundy in the décor as well as the simple yet hearty menu. James had begun to use the restaurant regularly. He felt very fortunate to have found a local restaurant where it comfortable to eat alone and anonymously. A rare find, and on his doorstep to boot.

He leant forward and, quite by accident, spoke to the waitress in English, as opposed to French, momentarily forgetting where he was. He'd just returned from an exhausting mission to the Middle East. When the lapse had been laughed off he heard a gravelly Germanic-sounding voice emanating from a gentleman perched alone on a stool to his left.

'So you are English?' the voice said.

James turned. 'Indeed I am… for my sins, yes,' he replied, to the amusement of the fellow diner asking the question who raised a wry smile.

The man James turned to glance at was a good deal older

than himself, perhaps in his mid to late seventies: elegant, very dapperly dressed, even sporting a silk cravat, very old school. James had clocked him before. He was compact and wiry with sharp features that seemed to have been stretched by a rack over his hooked beak. He had only faint wisps of grey hair that were oiled back over his crown, starkly exposing his jaundiced complexion. His head resembled an exotic bird of prey.

Sadly, it was obvious he wasn't well. That aside, his ferociously steely stare couldn't mask any lack of resolve. There was no pitying this man. It was glaringly obvious that whatever physical illness he may have had could never touch the man within. That was evident, and it startled James. Here was a man who was unquestionably a power-pack, as resilient and literally as tough as old boots. His illness seemed somehow removed from him. It was as if his body and mind were two different entities. His body was simply a vehicle, a carcass for his soul, about to be discarded.

James returned to the here and now with the stranger's voice in his ear again. 'I could tell from the accent you are English,' he continued, leaning across slightly. 'My name is Wiktor, Wiktor Foukes. Call me Vick. I'm local, I live just around the corner.' He spoke in a slow raspy tone that was surprisingly easy on the ear, and unexpectedly warm. 'I have been using this place at least twice a week for the past twenty years, ever since it opened.' He chuckled. 'It is like my second home now. I've noticed you have started to do the same.'

'Yes, quite right. You're very observant,' James replied, his interest piqued. 'I only moved into the area last year and found this place about six months ago. A great find. I can come on my own comfortably, the food is excellent and it's jolly good value. What more does a man want' He made sure to remain neighbourly yet had craftily replied without revealing his name.

That was how their friendship started, slowly and correctly, and before long James fell into a routine of using the restaurant, La Jolie Ville, that corresponded with Wiktor's. From then on they began seeing each other all the time. And soon, for James, it felt a bit like going round to a local pub in England, where he could sit at the bar and have a chat. The Jolie Ville had a warm ambience, a good atmosphere but… this was Switzerland, not home.

As it turned out Wiktor was a Polish émigré, not German, and without delving too much into his life by asking too many questions, James surmised that there was a hell of a story, a riveting past within this character. And he was looking forward to discovering what it was. All in good time.

James invariably drank a bottle of red wine and Wiktor sipped voraciously on whisky and water but never seemed to get even slightly intoxicated.

'Have you any children, James?' Wiktor enquired one evening, a month after they'd met.

'I do, Vick,' James replied, now on friendlier terms. 'Two, a boy and a girl both in their late teens. They live in England.'

'And… do you see much of them?' the old man casually asked.

Slightly irritated, James replied, 'Sadly not, no, I do not,' and stared into Wiktor's eyes, daring him to continue. The atmosphere tightened slightly.

'That is not good, my friend, not good at all, not just for you but, more importantly, for your children.'

Hey, hey, hey! Who the fuck do you think you are? James said to himself. His knife slipped on the steak he was cutting as a wound sliced open inside of him. His eyes flared, exposing his fury; they couldn't help it. The older man had probed, hit a raw nerve, and knew it. It was explosive.

Wiktor wanted to swerve the subject that had stirred up such gritty emotions, which his new friend obviously didn't want agitated. He considered the subject closed, for now. He knew he'd crossed a bridge, from casual familiarity to over intimacy, and it wasn't welcomed.

However, Wiktor immediately changed his mind. *To hell with it*, he thought, *I'm not happy*. James had lost respect in his eyes and, in turn, James felt that disdain. They sat in an awkward silence; both men wanted the balance restored. The lack of ease roared volumes.

James, re-composed, made the first conciliatory gesture. 'What about you, do you have children, Vick?' he asked, trying to sound as upbeat as possible.

'I did James, ya,' Wiktor replied in a quiet tone, his look fixed. 'Yes, I did, my friend.'

James registered the word *did*, spoken twice and, glancing over, caught the wave of sadness that inevitably follows memories of those held dear never returning. Fleetingly he didn't quite know what to say.

Wiktor saved him the embarrassment by continuing. 'They were killed in the war, my friend. My wife too, ya, but it was a long time ago now.'

Click, I get it. James instantly computed Wiktor's seeming previous indiscretion; if anyone had a right to pull him up for not seeing his kids, Vick did. That was the message that hammered home. 'Oh my God, Vick, how terrible, I am so sorry.'

James turned to face Wiktor and the two men looked into each other's eyes. Again, it was like mind reading. The eye movements, slight welling, the mouth drying and going tacky, the emanation of sentiments volleyed, said it all. There was no need whatsoever for words.

James had this acute ability to empathise, to feel another's feelings deeply, and it scared him, truthfully. On one hand it was an essential element of spy craft, he knew that, to read people, but emotionally, privately, it made him vulnerable. He felt that. Neither did he understand that side of himself, nor had he made any efforts to reconcile the difference between a professional and a personal life. As a result everything became professional. He still believed every aspect of life was pigeon-holeable.

This bottled sensitivity, he knew, had been a major factor in his choice to follow the unfortunate fashion in parenting which rejects emotional warmth towards one's children as a buffer against loss of control. His failings as a father, and the regrets he had, tormented him but he simply couldn't buckle to warmth. When he decided to leave his wife he had made the conscious decision that he was determined to remain cold and distant, and emotionally removed, completely. It was the safest course of action and was why he wanted the divorce. He was sure he felt it was weak to love. In reality, he simply didn't want to be hurt. The moment he left his family, James had suppressed all feelings and placed them in a cubby hole marked 'private'.

'Ya, it was dreadful, too awful and I never met anyone else or never wanted to, but as I said, James, it was a long time ago. In fact…' Wiktor continued, looking across and smiling, '…it seems like another world entirely, another time, James, and it was.'

'You have my deepest sympathies, Vick, how tragic,' James replied, moisture misting his eyes.

They sat for a minute in respectful silence.

James recommended the conversation. 'What did you do - in the war, Vick?' he said, kicking himself slightly for asking a question, knowing questions often spawn lies. As Dickens wrote in Great Expectations, 'ask no questions, get no lies'.

It's better to let conversation flow, but dialogue has to start somewhere.

The silver lining to the fractious words Wiktor had just spoken was that it was opening up a deeper friendship, a newfound intimacy between the two men. Some meat to the bone, as it were, whereby their affection was being forged on something more substantial than mere politesse. Far from telling a lie, Wiktor decided to reply with more revelations about his past. He looked up; the waiter was right there. He flashed a finger indicating a top-up. Richard noticed his hand and fingers were completely out of proportion to his body; they were huge, like talons.

'Can I get you one, James?'

James placed the palm of his hand over his glass. 'That's very kind, but no thank you, Vick, I'm fine with this.'

It was the first time buying each other drinks had been offered. When the waiter backed off Wiktor started.

'I was with the Polish resistance, James, and then moved across Europe soon after the invasion of my country. Actually, it was me who delivered one of the first German Enigma machines into British hands which my group managed to get hold of in Warsaw. As I'm sure you know we handed it over in Paris in 1940 to your ambassador there, a Duff Cooper. Have you ever met him?'

'No, I haven't,' Richard said, gulping.

'And then I mainly stayed in Paris for the rest of the war. Four years, based with the French resistance... and of course you British.'

'My God, how fascinating,' was all James could muster.

He now looked across at an obvious war hero, an unsung legend. Someone whose actions had helped save hundreds of thousands of lives, possibly millions of lives, and he'd certainly changed the course of the war. Wiktor suddenly sky-rocketed in James's estimation; he'd become a star.

It's hard to comprehend the unrecognised heroes, the ordinary guys who really won the war, were actually ever real and alive. They were fact, not fiction, and then to meet one of them, well… it now felt an honour for James simply to be in Wiktor's presence. Winston Churchill had said to the British king at the end of the war that it was Bletchley Park's ability to decode the Nazi leadership's communication through the Enigma system which was the key element that had actually won the Allies the war.

There had been no mention between the two men that James was in any way engaged in undercover work up until that evening. Spying, covert activity for James, was more background than underground. Behind-the-scenes work, pulling strings like a puppet master in the wings of a theatre. There was no popping out of the undergrowth with machine guns anymore. Well, only the occasional wet wipe. It's a job of prompting and encouraging the enemy to put their heads above the proverbial parapet, exposing themselves to the full force of law. Giving those you oppose enough rope to hang themselves with.

Whatever, James thought, importantly, they both shared a familial bond of being involved in occupations that receive no praise, nor reward for success, and no assistance whatsoever when in trouble. A thankless profession neither men would have changed for all the gold in Geneva's bank vaults.

It had only been three days since James had returned from a three-week trip to Iraq and Iran and he was having difficulty readjusting to the civility and tameness of Geneva having frantically dashed around the Middle East imploring Ayatollahs and dictators to see reason and avoid war. It was looking as if he and the delegation had failed. As a result he drank more than normal and after tackling a second bottle of wine he declared, 'I haven't told you, Vick, I am Chief of Security for *the* United Nations. The delegation I was with just got back from Iran and Iraq; there's going to be another ruddy war.'

After the slightest of pauses Wiktor spoke. 'Ach, don't vorry about it James, who cares! Let them fight it out in the desert; good luck to them,' he said in his calm, seen-it-all, done-it-all drawl which made them both sit back and laugh. Wiktor had completely ignored James's first declaration, knowing only too well how to keep a secret safe. He wasn't an idiot, he knew very well James was no businessman or artist.

Wiktor raised his tumbler high and said loudly, 'May the best man win, mabrook to them, good luck,' which made them laugh again. James added 'Fuck 'em,' under his breath, as their two flutes clinked. 'You're right, Vick, who really gives a monkeys.'

They strolled home together under a full moon, and a cool blue, alpine fresh sky. Wiktor was giving James a helping hand.

'This is mine.'

'Blimey Vick, I'm in the next ruddy block,' an amused James declared. They shook hands. 'See you for a bite at the Jolie soon, take care old boy and… go steady!' were James's last words as the two now firmly bonded friends went their separate ways.

CHAPTER 6

SOLO

On the Thursday evening following their walk, Will and Nelson sat in his old Audi estate, with the engine running, queuing to board the overnight ferry from Portsmouth to St Malo as planned.

Fortunately for Nelson, soon to be caged in the hold, it had been a beautifully clear, frosty autumnal day, one of only a handful of the year, so the English Channel, under moonlight, looked and felt as smooth as hammered steel.

Will gazed through the heat-blasted windscreen, transfixed by the colossal silver salver moon in front of him, hanging low on the horizon, creeping stealthily behind the ancient harbour's mass of masts and cranes as he waited to board. The moon's pearly-soft brilliance defined the ancient city's skyline perfectly in an eerie series of slow-moving moon shadows.

The excitement of travel, when it came to nearing actual departure, had temporarily evaporated for Will. The thrill was marred by the tension of packing, saying farewells and ensuring all the little strands of his life were in order before leaving home. It had even crossed his mind to make out a ruddy will himself. The buzz of adventure was only just starting to creep back in now that he was finally underway. There was nothing he could do about anything anymore, he was off; the key was just to relax, enjoy the ride, let nature take its course and… wish for only positive accidents.

But due to the ambiguous nature of the journey Will was embarking on, he was going through high-speed tidal surges of doubts as to whether the whole trip was a frivolous waste of time and money, a pie in the sky distraction, and whether there'd be any value to be had, any value at all, in the excursion. He was clinging to the career change he desired. He made some preparatory notes as he sat in the car, about to board, occasionally peering up to stare at the humbling moon, yet he felt anxious, apprehensive and nervous. There was no denying it. His bowels shifted, he expelled wind: an ill wind, which made the over-heated car intensely claustrophobic. He opened the window. Sharp fresh air met heat by his right eye.

He'd been miserable for the past few days. He'd felt the gloom of a man setting his affairs on order for the last time. As if there was impending doom.

Will inhaled the fresh air which seeped into the depths of his lungs. *Oh, to hell with it,* he concluded, as he exhaled, *there's no turning back now. Keep positive.* At the very least he would have a good walk somewhere new, get a bit fitter, tuck away a few decent meals and guzzle a couple of bottles of pukka wines in France. *Just keep positive. That's the way to think about this.* It was heading rapidly in the general direction of Christmas, too, so he could buy some decent pressies for the girls: quality wines, soaps and local goodies.

He was further cheered by the memory of the email he'd received the day before from one of the original antique dealers in Bordeaux. The email had said words to the effect that the dealer thought he'd found a collector who was very interested in Will's maps and would pay top dollar for them.

So the mini break he was off on may not prove too heavy

on his pocket, either. He'd simply have to make sure the jaunt wasn't going to be a complete waste of time.

Perhaps it was frivolous, but holidays, trips away, should be without meaning. They're a time to go off and get lost somewhere new; a time to leave the familiar behind and squelch the routine for a while. Society herds us into being mature, taking structured holidays from structured lives when, in reality, we are only being safe and boring. We're told it's the respectable thing to do, but it's cowardly. Life actually wants us to let our hair down and to go off and take chances, go off piste, have a laugh, get lost and taste the spirit of adventure. If you're bold in life, nature will never conspire to trip you up; it will help you. It only lays traps for the complacent.

'Just enjoy yourself darling, eat some good food and don't pin too many hopes on finding anything particular on the map. Don't allow your father to let you down anymore,' Sophie had repeated as they kissed farewell. Her words rang in his head. 'Promise me?' she'd said emphatically. She could tell he was in a sensitive place.

Forced to sit still with his thoughts Will now felt incredibly juvenile for even having decided to do the walk in the first place – surely that was the reason he was feeling this anxious. It was because he didn't need or want to reopen old wounds that seemed to be curing themselves. The scars of bad parenting were healing of their own accord. What did he think he was doing - off to come to terms with his neglectful father on some spurious walk - what a prat! But again… what the heck. Will sighed. And then out loud he said, 'Fuck it, you're underway now.' He pulled himself together, fired up the engine and edged on-board.

Will stood on the open deck at the stern of the ferry, smoking, as Portsmouth and, with it, the British Isles receded into darkness.

He stared at the ferry's wake, a churned white herringbone trail on the black sea below, fizzling into the distance. To Will, the engine's whisked froth on the sea's surface resembled a milky way of reflected stars sparkling off into inky parallel heavens. The rhythmic flashing of The Needles lighthouse beckoned on the horizon like a distant satellite. It looked as if the night sky had momentarily been transposed onto earth. The heavenly star-studded velvet curtain had dropped. What was vertical had become horizontal and Will was now, not on a boat on the ocean, but on a comet hurtling through the universe, bound for a distant galaxy. He craned his neck right back, and exhaled a big plume of smoke up into the night sky and then took a deep breath in, drawing inspiration from the wind and spray. The sound of ghostly wave-crests rode up out of the void, and whispered a low thrilling chorus in praise of exploration.

Will re-entered the ferry, had a leisurely meal and then popped down to the hold to check Nelson was settled before retiring to his cabin. He fell asleep on his tight little rack-like bunk to the rhythm of engines propelling him forward, towards the new.

Mid-Channel the weather turned nasty, and the sea became angry. Will was woken by the turbulence and, unable to get back to sleep, tossed and turned and worried about his caged dog down in the groaning and creaking hold. Thus he arrived in bad shape when the ferry docked at dawn.

With a slight hangover and feeling a tad seasick he hit the auto-route in the pouring rain, having driven like a bat out of hell through St Malo's walled city to wake himself up. Nelson, however, with no visible signs of wear and tear, was up, bright as a button, riding shotgun as usual.

He did, against the odds, manage to get down to Blaye, the actual starting point on his map by three o'clock that afternoon having spent six hours on the road with a fifteen-minute power nap en route. By then, poor old Nelson was a bit bamboozled too but, the moment the car door opened, he was off like a spring-loaded bolt, revelling in new scents and smells. Will checked into the charming hotel he'd found on the internet, had a quick peep in his room and then immediately set off for Bordeaux, half an hour away, to try and sell his maps.

Will's bearings from his one previous visit to the city returned intact. He knew exactly where to park in the ancient Chartrons quarter down by the old riverfront docks where all the antique shops were. He set off on foot, his bundle of maps in a plastic bag under one arm and Nelson dominating the other's use. He always pulled hard.

Will thought he'd just try a few other shops before going straight to Monsieur Degas, the man who'd responded, to get an idea of value. The first shop he went in to said 'non', the maps weren't for them, but go to Mr Degas at such and such a shop: this was his area of expertise. Okay. The second did the same, as if primed. All roads lead to Degas, Will concluded. So within half an hour of arriving in Bordeaux he pinged into Mr Degas's ill-lit shop, dog in tow. His musty premises were lined with old folios and hung with fading prints. *This is the place, I can smell it*, Will thought. Degas's shop had an aroma, peculiarly similar to the maps and the family painting he'd been sent.

As Will entered he could see Degas sitting at his desk, peering intently at an ancient book through a large magnifying glass like a beady-eyed toad. He looked up dreamily, lost in his work, and then startled himself as reality blinked back in. The Englishman had arrived. Blink. Will noticed his forehead suddenly glisten, erupting into a scream of sweat. Like a lamp being switched on, old Degas's head began to glow.

All recesses of the shop itself were pitch dark and hid many invisible corners. The only artificial light source in the shop came from Degas's flaring desk lamp. The harsh light fully illuminated the work area and splayed out to reveal the older man's moist complexion, shimmering in the spotlight, every pore magnified. Dust particles swirled around him in the definite shafts of light, as if a smoke machine was discreetly emitting an effect.

'Bonjour, monsieur,' Will said, as he approached. 'I am the Englishman who has the old maps to sell,' he managed to say hesitantly, in his simplest French.

He had picked up the language quite well after school when his parents had moved to Geneva, in the French-speaking Swiss canton of Vaud, and he'd tried to keep it up since, but it was only a pretty basic grasp. He was still glaringly English.

'Ah yes, I remember. Will-i-am, is it?'

'That is correct, monsieur. That's me,' Will said.

'Is it possible to see them, please?' Degas asked, with a toady grin.

'Yes of course, monsieur,' Will replied, and proceeded to unwrap the bundle, issuing a sharp order for Nelson to sit; the dog immediately obeyed, craning up at his master expectantly.

Will unfolded the bubble-wrap covering to reveal the tall pile of maps in their red ribbon. *This shop in France, this smell, does match, it suits them perfectly*, he thought. *They've arrived home.* Sitting on the old desk, in the shafts of light, they looked like a present, a gift. A farewell gift from his father. Will consciously passed the pile across to Mr Degas who made space on the desk for them and began to finger the bundle carefully, first opening the top one. He began to rub the parchment with his stubby little fingers. Will saw him actually bend forward and sniff the paper as a sommelier would, decoding a wine. Then he put a magnified monocle to his eye and peered even more closely. His eye pulsed to a greater dimension. *I hope it doesn't pop*, Will said to himself, stifling a giggle. Finally old Degas began to nod approvingly as he studied the ink with which the maps were drawn. He began to make noises as if he were tasting the finest of vintages. Ooh's and aah's came from his lips. 'Oui, yes, they are originals, from the 1930s,' he finally said as if to himself and then looked up at Will. 'Only part of a much bigger set but they are interesting. Have you any more?'

'No, I haven't, that's all,' said Will.

'Can you please wait here? I am going to do a little test in my back room, is that okay?' Degas got up and pointed behind himself.

'Of course, no problem,' Will replied.

Most of what old Degas said Will understood, the bulk of words being the same as English, with just a different accent.

'I will return in two minutes, monsieur.'

With that Degas lifted up his barrel-shaped bulk and nimbly rolled away behind a curtain towards the rear of the shop with one of the maps and closed a door behind him. Now alone, Will began to feel dizzy, really wobbly, and kept swaying as if he was still on the rocking ferry-boat. He even had to put one hand on the desk to stay upright. Degas kept to his word and reappeared within the allotted time. Shuffling up to his desk but not sitting down, he said, 'Okay, Monsieur Will-i-am, I am very interested in buying the maps and I will give you fifty Euros for each of them; that is my best offer.'

Shit, Will thought. He never dreamt he'd get so much for them. Fifteen odd Euros each he would have readily accepted, even one or two hundred Euros to get rid of the lot and chip away at his expenses on this trip. But this was just under two thousand Euros. Not too shabby at all. He decided he'd hold his nerve though and try and push his luck a little further. If you don't ask in life, you don't get.

'Another dealer told me not to accept less than eighty each, Mr Degas, I think you can do better than fifty.'

Degas hummed, harred, tut tutted, shrugged his shoulders and waved his arms about in true Gallic fashion and then finally curled his lip like a professional haggler, defeated. 'Okay, I can give you sixty-five each – that is my very best offer,' he said, bowing his head. He leant forward, tapped on his calculator and, with the same hand, held it out saying, 'I will give you two thousand five hundred Euro now; have we got a deal?'

Damn fucking right we have, Will thought, wanting to kneel down and bite his hand, arm… and leg off but instead he mimicked Degas, shrugged his shoulders, and faked defeat. 'Okay, Mr Degas, you win,' he said. *Vous gagnez*. 'We have business.'

Will then lunged for old Degas's hand, clenching the clammy little offering he'd held out, squeezed nice and hard, and shook his arm violently, cementing the deal. As a result of his coup Will's nausea vanished immediately, and was replaced with euphoria.

'One moment, please,' Degas said, and shuffled back behind the curtain.

He reappeared clamping a crisp wad of notes in his left hand. And then, having licked his fingers, he proceeded to count out the notes on the illuminated desk. But before he picked up the pile and handed it over he counted the pile of maps again, pretending to be thorough, and then looked at Will.

'I will need you to fill out a receipt, I'm afraid,' he declared. Then shrugging, he stupidly added, 'For the tax, you understand?'

Alarm bells. 'Yes of course, no problem.'

The old man passed Will a docket and pointed where to write his name and address. Will happily wrote it down, naturally giving a false surname and a made-up location in Farnborough, thinking, *bugger the taxman*.

With that, the deal was done. The two men shook again and Will hotfooted it out of the door. He couldn't believe his luck as he half trotted, half skipped on the cobbles as quickly as he could. The wad of cash in his pocket made him want to gallop but, not wanting to look dodgy, all he could do was yank Nelson, who wanted to pee everywhere, along at a sensible clip. As he cantered down the ancient lane, it even crossed Will's mind to thank his dead father. All was temporarily forgiven. What he hadn't noticed, was a man in a gabardine coat pull his collar up and fall in behind.

Will flipped out his mobile phone and dialled as he walked. 'Hey, hon, Soph, it's me, darling. How's it going?'

'Fine, thanks,' she replied, a little hesitantly. 'Just got back from school and settling down to begin the big marking session – and you, you sound giddy, are you alright? How was the journey down?'

'Well, it was a rough old crossing in the end and then six and a half hours in the car today,' he said, panting. 'I feel exhausted to be honest, hon, but…' His voice became louder. 'Good news, in fact, great news! Guess how much I got for the maps?'

'I don't know – three, four hundred Euros?'

'One thousand five hundred,' he burst out. 'Hey, hay, hey, can you believe it?'

'Wow, that's amazing!'

'Yes, absolutely fantastic, I'm going to give Louise half, though, which will pay off the grand we had to pay to have

James's stuff sent over and a bit on top - will you give her a quick call and let her know?'

'Yes sure – I'll do it now. How's our little boy?'

Will looked down at Nelson, trotting along. 'He seems alright, but the poor fella was down in the hold last night. It was a rough one but he seems chipper enough. Hey, look, hon, I'd better get off the blower; it's costing a fortune. I'll call tomorrow night after my day's hike. Have a good evening, all love.'

'Great news darling, well done – that'll pay for the trip too. Enjoy yourself. Eat well, bye, big kiss.'

Will thought he'd keep quiet about the extra grand in his pocket so he could spend it on some decent Christmas goodies for everyone and perhaps have a bit of a blow-out himself, get a stupidly priced bottle of wine, or even stay an extra night and sniff out a bit of mischief if he was up for it.

Will had hung up just as he arrived at the ticket machine. Having fumbled with change then found his Audi, he got to the actual barrier, to get out of the car-park onto the thoroughfare, when a suitably drunk man stumbled in front of the car, actually tumbling onto the bonnet which made Nelson bark furiously, right in Will's ear. Will laughed out loud. Professionally distracted, neither he nor Nelson noticed the man in gabardine sweep in behind, crouch down and place something under the boot by the exhaust. Having swore and cursed and jabbed a finger at Will's car the drunk stumbled off, seemingly refreshed, and Will headed out into Bordeaux's Friday evening traffic thoroughly amused and none the wiser.

Meanwhile, back at Degas's shop Reynard had lurched out of his hidey hole and, having stretched, he lumbered across, leant over the desk and tore the receipt off the pad. He'd arrived at nine that morning and had sat all day, perched in

Degas's back room, and had never come out once. He hadn't even read anything and had sat motionless and silent in the box room for seven hours.

'Lock the door, Degas,' he ordered. The dumbfounded proprietor, goggle-eyed, simply stared up at him. 'Now, Degas.'

'Oh, yes, of course,' Degas mumbled, coming to, and then got up and shuffled to the door and flipped the sign.

While he was doing this Reynard opened each map out on the desk slowly and looked at them in detail, wondering how on earth his boss could be so excited by them.

When Degas reappeared, Reynard continued, knowing what he had to say now would ensure the antique dealer's absolute discretion in this matter. 'My employer informed me that your Lodge, the Brethren of Sion, has been made aware of the service you have done for him,' he said, craning around. 'We require your complete tact in this matter. My employer has asked me to give you a thousand Euro as a small token of his appreciation. I trust this is not an insult to you?'

'No, Monsieur Reynard, not at all, that is very generous,' Degas said, perking up. It was turning out not be such a bad week. He added, 'You have my word that this transaction never occurred.'

'What maps, eh, Degas?' said Reynard, not an inkling of humour in his voice.

'Exactly, I know of no maps,' mumbled the ruddy-faced antique dealer, forcing out a feeble laugh, dying for the odious individual from Marseille to leave.

'Very good, you have done well.'

And with that they shook hands in the dim light. Reynard swiftly departed leaving the thousand Euros on his desk in a neat pile of fifties, having picked up the stack of maps and placed them in a very tame-looking leather satchel.

He got on his mobile phone as he walked over the same cobbles as Will had done ten minutes before.

'Jacques, it's me,' he said into the mouth piece.

'Yes, sir.'

'Talk to me.'

'The tracker has been installed. Audi, UK plates, right-hand drive. Old, a rust bucket. We've tuned into it and are about to follow the car now.'

'Good, well done, *mon brave*. I will call you in an hour – don't lose him.' He hung up and dialled another number. This time his voice had the hint of submission about it. 'It is me, sir, Reynard. Have I caught you at a good time? Very good, to let you know I am now in receipt of the thirty-nine maps. The Englishman I told you about is called Sawyer, Will-i-am Sawyer, and is about thirty years old. We don't know what he is doing in Bordeaux yet, but we are following him with a tracker device as we speak. English number plates. None of the thirty-nine maps I now have in my possession are of this area. That is all I know for now.'

'Okay, Reynard, this is wonderful news, absolutely incredible news,' Reynard's boss gushed. 'Make me another list of the areas that the new maps cover this evening and email it to me immediately, and then courier the maps to me first thing in the morning, unless you come to Paris yourself tomorrow. And Reynard, make a note to be back in Marseille on Thursday. We have a delivery from Cyprus. Phone me later and let me know where this person goes and if you need more men just ask.' He hesitated before hanging up and added, 'Oh Reynard, one last thing, have you had a close look at the maps? Are there any markings on any of them?' He couldn't help himself.

'Markings, sir, no sir, I don't think so; not that I could see.'

'Okay, *dommage*, Reynard, Shame. Call me in two hours. Good man.'

Reynard was known to everyone by his surname only. And it seemed natural, in his case, to drop the Y, so it sounded like Renard, Fox. Mr Fox. He liked the sound of his own name. He knew it suited him and his nefarious profession perfectly and added a bit of gravitas to his already formidable demeanour. The fox, having sniffed out his quarry, headed to his hotel as Will negotiated his way out of one of France's ten largest cities through Friday rush-hour without too much difficulty and then booted the half-hour drive back to Blaye, spurred on by the wad of cash in his pocket.

On a monotonous stretch of motorway his thoughts shifted to think about his father coming down here on the same mission and Will began to try and get into his mindset. The value put on the maps now encouraged him further; the maps had an intrinsic value. They were originals of some sort, Degas had made that obvious, and the one he still had in his possession, the only one with any markings, was the only one that had any added value: something more. A certain *je ne sais quoi*. It definitely had a story attached to it, Will had sniffed that with his eyes, and he now determined to get a proper grip with it, to understand it, to unravel its story with his more subtle senses. The original map he had was tucked away safely in the secret compartment in his ancient Bedouin wooden chest back in England. He'd only brought over his Series Blue map with him onto which he'd meticulously superimposed all the original's markings.

He was excited. The doubts he'd had over the past few days had vaporised. He was now a man on a mission. No better feeling than that. He knew exactly what he was doing.

However, as soon as he pulled up outside the charming, authentically French, stylish little townhouse hotel, and switched off the engine, he felt deflated, exhausted, his adrenalin all used up. It was only six thirty. He went straight up to his room, fed Nelson, washed his face vigorously with cold water to keep awake and went straight out leaving his faithful companion in the room. He was a hundred percent confident that Nelson wouldn't whinge or whine and would settle easily. Will couldn't stop now; if he lay down he knew he'd crash immediately and wake up at two or three in the morning, plus he hadn't eaten all day.

It was a bitter winter's evening which greeted Will when he stepped back out onto the pavement. The bracing cold numbed his fatigue. The proprietor had told him that no restaurant would be open until 7:30. He had half an hour to kill.

Will walked down to the nearby bank of the vast Gironde and peered out across the dirty expanse of water in the dying daylight. He couldn't see the other bank on the far side, the river was that wide. Like one gigantic industrial conveyor belt the enormous body of water swept past him relentlessly at great speed. He could see tides collide in silhouette out in the slip stream where they ripped diagonally across towards the horizon, pushing up tongues of surf which met and fused. The threatening river seemed to be baring its teeth to him, showing him its fangs.

Will stood transfixed as he noticed a groaning coming from the river and then, peering out, he could see the hulk of a car ferry appear out of the gloom, looming large out of the brownness, struggling with the current; then it docked and unloaded two hundred metres upstream. The scene made Will think he'd entered another continent altogether. It could well have been America's wild west or Africa's Timbuktu.

Will turned around and could see a group of men playing boules in a shabby, spot-lit, windswept sand pit. Their balls threw up occasional puffs of red dust which drifted ominously low across the park. Will shuddered and turned towards them. He pulled the lapel of his coat around his ears and walked the short distance back up to the beautiful castellated old town through an applause of white doves which clattered up before him. He was walking illuminated by phosphorous-orange lamps through an avenue of huge poplars, shedding their massive leaves. The wind rustled bass tones through their boughs as Will's feet lightly crunched the discarded foliage beneath their branches. He could hear the boules players' balls clack sharply behind him, and then loud exclamations emanated from the players which faded and merged with the swirling flora as he left the influence of the menacing river behind him and headed towards civilisation.

There was a little more time to kill until restaurants began serving so Will popped into the first bar he passed. He stepped into a spartan, too bright, neon-lit café with a long zinc bar and uncomfortably ordered a stiff drink beneath the glare: a vodka tonic. He stood, shuffling uncomfortably in this stark new environment; he was used to drinking in the cosy warmth of British establishments. As he gulped his powerful, ice cold drink he thought about how meal times are sacrosanct in France, particularly lunch, which is more of a religion than a meal. He looked at his watch and ordered the bill – nine and a half Euros. *For a flipping V&T in a shitty little bar in the arse end of France? They're having a giraffe*, he said to himself as he left a ten euro note and vamoosed.

Meanwhile, outside in Blayes's traffic system, an innocuous little car circled with two men up front. The passenger crouched low over the glove box, his eyes transfixed on a small computer screen, up-lighting his face in a morbid green colour. The car pulled up and parked.

CHAPTER 7
FADING AWAY

Geneva, nine years earlier.

James Marshall was sitting at the bar of the Jolie Ville, alone. It was only when he'd finished his meal that he asked the waiter if he'd seen Wiktor.

'Jean, has Monsieur Foukes been in recently? I haven't seen him for a few weeks. Have you?'

'Non, monsieur, I have not either.'

That news had played on James's mind overnight, so in the morning, before heading to the office, he called around at Wiktor's adjacent apartment block. He buzzed the concierge and explained that he was a neighbour of Mr Foukes, and that he had not seen him at their local restaurant for a number of weeks and was wondering if he was away.

'Non, monsieur, unfortunately he is not well, and has not left his apartment for two weeks.'

'Oh dear, I am sorry to hear that,' he said, handing over a card. 'Please say that James, James Marshall, came by and I will return this evening. I would like to see him if possible.'

'Yes, of course, monsieur.'

That evening James returned clutching a bag of grapes and a bottle of whiskey discreetly tucked under his coat. The concierge said yes, Mr Foukes would be happy to see him and directed him to the lift and gave him the apartment number.

James found Wiktor looking ashen and skeletal when he answered the door; he'd aged considerably. He was draped in an oriental satin dressing gown, his neck was wrapped in the obligatory silk cravat and on his feet were a pair of ornate eastern slippers. To James, his jaundiced pallor resembled candle wax in the shadows, and in the light, because his skin had been stretched even more tightly over his face than normal, it made him look as translucent as a lemon jelly.

'Not feeling too well, old boy, eh?' James said as he entered the flat, trying to sound jovial. 'This should cheer you up a bit.' He handed Wiktor the bottle of scotch.

'Come in, James, come in, please, I've been vanting to see you, that is very kind,' said the older man, taking the bottle, and proceeded to lead James through the hallway in a trail of swirling, pungent French tobacco smoke, curling mysteriously around the host like the vortex in a wind tunnel.

The apartment James had entered was luxuriously spacious. Although almost devoid of furniture, what was there was exquisite. There were magnificent oriental carpets, not just on the marble floors, but hanging on the walls too. James commented on their beauty, touching them as he passed; he'd bought a number of them himself on his frequent trips to Afghanistan, Iran and Iraq, and was beginning to build a collection. Apart from four delicately carved ornamental chairs in the corners of the spacious sitting-room the only usable pieces were two comfortable well-worn tan leather sofas facing each other, divided by a long dark carved Javanese coffee table. On the mantelpiece there was only one object: a tiny old black-and-white photograph which sat imperiously encased in a huge, highly decorated Eucharistic object. The photograph's setting was a metal-worked splaying sun, inlaid with semi-precious stones. The shiny silver sun beams caught any available light, making it flash, and it winked at James as he sat down. He thought it looked more like a valuable religious object housing an ancient relic than a photo frame.

'I have cancer, James,' Wiktor said matter-of-factly, as he too seated himself. 'My liver is not working, I have not long to live. The doctors say it is a matter of only a few months… at most.'

'Oh Christ, Vick,' said James quietly. 'I'm so sorry.' He looked up at the wizened old man before him. 'Thank you for telling me.' Slight pause. 'Is there anything I can do for you? Would you like anything?'

'What!' the older man said, chuckling. 'Like strawberry's and cream?'

'Exactly, my friend, anything like that,' James replied. 'Or a run out somewhere. Anything, anything at all, just ask.'

Wiktor leant forward, deadly serious now. 'Actually, James, I would like you to do something for me,' he said, as he reached for and lit another cigarette. 'That is the reason I have asked you to come up this evening, but let us open this bottle first. Fetch a couple of glasses from the kitchen, would you, and a jug of water; it's all on the sideboard, there's a good man.' He flicked one of his massive wiry talon-fingers towards a closed door.

While fetching the glasses James thought Wiktor must have thought about this visit and wondered what it could be his friend wanted. In the half light, surrounded by objets d'art, dressed as he was, Wiktor looked more like the caterpillar on top of the mushroom in Alice in Wonderland than an old soldier; he now looked very wise, like a magician or a high priest.

Having poured the drinks Wiktor started talking. He didn't ask whether James had other plans that evening.

'James, I wish to give you something, something rare and a little strange,' the elder man said, taking a draught of his whisky.

'Oh!'

'Yes, it is indeed. My doctor is coming around in an hour, ya. I am going to hospital for some treatment, but I want to tell you the story behind this gift as quickly as I can. I was going to call on you anyway. I am so pleased you have come tonight. I am going to start this story at the beginning, and you must listen carefully. Come closer, come on, closer.' He coughed, a bilious hack, and swallowed. As James put his elbows on his knees Wiktor leant back. 'My wife's family are part of a distant Polish royalty, James,' he said, starting his story, 'and they have looked after me these past fifty years. This apartment, and all the furniture, are theirs. I myself have nothing, and no one to give anything too, but I do have something in my possession, which I want to give you. I acquired them at the end of the war and I want you to have them. You are exactly the person who should have them, as you will see.' James came off his knees and sat back. Wiktor continued. 'I've mentioned this to you before but in late 1939, not long after Germany had invaded my country, we very quickly formed a large partisan group, under the name of F2 Network. You may have heard of us. Anyway, I remember telling you we overran a German command centre in Warsaw and captured an Enigma encoding device. I was commanded with taking it out of my country with two code breakers and delivering them to Allied hands. In this case it was you chaps, the British. I travelled firstly to Romania, over the Carpathian mountains, it was a very hard brutal winter. It was slow. Finally I paid a big, ya, a very big sum of money to a family of gypsies who smuggled me and the two mathematicians into France as part of their… their… annual springtime pilgrimage to Vaccares in South of France. Well, it took us just under a year to reach Paris in the end and deliver the Enigma device and the two code breakers to a Duff Cooper at your Embassy in April or May, I recall, in 1940. I was only twenty-five. The device and the two Polish mathematician code-breakers went to Bletchley Park in England, and the rest is history as they say. I never heard from them again. Back in Poland, the Germans arrested a number of our cell and one member must have broken and my name was given. I was on my way over the mountains so I didn't hear about it until I reached Paris, six months later. This was when my wife was arrested and she and my children were taken to a concentration camp. They were in Dachau for a time, we know that, and then… nothing. And we never found out exactly where they were taken from there or where they died. They disappeared, James, and they never returned. Like two million of my fellow countrymen. We looked everywhere and tried so hard to find them after the war, and spent a great deal of money searching, for years, but nothing. They just disappeared. This here is the only photograph I have of them, my angels,' Vicktor said, sombrely turning and pointing up at the sparkling silver frame above him. 'I don't know whether your government ever wanted to give me recognition for delivering the Enigma device, ach, I used a different name during the war anyway, so I can't blame them. What the hell!' Wiktor shook his head, and took a long draught of his whiskey. 'I told you before, I then ran F2 from Paris under the name of Tadenz Jekiel. Tadenz Jekiel was my war name. And, in fact, James,' he said with a smile, 'Wiktor Foukes isn't my real name either. Anyway, I ran cells all over France: Lyon, Toulouse, Marseille and Bordeaux, all from Paris. Most information from my agents was transported to me through the sleeper trains, the wagons lit. The railway men in France were the keenest resistors, an amazingly brave group. Much of the time I would go myself and collect the information. I was driven by the anger over my wife and children's incarceration, you see. I didn't know the brutal truth until the war was over. I thought they were just in prison. I would transmit or transfer all the information I'd gathered and give it to your British MI6 agency - they were called SIS then. It was mainly about Nazi shipping, submarine and troop movements, that sort of thing. What was happening and where. I only dealt with one man for the whole war from M16, whom you remind me of, James; he was called Billy, Billy Dunderdale. Ring any bells?' Negative. 'A great fellow. Well,' Wiktor continued, 'the Germans managed to break up our cells little by little as the war went on but we kept the main network working right up until the Germans finally left France. I am sorry to bore you, my friend, but I am getting to the point now. I spent about six months, very early in the war, establishing an agent in Bordeaux, one of my best, and it was there I came across one of the worst of the German collaborators for the first time, a Maurice Bousquet. Remember that name, James: Maurice Bousquet. It was back in 1941, when I first came across him. He was then the chief of police in Bordeaux before he moved to Paris: a complete bastard; all he was interested in was the money. This guy even worked for the Germans *before* they invaded France, can you believe it, sending the Gestapo information from Bordeaux, France's main bulk wine-producing region, about exactly whereabouts on the Maginot Line wine was being sent. Through this information the Germans knew precisely how many troops were based where. You see, James, it is simple; every French soldier has a set allocation of wine per day, a wine ration, and so it is only a basic equation to work out how many soldiers are positioned in a particular place. The Germans could then work out the weak points on the defence lines and Blitzkrieg through them. So he actually helped the Germans to invade his own country. He was the worst of the worst. He also organised and oversaw the transportation of Jews and prisoners of war, firstly from Bordeaux and then, I assume as a reward for all that efficiency, he went to be the Paris Chief of Police. My hatred of the Germans somehow focussed on this one individual. I kept bumping into him, so to speak, so I then began to trail him throughout the tail-end of the war – it was *my* great hobby, James. I was waiting for the moment to strike. I knew a lot about him just by following him here and there for a few years. I was hunting him, you see, James, like killing a beast by hand. I had to get inside him. To know exactly how he ticked. It became an obsession, to be honest.' He paused, lit another cigarette and sat back, slightly calmer now. 'Anyway, James,' he sighed, 'to cut an even longer story short, when the Germans eventually left Paris in 1944, and the end of the war was just a matter of time we decided to strike; that was me and the French resistance.' James now leant forward slowly and took a slurp of his drink as Wiktor continued. 'In 1944 in Paris there were a lot of resistance groups such as the Maquisards, all setting up hit squads to eliminate resistance to liberation. Crooks, bank robbers, explosives experts, all those sorts appeared out of the woodwork. But there was no way I was going to allow this character Bousquet and others to escape to the other side of the world or reinvent themselves and live peacefully ever after, you understand that. James? So I chased him and his fellow high-up Malice collaborators through central Paris as he tried to escape when the Germans fled. We were in a fast Fiat and he was in a lumbering armour-plated limousine. I caught up with Bousquet near Pont Neuf and I shot him, as easily as the rabbit in the headlights, and the local resistance I was with killed the two men with him. The others were officials too, public servants, part of a pro-Nazi militia, and all clutching identical packages. Because I led the resistance to them and I killed Bousquet, I got his parcel. The Resistance guys took the other two. The maquis I engaged for this were part of a Mafioso-type network from Marseille, a criminal underground. I tell you, James, these guys made the actual Mafia look like boy scouts. They were hard men, utterly fearless. I never had any more contact with them after that moment: never again. The main man was called Lafarge - remember that name also. Le Dom Lafarge.' Wiktor repeated the name, and visibly shuddered recalling these memories. 'God know what became of him, he must be dead by now,' he continued. 'Basically, these were the guys who could get things done that nobody else could; they were a necessary evil at the time. It was all chaotic and fast-moving as you can imagine; France was being liberated, the Allies and the Americans were coming through the country from all directions. This guy Le Dom - to illustrate my point, James, once I had executed Bousquet and grabbed his bundle I saw Le Dom shoot the driver. Poof, gone, as easy as that. Innocent guy. It upset me greatly. What had the poor French driver done? He then dragged the other two collaborators out of the car, got them on their knees and put his gun to their heads demanding to know what these packages were all about.'

'Bundles, packages, Vick?' James interjected.

'Ya, ya, I'm coming to that, James, hold on. Let me continue.'
'Of course.'

'These two guys were yelling to be saved. Le Dom executed one straight away, bullet through the head, paff, and then the other guy really began to talk. As I walked slowly away I heard him saying he'd show Le Dom where their treasure was hidden if he let him go. They tore a map out of the bundle as I turned; I'd had enough. At a corner I stood and looked back one last time and saw the fellow on his knees pointing furiously at the map. Then Le Dom shot him and, Jesus Christ, James, I swear I saw him then turn, quick as a flash, and shoot his two associates. Can you believe it? The bastard didn't want his own men to know a damn thing. Lafarge, James, as tough as they come, as hard as they come, a brutal man,' Viktor said, panting and wheezing at the excitement the recollections were generating. He gathered himself. 'The last thing I remember was him look around furiously, I presume for me, but I was gone. I threw myself into the crowd and rushed over to Gare du Lyon, jumped on a train and headed south. I came straight here, where my wife's family had sought sanctuary thirty years before that war. And that was it, James, my Second World War was over. I never used the name Tadenz Jekiel again and I don't know what happened to Lafarge after the war.' The two men simultaneously picked their glasses up and gulped. 'I knew I had done wrong, James, believe me. I had gone against *the* Geneva Convention but - and I hate to say it, James - it felt good. It felt so good to extinguish this vermin Bousquet from the face of the earth, very good indeed, ya. I remember it as clearly as if I did it yesterday. I can see the look on his face when he realised his time had come; his life flashed before him. I was like God on Judgement Day. I held my pistol at him for a long time, watching him squirm in his own juices, ya. I'd do it again one hundred times, I have never lost sleep over it. It was the highlight of my war actually, ya, it was.' Wiktor laughed, a high-pitched laugh, more like a call to the valkyries. He took another mouthful of his drink to calm himself. 'And here I have lived since, as quiet as a church mouse. So there you have it. That is my story, my life. There has been nothing since, and now it is over.' He looked up reverently at his most treasured possession on the mantelpiece before continuing, more serious again. 'I am going to give you this pile of maps, James. This is the package Bousquet was clutching when I shot him. They must have had some major significance for him. He was fleeing Paris with only a small bag of clothing and very little money. I searched him. I don't know where he was going, we just stopped his car, I told the chauffeur to run but he didn't and then I shot Bousquet sitting in the back seat, in front of his friends, no questions asked. I have done nothing with them, the maps. I have never even opened them. As I said it felt wrong to have taken them, and in no way did I want to be traced to the murder of Bousquet, so I have done nothing except think about them a great deal. This was nearly fifty years ago now, my friend. A world away.'

During the story the two men had worked their way through the bottle of whisky. James was in need of the toilet. Whilst he was relieving himself Wiktor disappeared into another room and reappeared with the pile of maps tied up in a thick red ribbon.

As James came back into the room he could see the light outside had faded almost completely. Only the faint outline of the Alps' snow-capped peaks remained, rippling into the far distance. Wiktor had switched on a lamp. This spray of ambient light really made Wiktor and his plush furnishings come to life. The photo frame above them began to animate as if a lamp itself and the embossed golden dragons on Wiktor's dressing gown began writhing into existence whenever he moved. James felt slightly bamboozled, woozy even. Whether it was the effect of the whisky, Wiktor's story or the ecclesiastic atmosphere that was hypnotising him, he wasn't sure. He gazed at Wiktor, slightly goggle-eyed, as he leant forward, untied the red ribbon and took a map from the top of the stack.

CHAPTER 8

THE TRAIL

'*Non*, Monsieur Renard, the car is still 'ere, it hasn't moved. We've found him, though, he's having dinner in one of the local restaurants alone. That dog is not with him nor in the car. We think he must be staying overnight in Blaye.'

'Okay, that is fine, good,' Reynard said calmly. 'Find out where he is staying. Follow him. One of you go and find a cheap hotel nearby for yourselves. Wait an hour after he gets back to wherever he is staying to make sure he's gone to bed and then be back at his car at six tomorrow morning. It will still be dark. Set the tracker to alert you if the vehicle moves. And Pierre, get this into your skull, you cannot lose touch with him or the vehicle at any cost – believe me, I cannot tell you how important this is to the boss. Your life won't be worth living if you fail. Do you understand?'

'Yes, sir, perfectly.'

'Good. I am getting other men sent up to assist you. They'll be leaving Marseille within the hour and be with us as soon as they can in the morning. Text me the Audi's registration number. I'll phone you back in an hour. He is to suspect nothing. Am I clear?' With that barrage of clipped orders delivered Reynard hung up and phoned his boss.

'Monsieur Lafarge, sir, sorry to bother you but the update is that the Englishman, we are sure, is staying the night in

Blaye, a small town twenty minutes outside Bordeaux. He is eating now and we know where his car is parked. I have two men on site and have sent for two more men to relieve them in the morning. Is that okay?'

'Yes, yes, Renard, get them up now. Whatever you need,' Henri Lafarge said excitedly. 'Call Marseille though, get the brothers to join you.'

'I did, sir.'

'Excellent. I have a change of plans myself. I am going to Marseille tomorrow and I will get the plane to stop at Bordeaux on the way. I'll pick the maps up myself, so don't bother sending them. Book a table in my name for just the two of us at La Tupina at 8pm – a private table. I'll be staying at the Grand Hotel. This is *incroyable*, my friend.'

A little confused, Reynard simply said, 'Yes, sir, that is good.'

'*Mon Dieu*, I can hardly believe it. Keep on to this, Renard - like your life depends on it. Did you find out who this Englishman is?'

'Bad news there, sir; our man in London says that the name and address he gave don't add up. I will see what I can do in the hotel where he is staying tomorrow and I will forward his car registration to London now. They will look into that.'

'Mmm interesting. Okay, Renard, stay on it and call me at nine tomorrow morning. Oh, and if anything dramatic happens tonight call me anytime, we cannot lose him. Get me that list of the maps emailed urgently, do you hear?'

'Of course, sir, I'll do it straight away. *Bon soir*, sir, Good night.' When Reynard hung up he looked at his phone, bemused. He'd never heard his boss as animated or excited as he had been over the past week. Never like this. Ever since he'd known him, and that was thirty plus years. It was strange, very strange.

The raw cold Will stepped out into the following morning, at 8:30, was a hell of a lot sharper than he'd expected. The frost tore into his throat. He was suitably attired though; a thick woolly hat capped his fully kitted walking gear. His new socks came up over his mustard coloured corduroy trousers to his knees which he thought made him look the part of a serious walker. The reality was, to one of the locals who could see him, Pierre, he bore no resemblance whatsoever to Belgian's revered Tintin, which Will thought he did, but more closely to some sort of a nutter, a clown.

He'd filled a small Thermos with coffee and had his hip-flask fully loaded with some sweet Metaxa brandy a friend had brought back from a holiday to Corfu earlier in the summer. On the way out of town he dumped his overnight bag in the boot of the car with his wad of cash stashed in the side pocket and continued on foot as planned, map in gloved hand. He knew it was a bit early, as UK was an hour behind, but he thought he'd give Sophie a call anyway.

'Mornin' darling,' he chirped. His breath visible in the chill air. 'I'm underway… brrrgh, it's bloody freezing here but dry, so… *on y va* as they say, let's go. We're off. And you, love? Did you sleep well?'

'I'm okay,' Sophie groaned, yawning, 'I was up marking until eleven though and have got the whole day of it again, and tomorrow, yuk!'

'Oh, poor bunny,' he said. 'Did you call Lou?'

'Yip, I did, she was chuffed. Call me later, would you Will, hon? I'm just getting up. Have a good day out there – keep warm, go steady. Big kiss.'

'Yeah, yeah of course, I'll call again this evening and let you know how it went. Have a goodie yourself, byeee.'

'Boss, it's Pierre, the Mark has left Blaye - walking, *a pied*, On foot, with the dog! It is freezing,' one of Reynard's underlings said into his phone, smirking, looking at Will heading up the road. 'The guy must be a fool. He is dressed for a long hike, I think. He put his valise in the car and is now on his mobile phone.'

'Okay, Pierre, whatever. Calm down. Listen, Philippe and Jean, the brothers, should be with you soon. For now, just keep going up and down the road in your car, every twenty minutes and keep track of him. They will get in touch with you when they arrive in Blaye. Just keep swapping over and see where he goes. What direction is he heading in?' Reynard asked, standing in his socks, string vest and underwear before his hotel room window, looking out over the beautiful bustling Bordelais river frontage, the Quai Richelieu.

'Towards Bourg, sir.'

'Okay, fine. Just don't lose him or make him suspicious in any way. Do you hear me?'

'Yes, sir.'

'I will come out and join you myself later. Phone if there are complications, otherwise I will call you back in an hour or two - oh, and Pierre, from now on we call him "le lapin" – the rabbit, have you got that? Let the boys know.'

Will and Nelson walked out of Blaye through the shabby, industrial end of town. It was a long, straight desolate start to their day: derelict terraced houses on one side of the drag and dirty factory units of various sizes backing onto the river the other. The depressed road Will pounded, alongside the early morning traffic, housed only an occasional inhabited dwelling. All the rest were boarded up and seemed empty. Within one decrepit terraced cottage he caught a glimpse of an old lady crocheting or peeling potatoes, he wasn't sure. They passed alleys leading up around the back of the houses where, at one point, Will noticed the outline of a slender black cat peering wide-eyed and unmoving high up on a dank wall.

Nelson missed it. They squeezed around endless wheelie bins as trucks and cars rumbled past very close to them. Right at the edge of Blaye they skirted a huge grubby industrial wine warehouse and bottling plant with vast dirt-stained concrete wine vats that loomed over them like grain silos. Will saw this was all owned by a company called SCREG. *How*? he thought. *How on earth can they sell wine called that? God only knows.* He had to laugh. Certainly a massive challenge for any marketing man wanting to sell their wine - called SCREG! Screggy wines. More suited to a Bond villain's company name than a wine brand. Obviously the very bottom of the wine production scale. The industrial stuff. Vinegar perhaps.

On the very edge of Blaye, bonfire smoke and the heady smell of burning leaves swept down from a villa's garden on the rise above and curled around a very old, blind, emaciated tethered-up Boxer dog in a filthy front garden. It began to howl mournfully. It was a hauntingly sad sight and sound to leave the town with: impotent yowls breaking up and fading away into the smoke-swept distance as our intrepid duo marched forward, out of Blaye and along the side of the pavement-less main road. Cars began whizzing past them, a hair's breath away from fatal collisions.

Now they were now out in open countryside dominated by vineyards. The winter vines were leafless, bare and scrawny, bound and crucified to wire fencing. It was here, in a pull-in on a rise, that Will finally met France's greatest river in daylight. The river he'd been studying for these past weeks. The mighty Gironde, splayed out majestically below him. Its vast, still-looking body of water was half a mile wide at this point. It looked motionless in the morning haze, the dirty tan brown colour of its brackish water seamlessly blending with a golden mist which hung above its surface. And that too, merged perfectly into the muddy sky above. Will stood, staring at the monstrous, weighty river – the immovable force - and smoked a cigarette. His feet began to freeze; he marched on the spot and then moved off.

After an hour of tramping the unforgiving tarmac road they passed the first point marked on the map - a red cross. At the exact point on the map's indication point Will could see huge boulders and old blocks of dirty concrete piled up on the side of the carriageway - a mouldy black - and he wondered what on earth they could be. They were out of place. Having taken a couple of photographs he carried on. They passed no one at all on foot, only occasional cars, going incredibly fast. The countryside was utterly devoid of humans. There was no one around. Not a soul. The vast majority of the houses he passed were empty – all holiday homes. It was ghostly.

Will force-marched himself, pressing ahead, battling the cold and the tedious asphalt. He had to get off the road as quickly as possible. He barked at Nelson to stop pulling and to keep in as cars flew past in either direction at speed. It was thoroughly depressing and Will's feelings of idiocy returned; he felt dumb for being on such a pointless mission, a fact drummed home as he passed two mini roadside shrines to lives lost. These memorials were for grieving families and acted as alerts to fellow drivers of the tragedies that had occurred at those spots and the dangers of the road's contours. These warnings seemed to go completely unheeded; car drivers flew by at dangerous speeds. You could only appreciate the risks on foot.

Just as he began to feel like a tramp, two hours after setting off, a relieved Will finally reached a crossroads. This was the point of a second red cross, where again mouldy concrete slabs were unceremoniously dumped into a ditch by the carriageway. He took more photos of this vicinity.

It was here, too, that the green arrows commenced their imprint. The markers indicated took a riverside byway as opposed to the main road he'd been on. A hugely relieved Will took the green, riverside route and collapsed on the first bench he came to in the quiet crossroad hamlet of Roque de Thau. He poured himself a cup of coffee from his thermos and then unscrewed his hip flask, and took a neck-craning slug before handing over a few well-deserved bickies to Nelson.

It was at this point that Will first noticed a black 4x4 Mercedes M4 turn around abruptly just ahead of him and roar back for no apparent reason. *What a prat*, he thought.

Reynard, still in his hotel room, picked up his mobile phone. He was now dressed and lay on top of the made bed, socks on, toes twiddling.

'Pierre, have the boys arrived?'

'Oui, sir, yes they have. Philippe and Jean. They have just done their first run past le lapin, the rabbit. The guy has walked along the main road since we spoke and has only just turned off down towards the river.'

'Good. Just keep a trail on where he goes. Buy a map if you can find one, mark the route he takes and just keep swapping over with the other car so as not to scare our little bunny rabbit. Try the tourist office. And Pierre, where exactly is he now?'

'He has just stopped at a place called Roque de Thau. He's nearly been killed a few times by cars,' Pierre said, and began to snigger. 'Do you want me to run him down, finish him off, sir? It'd be a *morceau de gâteau*, a piece of cake, sir.'

'No, no, no, not yet, you damn fool. That is the last thing you will do, you idiot.' Reynard sat bolt upright and put his feet on the floor. 'For Christ's sake keep him alive until the boss says otherwise; just stay with him, do you hear me? I will be out soon.'

Reynard hung up and immediately called his boss in Paris.

'Bonjour, monsieur, just to let you know Jean and Philippe have arrived. Our man has set out on foot from Blaye.'

'He has what?' exclaimed Henri Lafarge.

'Yes, sir, he put his suitcase in his car in Blaye and headed off, walking with his dog. This was over two hours ago. It is freezing cold.'

'Mmm, this is interesting, very interesting. I wonder what the hell he is up to.' Then a pause. 'Do you know exactly where he is now?'

'A place called Roque de Thau I think, sir.'

'Roque de Thau, yes, yes, I remember it, I know it. I've walked there myself.' Henri began to animate. 'In fact, it was with my father, Renard, a long time ago, yes, a long, long time ago.' He snapped back to the present. 'Renard, call up and hire a helicopter. You can get them at the airport. He's getting close.'

'Close, sir?'

'Just tell the boys to ease up a bit for now, that's all. Just do as I say. We don't want to unnerve him at all. Get on that chopper and you direct the lads from there. Tell me exactly, and I mean exactly, where he goes from now on.'

'Yes, sir, I am onto it.'

'Is he following a map like the ones you got yesterday?

'I'm not sure. I'll find out.'

'Call me in an hour, I will be waiting. Any problems let me know.'

'Of course sir, *au revoir*.' Again, Reynard looked at his inanimate phone and shook his head when he hung up. He too had been down here thirty years ago, and he recalled that trip had seemed a bizarre, inexplicable waste of time then. It was when he was a young man and had only just started working for the Lafarge organisation. As confused as Reynard was, his boss hung up thinking he knew exactly what was going on.

Ever since the maps have shown up, Henri said to himself, *my life has been turned inside out.* Memories kept gushing back but with such clarity. *Keep calm*, he kept repeating to himself; *it must be the hangover.*

Henri, the only child of the legendary Dominique Lafarge - Le Dom, the original founder of the Lafarge criminal organisation - now sat back, plonking his feet up on the Louis XIV desk in his salubrious Parisian office. He had to calm himself. He closed his eyes, forced himself to breathe gently and - thank God - warm feelings returned. He smiled, reminding himself he was un *cochon en merde*, a pig in shit, wallowing in his destiny. He opened his eyes slightly and gazed out through the large Haussemann windows at the relentless traffic fuzzing around La Bastille below.

Henri had lived with the legend of Bousquet, the notorious collaborator police chief, and finding his stolen wines, ever since he was a boy. He had inherited the obsessive quest from his father, and now, at last, after many decades of patience and perseverance the dream was on the cusp of being realised. He could hardly believe it. Finding Bousquet's wines had become, not simply a hobby, but something much more; something between a sport and a religion for him.

He knew that the vast collection of vintages stashed by Bousquet had never turned up. He, and before him, his father, had made it their business to know if the wines ever came to market, or even if they were offered on any French menu. They had acquired lists of what was in the cellars Bousquet had thieved before and during the Nazi occupation. The wines were still at large.

Henri had been up around the Bordeaux area a few times alone and also with his father ever since he was a child in various attempts to uncover Bousquet's wines; as a result he was familiar with the region Will now tramped.

Henri's heart began to beat ferociously again; he pictured uncovering the vast collection of wines, the fortune they'd bring, at last, at last... *this is my family's ticket out of the scuzzy business I am in.*

He felt a sudden charge in his marrow and twitched, as if his father had sent him a messages via his DNA from the grave. His genes were talking to him.

Henri had forever kept his deceased father's dream very much alive; the quest to find Bousquet's maps, and the one treasure map that would lead to his spectacular wine cache, lying hidden out there, somewhere, for all this time. The traffic hypnotised Henri. Round and round it went. He stared at the organised chaos in a pleasant warm daze, lost in the revelation of a dream coming true.

The other maps from this series, which his father had acquired from Bousquet's fellow Nazi collaborators at the end of the occupation in 1944, would be ritualistically brought out of their special armoire, which sat in pride of place in the family home in Marseille, and pored over. He clasped hold of the golden key which hung around his neck and recalled his father locking the sitting-room door with just the two of them inside and carefully removing the maps from their secret compartment as a priest does the Sacrament. Every time he'd perform this act his father reminded Henri, sermonising, that these maps were the real source of their family's great wealth. 'My son, if it weren't for these maps, we'd still be gutting fish, eating shit,' he said on each occasion. His father had told Henri he'd been given them as a thank you for his war efforts which couldn't be officially recognised. And that they'd led him to two great treasure hoards that Le Dom had uncovered before Henri was born and had sold off piecemeal. These were the very fondest memories Henri had of his father. It was the one really private matter that only they shared. The maps and their provenance were their secret. Only theirs. The source of the Lafarge fortune was a mystery to everyone but Henri and his father; and Henri had never shared it with anyone. Not a living soul. He knew the mystique surrounding the origins of the family's meteoric wealth was vital to their aura of power. It gave them a magical quality. Something divine. It was now essential for Henri to reinforce that dwindling status. He had to reinvent, reassert and put himself in pole position. Really he'd always been just the son of Le Dom, he knew that. Bousquet's wines would, without a shadow of doubt, elevate him to being a man in his own right. They'd cement his name firmly at the top echelons of French cultural life for decades to come, and he'd be able, at last, to legitimise the business.

Henri began pacing around, itching to get out of Paris and return to Marseille with the other thirty-nine maps in Reynard's possession and complete the family jigsaw. He just couldn't wait to see them, to touch his precious maps. The others in the set were his father's; these ones were his.

His housekeeper knocked and popped her head around the office door. 'Coffee, monsieur?' she asked sweetly. He flicked her away with a contemptuous forefinger, not saying a word, too lost in his daydream and not wanting the caffeine to make his heart beat any faster.

Henri now began to picture himself the following evening, in his Marseille mansion, locking himself in the grand map room. He would move the sofas, roll the carpet back and remove the other maps from their locked case, just as he'd done with his father, and alone on many occasions since Le Dom died. He always did this ritual on the anniversary of his father's death. It was something he did, too, when he had a problem to solve. The act of assembling the jigsaw of maps into a cohesive pattern on the beautiful parquet floor always succeeded in rearranging his mind, and finding solutions.

He just couldn't wait to construct the new one hundred and nineteen map collection, which would make up the complete map of France. The excitement was childlike. The last map, the one little gap in the whole puzzle which would be missing, would be revealed. The map of his beloved France would be ninety-nine point five percent complete. He now knew for definite where that final solitary gap would appear - it was the small area between Bourg and Blaye.

He'd received the email from Reynard the previous evening listing the thirty-nine areas which the new, unmarked maps covered, and he'd pictured exactly where the sole missing link was – the area he and his father had always suspected. Henri had a crystal-clear mental picture of the existing assemblage of maps and where the gaps were, and so last night he'd mentally filled in the holes from Reynard's list and completed the Lafarge family crossword.

His father had always pointed at the only two maps with markings out of the eighty in their possession, as they laid them out on the floor. Both of these other maps were at opposite ends of western France, identically marked to Will's, which had led to the two enormous treasure troves. Henri loved these beautifully illustrated maps, like ancient battle plans. His father had told him one stash was uncovered in a coastal farmhouse in Brittany and the other in a mountain retreat in Corbieres. The founding of the vast wealth Henri had now depleted had come from these two hoards. His father had found the most spectacular artworks, wines and jewels that the collaborators had stolen and hidden in these two locations. The black market had then turned them into cash. Bousquet's wines, however, were the prize of prizes. *La cerise sur le gâteau*, as his father had said repeatedly. Finding them would be the cherry on the cake to the name Lafarge.

Henri had maintained continuous contact with antiquarian map specialists and fine wine merchants after his father's death, constantly reminding them of his search for these particular maps and certain vintages. Willing his dream to life. Henri just knew they'd crop up one day and then, to get a message from one of his contacts in Paris ten days ago, saying that the maps had possibly appeared in Bordeaux - well, it was an incredible sensation for him. A delightful combination of relief and excitement had surged through him. He was experiencing sensations he'd never known possible. He'd always felt, in his core, the maps were coming to him one day. He strongly believed that was a given. These maps and Bousquet's wines were his destiny. He couldn't articulate it any other way than acknowledge he was in the throes of having a spiritual experience. He was feeling divinity for the first time in his long life. *Dreams do come true, if you truly believe*, he thought. For over fifty years I've been waiting for this moment to arrive. *My date with destiny has arrived.*

It was as comforting as it was disturbing. He wiped a ripple of sweat from his beading brow with the tips of his chubby, gold-ringed fingers.

The news of the maps' reappearance had rejuvenated him, he couldn't deny it. *I feel young again*, he admitted.

Undoubtedly it had put him on an emotional rollercoaster, but the excitement of vigorous life surging through his compact frame, his heart beating furiously within its cage, with purpose, was immense. One moment he was excited and alert, the next dazed and desultory.

When he'd received the list from Reynard confirming the missing areas last night he'd opened one of the last remaining really great vintages from his Paris cellar. He had none left in Marseille. A bottle of Romanee-Conti DRC 1929, worth over ten thousand Euros. He'd have to pay at least twice that in a restaurant. He'd sat alone in his vast, darkened Paris apartment and had drunk the entire bottle himself. He'd told his staff to leave, had decanted the wine and sat before a roaring fire sharing toasts with his dearly beloved dead father. As he'd become drunk he'd talked out loud to his father's spirit, exclaiming, 'We've done it, Papa, we've done it! We have always known the maps are our family's, ours, yes, ours.' He'd sunk deep into the sofa's cushions before the dancing flames, shadows swirling, and wept for the first time since his father's funeral. He'd blubbered, in fact.

When Henri had woken up in the morning he was perfectly calm and lay in bed convincing himself it was just a matter of waiting for the correct moment. He pictured his hand, in a dream-like state, reaching out as if for an olive branch. And he'd stretch out just that little bit further and pluck the map out of whoever's hand it was in, ever so gently. As if saying, thank you but this is mine. The wines were all but his. He sat up and looked admiringly at his heavily ringed hands and then slowly clenched his boxer's fists tight, taking huge pride in a couple of bones crunching.

CHAPTER 9

THE WALK

Having had his coffee and nip of brandy Will now sat in complete silence on the bench beside the Gironde. The enormous river swept past him in absolute hush. It was a breathless day; there wasn't even bird song or a breeze to rustle leaves; it was total stillness. So tranquil, in fact, that all Will could hear was the ringing in his ears and the cracking of his neck when he moved. This must be better than music, this unusual quiet. The harmony of peace was completed by warm rays of sunshine, some of the first of the day, bursting through the orange mist to bathe his face. He doubted if great rivers could ever sound as beautiful as this.

Will looked across and stared closely at the river now. Occasional, imperceptible wisps of wind merely made the smooth-as-glass surface purr gently. The Gironde, at this point, resembled what Will presumed the Mississippi to look like; it was especially wide here and he could see vast mud banks extending into the far distance, and sandbanks, savage and shifting, all bordered by a rash of low scrub. Although the body of water was serene at this particular moment Will knew he was looking at one of Europe's mightiest rivers, the widest estuary in Europe, in which hostile tides fluctuate fifteen feet or more from high to low tide - and this was all over sixty miles from the sea. One moment it could be a lumbering, lazy river as now, the next a maniacal surging body. Just as Will thought of that, all of a sudden the silence was rudely broken by a constant ripple of quick-fire flaps which broke onto the sandbanks below him, reminding him of fast canoe strokes, ghosts of the Cockleshell Heroes of Operation Frankton.

The Cockleshell Heroes, as they are now known, were a band of British Royal Marines who, in 1942, led a daring raid to sink German shipping in Bordeaux. Twelve British marines had set off in six canoes in open seas from an Allied submarine in the Atlantic Ocean, seventy miles from their target. It was at this time of year that their canoes, laden with limpet mines, embarked on their week-long journey upstream. Four marines had died almost immediately, in open seas, before they even entered the Gironde, and only two teams, four men, managed to paddle to their targets. They had passed where Will now sat seventy years before, maybe to the very day.

The cold had started to penetrate Will's feet. He was up on them again and began stamping. Then they hit the road. This particular bit of the route was somewhat familiar as he'd scrolled it endless times on Google Earth. The lane they walked took them along what is known as the Gironde Corniche or Little Switzerland: a thin strip of low-lying land one hundred feet wide at most between the river and a great ridge of south-facing limestone. This narrow belt of land had a micro climate all its own, somewhat Mediterranean. Will could see the cliffs and dells to his left dominated by ash trees, their white bark and pearly highlights shimmering in the haze, and the foliage punctuated by holm oak, wild cherry, downy oak or occasionally the familiar hawthorn of home. As he trudged Will even noticed some sloes poking through. He passed gelatinous mud banks fringed with reeds and a deep yellow nutgrass that blended perfectly with the colour of the sandy river in which it thrived.

This stretch of Will's walk, lasting for another hour, along the narrow lane beside the river, was marked unwaveringly with the green arrows on his map as the route to take, seemingly opposed to the main road running parallel, behind the cliffs, half a mile to his left with the red crosses. Stunning houses were tucked into the base of the long cliff, each with direct river views. They were built in the local stone that had been quarried for thousands of years from the hills right there. Will had read that the stone, called 'Bourg' stone, was mostly a light honey colour but it could also be pure white or cream like rich Jersey milk, and was sometimes textured like honeycomb or coral: very clean and bright with a definite uplifting effect on the eye. The open cast quarries were now generally redundant with the bulk of extraction ending with the virtual complete rebuilding of Bordeaux in the early 1700s. The old quarries were now used for growing mushrooms as the limestone had a mineral quality, formed by marine deposits, which, for some reason, suited the edible fungi. It was as if the stones were active and alive, harbouring a life-giving energy.

All along the river bank, every hundred feet or so, Will could see fishing huts perched on high platforms, way above the river, accessed by precarious individual bridges. They rose up out of the riverbank on incredibly long stilts and housed wide square nets on frames that could be lowered into the water to hoist out a range of crustaceans and small fish. All along were deep gluey inlets with small pleasure boats sunk deep into the mud. Will pictured the Cockleshell Heroes fumbling blindly into these creeks at dawn to take refuge and hide away in during the daytime on their nocturnal mission down river, in the same direction as he was going - all that time ago.

Will began to envisage his father on this very route, too, which he hadn't considered when he'd swept it online.

He now knew he was almost certainly looking at the same things as James had seen and probably, as a result, the views he now enjoyed would have triggered similar thoughts. He hoped so, anyway. The moment that reality swept in saddened Will – he thought they should have done this sort of thing together, shared the experience. *It's what fathers and sons do, isn't it*? He felt the rawness of shame. Ashamed that his father had remained remote and cold in the vain hope that this would keep his children in awe of him. That approach to parenting had only made James's children, in the end, lose respect for him, and actually made him look ridiculous. He'd precociously tried to foster the image of an international man of mystery, and had failed, as opposed to just being a dependable father. Not a great epitaph to have from your children.

An hour from where Will had his coffee he passed a memorial, a gigantic blue bulbous metal mine the size of a family car. He'd researched this online: found in 1990, out in the mud, it was one of a hundred and thirty-two horror-inducing bombs deposited into the river by the Nazis in 1944 when the war was lost to them as a parting gift to the locality. A mine field laid to ostensibly disrupt shipping. And just a little further he stopped and stared, because thirty feet out in the river, a wheelhouse, the mast and bow of a rusty old hulk protruded out of the fast-flowing water. The dead vessel was partially submerged in the mud. This must be MV Fujiyama which was scuttled by the Germans, again in 1944, to stop the then state-of-the-art 6,244 ton transport ship falling into Allied hands. It was a great photograph: a richly patina'd, rusting copper-coloured skeleton, appearing ghostlike out of the mist with soupy water swirling around it. The mast shot some twenty-five feet up in-to the haze.

Will noticed the tide change now. The surface water began to unsettle as fresh water and sea water met and began to fuse. He had to remind himself this was sixty miles from the sea. A tidal surge sixty miles from the sea! Opposing forces were convening. They momentarily halted the river's flow in a stalemate. The surface went flat as the conflicting currents clashed below the surface. Then a vast sheet of still mosaics appeared. And it was only then that the river sorted itself out and, having ruffled its feathers, began to make noises. Tiny quick-fire waves broke and slapped onto the mud, as if the river was applauding itself for successfully resuming rhythmic headway.

Looking onto the shoreline, for the Gironde is as much sea as river, and seeing all the flotsam and jetsam of low tide reminded Will of his childhood: walking various beaches' tide lines with his father, beach-combing, which they both loved, looking for the unexpected. He saw plenty of potential firewood piled up on the water mark which triggered memories of his parents and sister bonding most weekends, in Geneva, by going up into the pine-scented afforested Jura mountains and collecting branches and sticks for kindling which they would break up and neatly stack in the boot of their car to supplement the delivered logs. It was here, for a powerfully brief moment, Will actually felt as if he had his father back; it felt like another chance, a momentary reprieve before the melancholy of reality returned.

This is undoubtedly a special place, Will thought, looking up and around as he plodded on. *A very special place. Keep positive.* On the cliff face he saw evidence of troglodyte dwellings built into the walls which he'd missed on Google Earth. These ancient homes, thousands of years old, subsequently adopted by quarrymen, were carved into the actual rock. Doors and shuttered windows peered out at him from the cliff faces. He could see some were still inhabited today. One of the hobbit homes had smoke pluming out of chimneys carved within the cliffs, making the hilltops look alive, volcanically active.

Sadly eighty percent of all the wonderful properties Will passed here were empty, too, as was most of rural and coastal France, out of season. Actually, the whole nation looked like one big holiday destination shut up for winter. Will chuckled, thinking that the bulk of the country was mothballed for three quarters of the year, only coming alive over the summer and then shutting down again to hibernate for the rest of the year. He shook his head thinking just how incredible it was that this great republic and its local businesses could survive like that.

The lane abruptly snaked away from the river up onto the cliff tops and then wove through open countryside, planted with vines as far as the eye could see. Up here a bitter wind, unnoticed in the low riverside belt, became evident, making headway difficult and unpleasant. The three and a half hours Will had spent on tarmac were starting to take their toll on his feet and limbs, though this was certainly not the case for Nelson who maintained a relentless happy bob, pulling furiously on his lead.

Having forged on for another half an hour they reached an ominous-looking chateau which dominated a bluff. Will knew it was called Cheille. The mansion sat imperious, overlooking the mass of its monotone vineyards, commanding panoramic views across the Gironde estuary. This too was closed, shuttered up. He stopped to look around and could see the chateau had a perfect view of the river island, Bec D'Ambes. This was the point where the glorious rivers Garonne and Dordogne meet to become one, and form the actual Gironde. The island divided the two rivers.

Will stood on the road beneath the exposed chateau and took in the scene. The sun hadn't succeeded in winning the battle with the gloom. The day seemed determined to remain overcast, with only the occasional burst of sunlight. There was a wet, icy wind which bit sharply into everything. As Will ambled alone in the freezing shadows under the chateau's perimeter walls he was startled, and tensed up, hearing what could only be described as eerie screams or high-pitched, ghostly yells emanating from around the empty property. Perhaps it was merely echoes? He went to move. Then stopped and looked about anxiously. He had to reason. The sounds must be the sharp wind playing on the lifeless yew trees surrounding it - or could it be a desperate shanty performed by the most brutal ornate barbed ironwork fencing which wrapped around the main gates? Will shuddered goose bumps. In the shadows here, up on the bluff, he was chilled down to the marrow. This chateau was so out of keeping with all the delightful homes he had just walked past made out of the life-giving, gloriously bright, local stone. The contrast was shocking. He looked down at an unruffled Nelson, who, as always, just wanted to get on.

He'd read about the island of Bec D'Ambes, below the chateau, which had once been dominated by an extensive, sprawling oil refinery. It was one of Britain's first, and much needed successes early in the war: a positive newspaper headline. Will pictured Chateau Cheille, being in this position, having had the most startling view of the British bombardment of the plant. The chateau would have been centre stage for this bit of violent theatre, where the whole panorama in front of it must have been a phenomenal sight, lit up with a huge curtain of flames shooting up hundreds of feet into the air, erupting to generate intense waves of heat. Will craned his neck and could see there was some sort of a viewing platform attached to the property on top of the raised wall that hugged the road where he stood in its shadow.

This was where Bousquet held outdoor parties for his German SS cronies. They would celebrate seeing trade ships arriving from Japan mainly with much needed supplies for their industrial war effort. And indeed Bousquet himself had stood, alone, on that very balcony above, quaking in shock and awe, viewing the apocalyptic bombardment of the refinery in 1941.

Will looked beyond and could see, on the other bank of the river, Ile Cazeau. It was here, on the muddy banks of the river where two more of The Cockleshell marines died, shot by a German firing squad under Hitler's directive to 'annihilate to the last man' all commando's captured, contrary to *the* Geneva Conventions. As Will stood taking in the scene before him, and the stories it held, he looked up, disturbed by a helicopter buzzing overhead.

Although annoying on one hand, the throbbing rotors did complement the cold, post-apocalyptic scene of industrial dereliction on the island in front of him and the desolation around him, and impelled him to move again. The ominous growls of a helicopter never fails to induce unease. It's a big brother thing, an eye in the sky. In a war zone they are either coming to rescue or mow you down.

There was no reason for Will to stop here as the arrows on the map continued on, to enter the town of Bourg, which he could see on the horizon a few miles ahead. It was in Bourg, where he was heading, that his father had written 'Start'. So having taken a few photos Will set off again, down the hill in the dreary light surrounded on both sides by empty vineyards. Although most vines were completely bare, devoid of any foliage, some were, just, hanging onto a few bright, autumnal russet and yellow leaves.

The helicopter continued to hover and vibrate nearby and a little red car whizzed past as Will approached Bourg sitting on a rise above him. The rotors' throb was momentarily drowned out by screaming primary school children having a last rag in their playground as they waited to be collected by their parents.

Bourg, which he entered from below, was actually a fortified settlement clasped securely to rocks above a bend in the river, like a ship stranded on a hill. He hardly noticed the tops of masts poking up from the cluttered old wharf below. Tall amber, honey and yellow-coloured homes peeked above the ramparts, arched and galleried and bathed in a vague winter sun which rapidly faded through the giant avenue of plane trees. Due to Will's depleted stamina he decided to reconnoitre the town fully the following morning; he was too exhausted to look around now.

He found the B&B he had booked online quickly and immediately had a long bath. Then he settled down to relax and rest his aching bones and lay out to read more about The Cockleshell Heroes. But his empty, aching stomach soon forced him to venture out only an hour after arriving. He left Nelson sprawled, fully chillaxed on the bed: no interest in coming out at all.

Having walked around empty narrow streets and alleys and across the deserted market square, he stumbled into a large brasserie unexpectedly filled with people. He sat at the edge of the bar drinking a cocktail, a whiskey mac, to warm his cockles, absorbing the ambiance, listening to a rather good jazz pianist and chanteuse crooning to everything from Cole Porter to Frank Sinatra. Will knew his father, James, was a jazz man and wondered if he too had stumbled into this welcome oasis.

When Will had arrived in Bourg two hours previously, and the strawberry-coloured winter sun had finally melted into the sphere, only two people on the planet knew exactly where he was and both were now speaking about him.

'What? He didn't stop at the chateau?' said Henri Lafarge, questioning his henchman.

'No sir,' said Reynard.

'Where is he now?'

'He is staying in a local *chambre d'hôte* in Bourg.'

'Did we find out who he is?'

'Yes, monsieur, London called. Judging by his registration number he is actually called William Marshall, a British citizen and a journalist in the UK.'

'Marshall? Like a cowboy?' Henri questioned, his French not comprehending the Anglo Saxon name.

'*Oui*, sir, but this one, this cowboy - he can't run and he can't hide,' Reynard joked.

'Hungh, and a journalist, eh? Interesting. Okay, Renard, I am getting on my plane now and will be at the hotel in about two hours. Did you leave the maps at the reception and book the table?'

'Yes, the table is booked and I am going to your hotel now.'

Reynard still didn't have a clue what mission he was on or what its purpose was. He never asked questions, he just did what he was told. Perhaps this boy they were trailing was writing an article exposing their business - that must be it. Paff! Who knew? He was going to find out later by the sound of things. But Reynard wasn't too bothered; he liked his work and he was actually enjoying being in Bordeaux, away from home for a few days before Christmas. *Vive la différence*, he said to himself. Variety is the spice of life.

CHAPTER 10
THE TWISTED TALE

Reynard had waited for an uncomfortable age in a corner of the restaurant for his boss to arrive, sipping water. As soon as he saw his employer burst into the rustic La Tupina he edged out of the booth and stood up. He'd noticed his boss gesticulate through the glass entranceway, ordering his accompanying minder, Jose, to wait for him outside. Reynard studied him, albeit briefly, and was impressed; his superior still had a spritely, vital energy about him. He commanded respect. Fellow diners looked around as he swept past towards him.

Henri was a small compact man, immaculately groomed, with greased-back black hair with jet white fins of grey at the sides which seemed to be making him go just that little bit faster in his old age. His face was definitely scrunched up and rearranged like a back-street fighter's, with a half-flattened nose and tight lips. He was heavily tanned - Mediterranean, perhaps Italian to the casual observer – but in fact he was of Corsican origin like his lieutenant. He had the physique of Napoleon Bonaparte, a big man in a little man's body: something wild inside, taut and raw, ready to spring.

As Henri rapidly approached the booth he turned for Reynard to step forward and take his cream cashmere overcoat from his shoulders. And then, unburdened, he spun back around, demanding, 'Where are they, where are they? My maps?'

'Here, sir, they are here,' Reynard said, somewhat taken aback, and immediately leant across to hand over the satchel. 'I thought it was safer.'

'Do what I tell you, not what you think,' Henri said as he hurtled into the booth, and hurriedly took out one of the maps and began fingering and sniffing it lovingly. He looked up, wide-eyed. 'Yes, yes, my friend, this is them. This is them alright.' Perched on his banquette, he continued to caress the folded square of old paper. He looked at Reynard google-eyed, like someone under a spell. 'They are the same, I know it. At last,' he muttered, looking at, yet right through, the bemused Reynard.

If it was anyone else Reynard would have asked if they were unwell. 'The same, sir?' he enquired instead, raising his eyebrows. He didn't receive an answer.

The waitress appeared with menus. Henri looked down at what was handed to him blankly as if what was written was in hieroglyphs. Occasionally he'd giggle. Reynard looked at the menu politely, ignoring his the man in front of him. When the waitress reappeared Henri seemed to have recovered somewhat. When they'd ordered, both alike - La Tupina's famous crispy bacon entrée made with black pigs from the Pyrenees followed by locally preserved duck legs, and finishing with a tarte tatin and a bottle of 2000 Chateau Margaux - Henri sat back and composed himself.

'I am going to tell you a story of great importance to my family, Renard,' Henri declared. *Oh dear*, Reynard thought, *what is this going to be about?* 'This concerns wine, Renard, the life blood of France.' With that Henri let loose a baritone snigger at the memories the story was already triggering. Reynard sat impassively, bemused at his boss's continuing out-of-character behaviour.

Reynard only ever worked on a need to know basis and wasn't interested in anything but orders. He hoped his boss wasn't going to compromise him, tell him information he didn't want to know. Conversely, though, Henri was eager to share this story; he was positively desperate to tell someone about this long-guarded family secret. He couldn't contain it a moment longer. And he'd chosen the ever discreet Reynard as his victim. This was going to be an exorcism for Henri, something deeply cathartic. Just as laying out the maps and placing them in sequence put his mind in order, so talking about it to someone, at last, might ease his nerves. That's what he'd reasoned. Knowing something was the easy part; being able to talk about it, the hard bit. In no way did he want the story just to sound good; it had to make sense. He'd made the decision to ingratiate Reynard further into his world now that he was on the cusp of taking his business empire into greater realms. He either had to kill Reynard, for he knew too much, or bring him into the fold. He'd chosen the latter.

'I must start at the beginning,' Henri gushed. 'This is something you may have heard snippets about in the thirty years you have worked for me and my father but it all started back in the war years just before I was born. This is the story about the maps you have just given me. It began with my father when our business really took off during the war with the black market - trading this, stealing that - war was made for people like us. It was a great time, exciting and hugely profitable for organisations like ours. Everyone was poor but we were getting rich. My father, as you know, joined the maquis, the Resistance. The Allies needed us – we were the only ones who could get the things done that they couldn't do, and we had the balls to do them.' Henri gave a proud snigger. 'We didn't have to conform to soldiers' rules – oh shit, one moment.'

Their fabulous bottle of wine had arrived and was reverently uncorked by the sommelier. The two criminals sat silently enjoying the ceremony as all Frenchmen do. The ritual over, Henri Lafarge continued.

'So, my father spent a great deal of time in Paris towards the end of the war doing business and running resistance groups mainly up and down the railway networks from Marseille. Not only information, but sabotage, too, and he was in Paris when the Germans left. My father and his men worked closely with a strange Polish group of underground freedom fighters who were our direct link with the British Secret Service who all our information passed through. One guy in particular. The leader of this group - I remember his name because every ten years after the war my father, God rest his soul, made expensive searches for him and it plagued my father; he was called Tadenz Jekiel. I always remember his name because it sounds like Jekyll & Hyde. You know? The book. Ha, ha, you know?' A scrunched eyebrow response from Reynard. 'Anyway, we have never found this guy, I guess he died a long time ago now but he had been tracking Maurice Bousquet all through the war. Have you ever heard of Bousquet, Reynard?

'Yes, sir, I have – the infamous police chief and Nazi collaborator.'

'That's right, well done. One of the worst traitors France ever had during the war. Well, this Jekiel, the Pole, was given this pile of maps we have here, and my father others, as gifts for services to the state.' Henri hesitated for a moment and lifted his glass. 'Cheers, my friend, *santé*, you are the only person who knows this. No one else does – no one alive, anyway, ha, ha.

This was my father's and my secret.' Reynard's eyes narrowed momentarily as he lifted his glass. 'Now, come closer, my son. In each of these bundles of maps that subdivided France…' And then Henri sat back. 'Oh merde, shit,' he said. 'Renard, there are all these flies around me and one has landed in my damn wine. Call the waiter, would you?'

Reynard raised his arm. Immediately a waitress arrived at their side: a casually dressed, pretty half-caste girl of about twenty. '*Mademoiselle*,' Reynard said. 'We are sitting here surrounded by these little fruit flies and one has landed in my friend's wine.'

'Yes, unfortunately these flies are from the wine harvest, monsieur, I'm Sorry.'

Reynard noticed a tremor of anger from across the table, as faint as the whispered ripple from a distant earthquake. He could see the force of his boss's grip on the handle of his butter knife was so tight that his knuckles cracked and shone more brightly than his rings. And then quite suddenly Henri released his grip and Reynard felt the moment pass. 'No, madam,' Henri Lafarge interrupted, 'these flies are here because your establishment is filthy. This is a one and a half thousand Euro bottle of wine!' he hissed. 'This is unacceptable.' He began jabbing and trying to extract a dead fruit-fly from his wine glass with his stubby little fingers. His rings grated on the glass. He began to growl, loudly enough for every diner in earshot to hear.

'I will get the manager, monsieur.'

Without looking up Henri said, 'No. Just tell him Henri Lafarge is not happy and I will talk to him later.'

The waiter skulked off, and Henri leant forward and finally managed to fish the dead bug out with his stumpy index finger.

'Anyway, Renard, back to the maps… yes, the Pole, Jekiel, was given Bousquet's pile of maps and my father received the other two piles. Now, with the ones here.' He tapped the satchel. 'The whole collection totals some one hundred and twenty of them. The map of France is virtually complete. We have just about completed the map of France. There is only one piece missing. Are you following me, Renard?'

'Sort of, sir, yes, I think so,' Reynard stammered, trying to sound positive.

'Good, good. I still have them - the other eighty, they are my family's treasured heirlooms and here is what I want to tell you. Well, these maps have been the source of my family's prosperity for the past seventy years - our wealth, the foundation of our influence has all come from them, ever since they led my father to these people's stashes of goods that they'd plundered during the war. Art, my father never bothered much with; he did uncover plenty which he sold straight away knowing they'd be returned to their owners. But jewels, my friend - trunks of the stuff, I believe. And cases of wines of course. Huge amounts of it; great vintages he uncovered through the maps in these people's houses. One hoard my father dug up from the soil in a vegetable garden and the other had been stashed at the bottom of a pond sealed in barrels. Can you believe it?' Henri began to giggle moronically again. He couldn't believe he was actually talking about this. Reynard sat, disappointed. The enormous respect he'd had for the Lafarge family was rapidly evaporating. It was that easy, was it? No hard work. Just easy thieving from thieves. He prayed Henri Lafarge didn't notice the disdain in his eyes. 'Yes, sir, how incredible,' he managed to blurt.

'Yes it is, isn't it? Anyway amongst the eighty other maps there were only two that led to any treasures, Renard, only two with any markings, so we assumed that these three guys got together and made a pact of some sort that if one of them got caught the others would secure their stolen collections. We are not sure why, but the upshot was that my father, amongst other things, was able to build probably the best wine cellar in the whole of France, and possibly, the world through this. He drank a huge amount of it, as have I.' Henri's mind drifted. His voice softened. 'And I remember Papa saying when I was a young man, "This is one less bottle that the Germans never enjoyed, my son." That's funny, eh, Renard?'

'Yes, sir, most amusing.'

Their starter, fried eggs with grated truffle on bacon rashers, was eaten half unconsciously, as if over breakfast. Henri mopped up his runny yolk with a morsel of bread.

'Now listen, importantly, Renard, these wines have bought our organisation the influence and prestige we've depended on for the past seventy years,' continued Henri, chewing and then swallowing the last of his entree. 'They have bought us our security, believe me. When my father used to, or indeed I entertain politicians or cops they drank the best wine they have ever had. Moments they cherish all their lives and talk about, and talk about my family, Lafarge, in the same breath. We've handed out vintages so rare it is unbelievable. It has been a massively powerful tool in making our organisation what it is. They have protected us. I am sure you appreciate this.'

'Yes, sir, I do.'

'Excellent. Well, these maps are identical to the others.' Henri patted the satchel again. 'This story has been with me since I was a child, comrade, and here they are. This has been a lifelong dream for me. I have been waiting for this moment to arrive as Bousquet was the main wine connoisseur and most prolific thief of the lot. These maps must have been his. You see, he was born in Bourg and was Chief of Police here in

Bordeaux before the war so he had access to everything – hold on, here is our main course.'

The beautifully copper-coloured portions of duck breast were served on a bed of gleaming celeriac mash with some honey-glazed pears and apples on the side. The smell and look of this fabulous autumnal rustic dish, which complemented their wine perfectly, momentarily distracted Lafarge from continuing with his summary of the facts. After a few mouthfuls of the tender bird, pink in the middle, followed by a sip or two of their spiced ruby nectar, he resumed. 'Now, this leads me onto here, Bordeaux, because, as I just said, this is where Bousquet was born and brought up.' He was interrupted again by the waiter, a different one now, arriving to see how they were enjoying their supper; he was summarily brushed away. 'Okay, sorry, I am running away with myself; when this old antique dealer whom you got the maps from put some enquiries out on the internet as to the value of the maps one of my network of experts, thank God, picked up on it and so I sent you down here. God bless the internet. This is the first I have heard anything about this matter for maybe ten years. We have always held out that Bousquet's wines are out here somewhere as we would know if this important cellar was uncovered or put on the market. We know he stole maybe the best collections from, amongst others, the Pont d'Argent restaurant in Paris – well, what they couldn't hide, and from the Rothschild family both from their homes in Paris and their chateaus here, and many more great cellars; he even stole the best from the Élysée Palace, for Christ's sake! Great vintages like 1867 and 1855, oh, la-la. Also many magnums of Chateau d'Yquem we know he stole from 1921 that are impossibly hard to find, which I could sell for twenty-five thousand Euro per bottle all day long. Or ancient brandies that sell for seventy-five thousand per bottle – can you imagine?'

Reynard nodded, staring blankly between mouthfuls. He was perplexed; he couldn't fathom why he needed to know all this now after all this time in the dark.

'Anyhow, Bousquet got a big chunk of this collection, five thousand bottles from the president's palace alone, we understand. It just goes on and on. He stole large amounts of vintages so rare that there are none left. A huge amount was recovered from the Third Reich in Germany at the end of the war which everyone knows about, but Bousquet's, never; no one has seen it. We estimate he stashed away at least thirty thousand bottles which today may be worth anything upwards of two hundred million Euros. Believe me; it is incredible, just incredible. And to be honest, my friend, our organisation could do with them now, as I am not only very short on the best wines but I am even having to start to pay for the damn stuff now myself - can you believe that? What is the world coming to?'

Reynard looked up from his plate to see his boss quiver at the thought of paying for wine. He didn't just have to start paying for wines; Henri could no longer afford the bills his organisation incurred. He was on the verge of having to lay people off and sack house staff. He was actually on the cusp of financial collapse.

Henri had thought that by sharing this information he was initiating his lieutenant further into the heart of his organisation, but it was doing the opposite. *So, we are not that powerful anymore*? This is how Reynard interpreted what his boss was telling him, and that conclusion worried him. His security was being jeopardised. He didn't want to spend the rest of his days in prison. He was being told that the supreme confidence which he believed supported him was really a crumbling castle in the air.

'Okay, so on with the story, Renard. Bousquet bought himself that chateau out near Blaye, which you flew over today, when he was the police commissioner here in Bordeaux, before he went to Paris.'

'I see.'

The waitress arrived with their desserts: another golden delight, a tarte tatin. The classic French upside-down glazed apple tart, which was slightly burnt on the top and had a delicate, unctuous crème anglais oozing down the sides. Soothing hot cinnamon and honey vapours rose up tantalisingly. A few reverentially silent moments followed whilst the two Frenchmen bit into the light choux pastry, salivating over this traditional treat.

'Well, we've searched that wretched chateau many times. Firstly, immediately after the Germans left in 1945 a big team from the French government went there and couldn't find anything, and my father sent teams regularly after that, to be sure. The last time was a few years before my father died. It plagued him, knowing that the wines were still out there, and he wanted to find them before he died. It was one of his last wishes. Bousquet had no children, thank God above, and he left this chateau to his sister, a widow who was a teetotaller. I cannot believe she knew where the wines were. She was a churchgoer and I am sure she would have turned them over to the state. She died ten odd years ago, broke and alone, and left the chateau to a cat charity who sold it to a Swiss industrialist which piqued our interest again. I placed a local man, a carpenter, there for two years while the refurbishment was going on to let me know of any discoveries but *rien*. Nothing.' Both men simultaneously scraped their plates. 'I want a quick smoke and to call my wife. Why don't you come out too and call the guys in Bourg and check on our little rabbit, see if he's tucked up for the night? I'll finish when we come back.'

'Will do, sir, I'll make the call here. Jose will look after you.' They both got up. 'Thank you for the dinner, sir, it was *formidable*.'

'Okay, Renard. Order two brandies and coffees. I remember they have a sublime Remy Martin Black Pearl Louis X111, get two of those, I'll treat you.'

With that Henri Lafarge rushed out into the narrow cobbled alley in the walled old town where he made his call under the watchful eye of his minder who shuffled in the shadows to keep warm. Inside Reynard called a waiter and ordered the drinks and could see from the *carte*, the wine list, that the brandies were a staggering one thousand seven hundred and fifty Euro per glass. It had to be a misprint. *Better get what the boss ordered though*, Reynard decided, wishing he could pocket the money instead. He was shocked; it was equivalent to his monthly pay packet. He sat and made his call. The plates were cleared, then the coffee and doubloons were arranged as he waited for Henri Lafarge, who soon rushed back in and sat down.

'All okay, Renard?' he asked immediately.

'Yes, sir, quiet as a snail. He's in Bourg for the night. We are watching him.'

'Perfect, I want to know every little move he makes, where he goes, even what he looks at. Do you understand?'

'Yes, sir. Rest assured.'

'Every detail. So, where was I? Oh yes, the new owner of Bousquet's old chateau, the Swiss guy. Well, he spent a fortune knocking the place about and nothing was uncovered: of that I am one hundred percent sure. We looked into him in great detail. So I am convinced that the wines are not in the chateau or in his possession but I am sure they are around here somewhere. Buried somewhere like the others: I know it. Anyway, Bordeaux, like Paris, received orders from Berlin at the end of the German occupation to destroy everything - to blow up both - but the city's commanders disobeyed Hitler's orders and never did it for some reason. I believe they were persuaded by Brits not to. So all the buildings and monuments were saved. Bousquet would have known that so I am sure he would have hidden his wines somewhere out of the towns, in the countryside somewhere near. And that is it – here we are. I know no more. I know for sure the wine collection is still intact and out there somewhere,' Henri exclaimed, shaking his head and fluttering his stumpy fingers around like a kaleidoscope of butterflies. 'But where?' His left hand clenched and slammed down on the table which caused aftershocks in their brandy doubloons. His tone became venomous. 'All I can think of is this fucking Englishman, this toy cowboy, Marshall,' he jeered. 'God only knows where he got the maps from. He must have the marked map. He must. All the ones we have here, as we know, have no markings on them. There are only thirty-nine maps, too – one is missing. I now know it is of the area between Bourg and Blaye for certain. And why else is he here? This is all we can presume at the moment. He knows something. I know it. I just know it.' Henri's jaw shot forward and he stared blankly at Reynard across the table.

'Is it not simple, sir?' Reynard said, trying to calm his employer, 'Let's take him, and squeeze the information from him.'

After a blank moment, having been brought back to reality, Henri Lafarge continued: 'Easy my friend, easy, let's just see what tomorrow brings. Slowly, slowly catchie monkey.' He picked up his goblet, swirled the amber nectar around and then lifted the glass to his nose to inhale the ancient fumes. 'Cheers, Renard,' he said, brighter now. 'I trust you appreciate how vital and worthwhile it is for us to get these wines. I don't need to tell you the rewards you will receive too, do I?'

'No, sir, I understand perfectly,' the underling replied. However Reynard knew instinctively and through experience he'd be the recipient of mere scraps.

The two men toasted their new-found closeness and reclined in wonder. Henri was basking in the warm feelings that the sublime spirit was giving him, content at having aired such a secret and revelling in the excitement of the incredible quest he was engaged in, yet Reynard sat back with his thoughts continuing to question his boss's behaviour.

CHAPTER 11
HALF A MINUTE

In a dank Bourg the following morning Will stirred to find the soles of both feet slightly blistered. And as he dabbed the calluses on his sore feet with the cheap Metaxa brandy, he wavered, seriously toying with the idea of calling a cab and forgetting walking the return leg of his journey. But having had a good slug himself, he was out the door before he could change his mind.

It had rained overnight but it was another very cold morning. A dense freezing fog had descended, somehow suspending the desolate town in a sort of aspic. Bourg felt as if were held tight, frozen in time. The deserted, mist-shrouded narrow streets and alleys looked like something out of a period film set, prepared and waiting for the crew to arrive and arc lights to pop on. Tall higgledy-piggledy terraced houses, shuttered and still, their rooftops shrouded, reflected in mosaics on the wet cobbles under Will's feet. He couldn't imagine there were any people sleeping within the homes; the town felt like a totally empty studio's back-lot, and in desperate need of rejuvenating action. He reached the village square virtually on tip-toes, as if trespassing, and slowly walked around it, not wanting to wake the living or the…

He began taking photos. The square looked incredibly photogenic; dawn's faint blue hints began to merge with orange highlights from streetlamps over the vapour-covered piazza. Electric Christmas decorations, blue neon waves with white stars, hung about, suspended and shimmering in the freezing morning mist. A red-lit sign for 'The Cosy Café' flickered on and off in the haze, encapsulating the desolate atmosphere perfectly. Many of the old shops on the square were not only boarded up but some actually had upper windows bricked in too. It was as if some of them had been closed since as far back as the war, ancient signs dangling about to fall, flaked sign-writing all but disappeared. Will peered through one or two of the abandoned shop windows: an old emporium and an ancient hairdressing salon's deathly interiors were illuminated momentarily by the x-ray flashes from the café's sign. He must have taken thirty photos of this urban decay, this faded glamour. He couldn't get enough of its ancient, dream-like charm. The click of his camera's shutter seemed to skim across the cobbles and frack the dense layers of hush.

As he aimlessly wandered around Will began to focus his mind on exactly what or where that something was, here in the town, that the map led to. Why had the markings led here? This was the place on the map where his father had clearly written 'START' but the actual ring around the town was in the original pen, and seemed to signify that this was the place where whatever ended up, not started. Will reckoned this was the place where the route finished. If it wasn't the beginning then, surely, it must be the…

He pictured his father wandering around, staring up and into buildings just as he was, trying to find the meaning of the map. Will pictured his father wearing his big, heavy sheepskin coat. It was here he tried to actually get into his father's mind, to think what he was thinking, and mine what he knew - but he didn't really have a clue.

He'd got no vibes when he came out last night, either, and he was struggling to pick up on anything this morning. Why should he, though? He didn't know what on earth he was up to, let alone looking for. Then a sign of life appeared. A car, no, a 4x4, crept around the far end of the square in the foggy gloom. He saw it clearly, momentarily, under a street lamp. Its headlights glowed like beastly eyes in the murk as it slithered by. He laughed to himself, thinking he might as well stop the vehicle and ask the driver if they had any idea what on earth he was doing here! Then he thought he recognised the car from the day before and stepped back, into a denser shadow, but he wasn't sure in the wet haze. And then it was gone.

Will wandered around the empty market square one last time as the mist began to lift, taking the mystery with it. He was reluctant to leave the square. He didn't understand what his gut was telling him. Against his wishes he was propelled by an unknown force through a passageway and out on to the ramparts which overlooked the shrouded great river far below. It was Nelson, of course. He was cold, too, and had to keep moving; it was below zero. Nelson was pulling hard, eager to get on, have a run and warm up. They ambled along the castellated walls and crossed a lime-tree-lined car-park high above the river and around to the front of the town's main church, its steeple rising up into the swirling gloom alongside a large evergreen oak, piercing the sky like ancient weapons through stone. One a manmade spire, the other natural, both forging upwards, heavenwards, in parallel.

Another vehicle wafted past yet still no human stirred. No shops, cafes or even a bakery was opening. No bakery open in France! Will felt he was left with no other option but to head out of town. There was simply nothing more to see in the compact little market settlement. Nothing more to do. He had taken lots of photos but he couldn't just start poking around any further, and he didn't have a clue what to look for anyway, and so he decided to just get going and do the walk back to Blaye. This time in the direction his father had taken. If he loitered around much longer, he thought, he might get arrested.

He walked down an impressive, wide medieval stone staircase towards the river's edge before the sun was fully revealed. He knew it was up, trying to penetrate the all-encompassing mist which seemed to be endlessly erupting from the river itself, as if the very water was boiling.

The day before he'd spied a shortcut path that avoided the looping road which he would rejoin just past the spooky chateau. He could see this was a more direct route. It would save an hour of walking on tarmac and would be easier on his feet.

He released Nelson from his leash and scrambled up on top of an earth embankment: a massive flood-defence mound that had been built all along the river's edge to halt the tidal bore waves from breaching and flooding inland. Will had read about this feature when he'd done his research. Great bores swept up the Gironde at certain times of the lunar year. Freak waves.

He could hear the water slapping and glugging on the muddy bank below but couldn't see the actual river, the fog was that thick. All sounds of moving water he could hear entwined with the river as naturally as leaves do trees. Rivers, large and small, are one of those profound mysteries. They are always the same river yet always contain different water. They flow relentlessly day after day, week after week, year after year and century after century. Always there but never actually the same. They always contain a completely fresh body of water.

The cold impelled Will to move, so he strode out with purpose on the thin path atop the ridge as the mist's colour changed from midnight-blue to rust. He hesitated a moment having felt he should go back to Bourg and sniff around a bit more but something else kept him moving forward. He was tide-tugged. The lure of hubbub, of gurgling water like a boiling cauldron, somewhere further on, out in the river, kept him moving onward. He couldn't tell exactly where the noise was coming from or the cause of it as the river was still shrouded with this dense light-brown fog. He slowed and walked with trepidation, nearing the source of the liquid disturbance. The noise became louder and more intense, like a roar, as if the volume was going up. He stopped and, shivering, peered out into the gloom but couldn't see the race, the cause of this noise. He'd read about these races which were fast-moving tides forced together over random sandbanks which created a multitude of waves, converging together, ferociously smacking and clashing from every angle. He'd seen and heard a smaller one yesterday but this one was mega; as loud as storm waves lashing onto rocks. This was no singing sand; this was operatic.

It was one of these races, at the mouth of the Gironde, which had caused the death of four Cockleshell commandos at the very beginning of their mission. For sailors these are frightful sounds, imminent danger, a likely sinking, they suck you in, but Will, on solid ground, cautiously leant forward and peered into the impenetrable fog, listening to this ferocious show of nature being enacted out in the river. He desperately wanted to see it. He felt that whatever was going on out there would suddenly burst out any moment and engulf him. A tsunami. The noise was so distracting, mesmerising and unnerving that, as he strained to pierce the gloom and could only recognise the dying moon reflected in the water in front of him, he suddenly lost his footing on the slimy mud. As his feet skated out from under him, he managed, just, to jerk and twist his body around in mid-air to save himself from falling into the river. His feet flipped right up before him; he could actually see his boots in front of his eyes. And then he crashed down to the embankment, hard, on his back. His hat flew away, gone. He was decked on the lip of the ridge, floored and winded, but there was still momentum. The backward action of his sudden mid-air acrobatic movement propelled him off the ridge and over the other side. He slid at sledge-speed to the bottom of the embankment, fast and furiously, crumpling, stunned into a gluey mess at its base. He'd banged his head on the recoil too and lay dazed on the ground for a few moments, coming back to life with the help of Nelson, standing over him, licking his face and wagging his tail. Will managed to get to his knees and then fully upright. Breathing heavily, hands on knees, taking stock, he could see he was covered in a green slime from head to foot. Having done the obligatory swear and curse he began to laugh: half annoyed, half amused. *I'm now a proper Cockleshell commando, camouflaged, caked in mud*, he chuckled to himself. However, the instant the adrenalin wore off, he began shaking again, feeling more like a bloody loser than any sort of hero. He was frozen. He saw himself as everyone else would: an absolute fruit and nutcase out in the fields in mid-winter covered in gloop – what on earth was he doing? He laughed out loud thinking of himself passing himself by; *look at that bedraggled weirdo with the dog*, he'd surely say.

'Good morning sir, have I woken you?' said Reynard, sitting back in the front seat of a big black off-road Mercedes near Bourg.

'No, of course not, Renard, don't be stupid. What update? What is our man Marshall up to?'

'He's left Bourg, sir, three quarters of an hour ago. He just seemed to wander around the town for half an hour. We've now seen him cut out across the fields by the river towards Chateau Cheille. It is so misty out here we don't know exactly where he is or what he is up to but we presume he will come out onto the lane that runs along the river back towards Blaye soon enough. He's gone off piste, sir. I can call you back in an hour if you wish, sir?'

'No, Renard, talk to me. Presume is not a word I want to hear. Facts, Renard. Talk facts. What did he do, what did he look at in the town? I must know the details. The details, Renard, where is he now? Remember the other two caches were found buried. Get with it, man.'

'Yes, sir, of course. He took some photos of the town square, sir, and then stood looking at the church. That is all, sir.'

'Okay, okay. The square and the church. Right, okay. That was all?'

'Yes, sir, that was all.'

'Are you sure?'

'Positive, sir.'

'Right, call me as soon as he reappears and send two of the muppets with you out on foot after him – one from each end. Come on, wake up. The fields are important too. Yes, the stash must be down there. Why else is he there? Get after him, Renard, get after him.'

'I see, of course, sir, I'll do that…'

'Get onto it now, Renard, do not lose sight of him. Details Renard, details, it's all in the fucking details.'

Henri Lafarge hung up and rudely shoved his phone into the pocket of a dense fluffy white dressing gown, then stomped about his suite cursing himself for being hung-over again. He gunned towards a sumptuous breakfast tray loaded with silverware and pastries. Shaking, he poured himself a coffee and tore the wing off a croissant. He slurped and then guffawed, remembering the scene he'd caused when the bill had arrived the night before.

'Don't you know who I am,' he'd said to La Tupina's maître d'.

'Of course I do, sir,' the quivering man had replied.

'Well, *garçon*, I'm not paying this bill. D'you understand?'

'I see, sir, I am very sorry for the flies.'

'So you should be, it's revolting. Your establishment is filthy. And the duck was old. Sort it out.'

He'd sent Reynard outside while he settled the matter. He did this all the time these days. It amused him. Since he was strapped financially he'd order the best, find fault and then tell them to fuck themselves when the bill arrived. Somebody had to do it, he reasoned. Added to this paying for wines, quality wines, was an anathema to him now.

He chuckled again, his mood restored, as he slipped the receipt into the satchel: just over five thousand Euros he'd saved. He'd add that to his collection of unpaid bills. He got up and went across to the window. *Mon dieu, it's an awful day out there*, he said to himself, having looked out on the pea- soup fog shrouding Bordeaux as well. *I wonder what on earth he's up to, our mad Englishman*, he muttered to himself. He pulled his phone out and pressed a button.

'Good morning, sir.'

'When can we fly?' Henri barked at his captain.

'It is still thick fog out here, sir. The control tower has told me it will clear at midday. We can leave then.'

'Schedule us for 12:30. Anything different I will let you know.'

'Yes, sir.'

Unbeknown to Will two men were bearing down on him from either side as he set off again, cursing shortcuts. He could have been strolling along the road quite happily, looking around, and instead he was edging forward slowly, caked in mud and not enjoying any scenery at all. All he could do was focus on every little step he took. And, as a result of the slipping and sliding, the route he'd chosen was no quicker than the road, but he was committed to it now, so he just had to slither on.

Due to his fall Will's thought processing had altered. He was now far away from his father. His mind had tempered. A mental transmutation had occurred from the intense cold he'd felt before the fall immediately followed by a meteoric heating up and then a rapid cooling again. He had gone from frozen to boiling to frozen again within minutes. *My dog loves me*, he thought pathetically, as he stumbled on. *He was there for me but my father - where the hell was he when I fell? He was never there for me. Never helped me up.*

Will did have happy childhood memories but that was it. His teenage years and now his adulthood were bereft of paternal memories. There was a void, a blank, a big black hole. It wasn't as if his father had died decades before or had even been in prison, which would have been fine; there wouldn't be any excuses. All he really had were memories of anger and pain and rejection knowing his father was out there somewhere but ignoring him. Access to his father's door was always barred. He wasn't actually ever convinced his father had really loved him at all. In reality, he was still in shock about it now. Will was desperate for some sort of emotional closure. Where was the love? That was the question he asked himself. Where was the goddamn love? His mind hummed. He wanted one clear thought but found a swarm of them. He'd asked himself one question and got a hive full in return.

However, within moments, he felt content to be alone with his buzzing thoughts. He couldn't cope with being with any particular one. He certainly didn't want his father around any more. That was a definite. Although he'd wondered just an hour ago what his father might have been thinking about on the walk, now his father was the last person he wanted with him. He kicked himself for being such a sentimental git. *Grow up, Will, for fuck's sake. Stop being so flipping wet.*

He stopped for a moment and looked up and around and breathed deeply. *You have to be alone in life to watch clearly*, he said to himself. *No distractions. Life's loners are the best at it. That's what's made me a journalist and why I want to be a travel writer.* It was being a loner which had made him observant. *Concentrate, Will*, he said to himself.

He wasn't sure if he was starting to feel lonely or just a bit freer after the fall. And if he was feeling a little freer, what sort of freedom was it? Was it a house martin's or a hawk's? A buzzy flightiness or soaring control?

Going past great rows of stripped vines he looked up to the bluff and saw the Chateau Cheille in its entirety that he hadn't been able to see clearly the previous day, looming above him ominously in the swirling mist. *Oh, fuck, it's this place*, he cursed. The gloom in which the building sat reminded him of the prep school he'd been sent to in England, aged seven: a sort of mini Colditz. A grey lump with towers on either side. More grief-tossed memories grubbed his littered mind. His addled brain zigzagged over abandonment, twisted discipline, beatings, cold, bullying… *Get out*! a voice inside yelled.

He stomped towards the chateau thinking it resembled the sort of place where children were still being educated for a world long gone. An old place where formality and submission rule, with creaking floorboards and horrid matrons and middle-aged men with sadism on their minds, who creep and crawl around. The confused abandonment he'd felt, having been sent to school at such a young age, had torn his fragile psyche apart. He'd felt rejected and abandoned by his parents back then, too, and didn't know why. He'd forgotten about that. Will had been sent to an institution without his parents having given the slightest acknowledgement of his natural inclinations. 'What have I done wrong?' the seven-year- old Will would have asked himself, over and over again. 'I must be bad,' he'd have concluded. 'I must be wicked, why else would I be sent here? This is a punishment, not an education.' He stopped and looked up realising that is was in such a place, just like this, where he'd learnt never to complain or ask for love, for he'd get none back.

Will winced, the chateau's towers reminded him of being in his housemaster's office, growing up, pulling his shorts down to reveal his bare buttocks to the elderly monk. He'd have to bend over and place his hands on either arm of a brown leather armchair. Then he'd tense as the phutkish sound of the cane whistled down, shoulder height, from the black-robed holy man. Four or six times the shuddering strokes thwacked into his bare buttocks. He'd then pull his shorts up, turn and shake hands with his assailant. 'Thank you, sir,' he'd have to say before scampering out of the office, clutching his corrugated and bleeding arse. His housemaster was so accurate that Will would be left with either two backside ridges for a triviality or three for a misdemeanour. The monk'd had the knack to strike the exact spot twice.

Oops! A slip made Will revert to the here and now. He decided he'd just slide on past this eerie building today. Enough was enough, it wasn't doing him any good. It was depressing him. *Come on now, be realistic*, he began to reason. *Exactly what sort of friendship would you have expected to have had with your father? James was your father after all, not a friend.* In reality having the perfect relationship with a father is one of the rarest friendships on earth, and therefore virtually unattainable. *Get real.*

But the only bugbear Will still carried, he now deduced, was the distilled fact that his father had disregarded his duty to his children, and therefore he was actually guilty of child neglect. He had reneged on his duty to life, to nature. He had given his children no guidance whatsoever. If it weren't for the youthful hurt and confusion Will felt about being banished, rejected and abandoned, then all would have been fine. It wasn't just the injured child and youth that Will's heart went out to, it was to all the bruised children's hearts out there in the world that were going through the same thing.

Being educated from an early age, away from home, at best pisses children off. Young kids banished to boarding school often feel tormented by not being able to pass through Oedipal or Elektra yearnings as a natural consequence of paternal and maternal indifference. Development therefore becomes arrested.

The henchman behind Will was ploughing on, equidistant from him, through the grime, and the one in front had given up completely. *Zer' is no way I am ruining ma shoes for zis sheet,* he'd said to himself and had slunk back to the road as soon as the Mercedes which dropped him off had gone. He now sat smoking fags, shivering behind a hedge.

CHAPTER 12
ALL COMING CLEAR

James Marshall, eight years earlier, had done this very walk, albeit half-heartedly, avoiding all shortcuts. Amongst many other issues on his mind, he had indeed addressed the subject of his relationship with his children. It was more in tribute to Wiktor's last wishes to restore a relationship with his children when he'd given him the mesmeric maps than anything else. It was on this walk that James had concluded that he'd not just tried but had actually given his children everything he had wished for from life.

James was eleven years old when the Second World War ended. He'd been born and brought up in austere, tough times. His parents were both economic migrants to England in 1920's, after the First World War, albeit from Scotland and Wales. They'd come from extremely poor stock. To have reached a position to be able to privately educate his children was a huge achievement for James, something he was immensely proud of and which obviously engendered a great deal of pride for his parents, Will's grandparents, too. It was a huge combined family attainment. To have sent his children to public school was a pinnacle triumph for the bloodline: a goal, a mark of somehow arriving, getting somewhere at last. His children would move with the upper echelons of British society. The Marshalls were going up the social ladder, the greasy pole. And it was all thanks to him.

He'd had high hopes for his children but James had felt they'd grown snobbish, a cut above him and, sadly, the reality was he felt uneasy in their presence. He felt undermined by them somehow. He felt he wasn't good enough for his children - not rich enough for them, or whatever. He felt he embarrassed them. The reality was he was jealous of them. He'd never considered that, or the fact he was unwittingly selfish but, importantly for him, he'd given his offspring all that he'd ever wanted, or so he thought, he was sure of that. *And yes*, he'd admitted as he walked the pretty French country lane, *he could have done better by them.* Doesn't every parent feel they could have done a better job? *Everything's clear in hindsight*, he reasoned. *I may be a bit cold and indifferent*, he admitted, *but I never orphaned them or completely abandoned them.* He had done what he thought best at the time and didn't think being around was of much importance, frankly. *Let them get on with their own lives. Fun only starts when you get shot of your parents anyway, surely? And my work, my goddam work, doesn't help.* He knew he'd hurt his children. 'But,' he whispered to himself, 'I was a hurt child once too, remember.'

He determined many years ago that he was actually happier on his own. And that was that. *Tough*, he decided, *I can live with my bit of sadness, so can they. And, anyway… there's plenty of time.*

It was when James had reached the viewing point below Bousquet's chateau, and stood staring at the Gironde splayed out in splendour below, that he recalled the last time he'd seen Wiktor alive. The night he'd given him the maps.

'Come with me,' Wiktor had said. They both got up in unison from their sofas and walked to the window of his apartment, floor-to-ceiling panes that looked right across Geneva, over the darkened lake with the Jet d'Eau firing its plume high into the air, to the bright, moonlit snow-capped Alps just visible beyond, silhouetted and glistening on the far horizon. 'What I want you to do, James,' Wiktor continued, 'is to do something for yourself, not me. I want you to do something important for yourself and others dear to you.' He had turned and looked directly into James's eyes. He remembered Wiktor's powerful hand clutching his forearm, wrapping completely around its circumference. It was the solidity of the clasp which James remembered most; the vice-like grip froze him. 'Please, do not be offended, James, as a friend I can detect your distress and I want you to lighten your suffering. I can see that the loss of contact with your children is a burning torment for you, the guilt you carry, I share.' James stared out at the icy, sterile city, bamboozled. Wiktor was deadly serious. 'I want your assurance that you will make contact with your children, James. And stop this pain which is slowly destroying you, eating you up and clouding your judgement. You see the loss of my children...' With these last words Wiktor released James and looked around, turning James with him towards the shimmering framed photo, the elegant forefinger of his free hand pointing, 'This tragedy has been the greatest source of pain imaginable in my life, and the greatest kind of guilt imaginable for me. I caused their deaths, James. Remember. My actions killed my wife and children. And there is no way I can change that; there is nothing I can do or say to make good or bring my family back to life but you, James, you can, and you must.' His hand gripped James's arm again, this time even tighter, as he handed over the pile of maps.

The following week James had gone around to Wiktor's apartment to be greeted in the foyer by the concierge.

'Mr Foukes passed away in hospital two days ago, I am sorry to inform you, monsieur; he will be cremated in Petit Sacconex next Thursday at 2pm.'

James attended the depressing crematorium at the appointed time. The only other people in the small anonymous chapel, where the coffin was laid out, were the concierge on one side of the aisle and a young waiter from the Jolie Ville at the front on the other side. That was all. James thought how abysmal this was, how sad, that this man could be allowed to slip out of humanity utterly ignored. A man whose bravery in bringing the Enigma machine to Britain, which firmly resulted in changing the course of the war and saved millions of lives, and a man who had sacrificed his wife and children's lives in the process of that action, could be so unrecognised or acknowledged. It was criminal. It was shameful. The man deserved a state funeral. A series of tears ran down James's cheek, not for the loss of his friend, but an angry flow of tears at his absolute disgust for society and how unjust life could be. How atrociously unfair life often is, that brave men go unrecognised in this world. And scum are glorified. James knew the likelihood was that would be his fate, too: a pathetic lonely unappreciated end unless he adhered to Wiktor's last plea to him and resurrected his relationship with his children.

James shook his head as, beneath the chateau walls, he recalled Wiktor's fate. *Sod this for a game of soldiers*, he said to himself. And immediately turned back towards Bourg and gave up on his walk. It was all too much for him.

Will was out on solid ground again. As he stood stomping his boots to free them from mud, he spotted a direct path which cut out a U-bend on the road below. This little deviation he took enabled him to avoid the lazy henchman chain-smoking cigarettes just off the road.

He joined the lane bordered with beautiful home after beautiful home that he'd gazed at enviously the day before but today they were all hidden from the world by the mist in their pocket Shangri-la.

It was still bitterly cold on the Corniche but it was calmer, the wind had ceased. Will was in the perfect state to fully empathise with the few surviving Cockleshell raiders who had dumped their canoes very near to where he walked after their successful sabotage of six vessels in Bordeaux harbour. The four men had then walked, ill-equipped, cold and desperately hungry, to the safety of the French Resistance some two hundred miles inland in freezing conditions like today - no doubt caked in mud too.

Will was a complete mess and was exhausted but he staggered onwards. With chin upwards and a steely determination he came upon the skeleton of the MV Fujiyama he'd seen the day before, fully revealed in the lower tide, sitting proudly, ghostlike, on its mudflat stage out in the river. Will stopped, resting the weight of his torso with his hands on a low wall, and stared at its rusting frame reflected on the river's surface like an ancient mirror's frayed patina. The hulk looked as black as charcoal at first sight and then, before Will's unmoving eyes, like a magic trick, a shaft of muted gold sunlight ruptured the swirling mist to transform the hulk's colour into all shades of greens and coppery browns. Algae had created a range of tones and textures on the rusting iron. The light and shade revealed the framework of the old ship's decomposing superstructure beautifully. It became three-dimensional.

As fast-moving tides began to slither around and overwhelm the hulk, Will's thoughts shifted to wondering where this river's conflict began. Was it in the clear mountain springs, at its source, or was it within the raging vast salty Atlantic Ocean beyond the Gironde's mouth? Whose fault was it, this persistent clash, and who would win this unconquerable, twice daily tidal battle? This mighty force of a river which at high tide, allowed the saline invader to dominate, swelled to full power. Then, when the Gironde reached the highest point in its tidal reach, it finally loosened its brackish strength, gave up, and began the retreat back to low tide where the opposite happened and fresh, pulsing, sweet, river-water prevailed. It was a daily Goliath and David battle.

As Will continued to gaze at the stricken ship, mesmerised, it began to disappear into the fast-rising, swirling current. He was seeing its transformation from darkness into shimmering light and depth before his eyes and something in his mind just clicked. The truth tripped through with the light and switched him on. A subtle yet powerful transmutation was occurring right before and inside of him. Life itself suddenly became clear. It was an epiphany. A rare insight. Will had simply shifted a gear, altered his perspective to see everything he'd thought about, which had been dragging him down, from a fresh angle. He stood upright, turned his back on the river and perched down again onto the sea wall. His head drooped and began to rock from side to side as he absorbed the shocking truth.

It wasn't only the combination of his fall an hour before and being frozen and exhausted, but it was the effect created by the hypnotic sight of the unmoving ship's mutation which had deepened Will's inner appreciation of life.

From this fresh outlook he immediately understood his lack of a long-term relationship with his father was simply a shame, that was all it was, it was just a shame. It was a private sorrow. It was a small issue if he wanted it to be. It didn't have to be a life-breaker. It was just one of those things in life which makes you slightly melancholic, that was all. It needn't be a festering open wound. *Hey, you can't have it all,* he shrugged. *Life's not a smooth passage, a waltz in the park, one long skip across daisy fields. And we shouldn't expect it to be either. Okay, I've suffered a bit of parental neglect, and hardly saw my father for ten years but in the end... whatever... no big deal, get over it.* So many people in this world had it so much worse than he did, Will realised. It didn't really matter if he didn't want it to. As simple as that. He could dwell on it as long as he liked, feeling sorry for himself, playing a poor-me card but that wouldn't change a thing. And anyway, it was all in the past now, fast becoming just water... under the bridge.

Will looked up, momentarily disturbed from his thoughts by a vehicle coming out of the mist and passing him by at an unnaturally slow speed. His eyes followed the now familiar 4x4 crawling by, this time going the other way. He could see it was the same two dark aggressive-looking individuals peering out at him. Who the fuck are you? Will's glare back said to them. This was the third or fourth time he'd seen them. What the hell did they want? Once they were out of sight, having disappeared into a wall of mist, leaving him alone again on the shrouded, deserted lane, he began to feel uncomfortable. Isolated. It was quiet and ghostly, he was weary and he didn't know what he was doing there anymore. Will was so tired, though, so cold and wrapped up in his own world, that he really didn't care who or what they were. Surely they didn't want to rob him? Right then Will simply didn't have the energy to be concerned about them.

He had walked for three and a half hours with sore feet in freezing fog, had had a fall and now, at his wits' end, he reached the conclusion that he'd achieved exactly what he set out to do. He didn't need any intrusion on that. Alone on a byway in rural France on a harsh winter's day, ragged and tired, caked in slime, William Marshall finally grew up. Through physical and mental exhaustion he'd arrived at some sort of a safe space within himself that he could happily live ever after with. An inner warmth zone. It was really an outlook in life that he'd found, a point of view, which reconciled his personal sorrows with his aspirations. He felt liberated, hang-up-free at last. Standing there, lost and alone, he knew he'd somehow conquered his demons. Come to terms with himself. Will was sure he'd be able to move forward, easier now, unencumbered by baggage issues. After a massive sigh, he craned his neck back and stared upwards trying to pierce the glowing mist but only felt Nelson jerk hard on his leash, which completely off- balanced him and brought him right back down to earth. He nearly fell again. Nelson was urging his master to just... get on.

That sharp tug back to reality was a wake-up-call moment. Will realised he'd mentally accomplished his mission. *Come on, that's it*, he said to himself. There would be no feelings of guilt or failure at not doing the final two hours along the main road. It would be plain stupid in these conditions. It'd be too dangerous, and Will felt there was nothing whatsoever to be achieved by it anyway. There'd be nothing new to see. Why on earth tramp along a main road for no reason? It was over.

He turned and put his hands on the low wall to look at the slow-moving Gironde close up one last time. It was almost black in the shadows beneath him: perhaps this was where his father's life had been lived? It might have been like a river always running in the shadows, never coming out into the light. A chill, a fear, gripped Will that his life might run on in darkness too. His nails scratched the stone.

And then, all of a sudden, a great new love for his father welled up and rose up out of the very same shadows and swept over him and, immediately, he felt euphoric, lifted up. He felt his father's arms wrap around him. Will knew this was the feeling. The feeling he'd been searching for. And that feeling was the knowledge that forgiveness is the only way to live life freely, without bitterness. Will now felt that dream come true. There on the banks of the great river, which symbolised the great march of life, he forgave his father. Reaching this point was what he'd always been striving for. Will continued to stare at the strange, mysterious river, sweeping forward. The body of water, which had given him the answer he had struggled to even know what the question was, pulsed on by regardless. He stood, head bowed for a long moment, before standing upright, turning and walking away.

He fast-marched up the lane for twenty minutes and, near the junction with the main road, just before Roque de Thau, he saw the small roadside restaurant which had been closed when he'd passed the morning before. The bedraggled tramp and his mutt stumbled into the hostelry, sank onto a chair, ordered a beer and asked if the staff could call him a cab. The attractive waitress, rushing to get ready for the lunchtime service, kept him entertained but she couldn't help much; she was too busy setting up for lunch. She only had time to give him the phone book, and asked him to do it himself; she was sorry.

Meanwhile on the other side of the Gironde Henri Lafarge's Cessna Citation private jet was still grounded at Bordeaux's

Merignac airport because of the fog which was, however, clearing fast. He sat onboard, sunk into a plush white leather armchair, waiting for immediate departure, his feet up on the seat opposite. He was half an hour by car from where Will sat slumped uncomfortably in the restaurant, caked in mud. Reynard called him for the third time that morning.

'Sir, it's me again.'

'Yes, yes where is he now?' Lafarge said gruffly.

'He's called into a restaurant along the lane that he walked up yesterday. Apparently he looks a mess, as if he had a fall or something – he's covered in mud. I am assuming he is going to have some lunch and then walk the remaining two hours back to his car in Blaye.'

'Covered in mud, eh! *Merde*. Come on, Renard, think man, think, you bloody idiot. Maybe he was digging?'

Reynard's head recoiled at his boss's unfamiliar choice of wording.

Henri continued. 'Shit, okay. Do we know what on earth he did on the riverside?'

'No, sir, neither men saw anything. It was foggy but he must have kept moving. He didn't have time to do anything. And he has no tools.'

'*Merde*! Well, we'll just have to keep following him. And then next we have to get into his car. We must get this final map.'

'That's not going to be straightforward, sir, his car is parked outside a florist, right by a hotel window, and it's on a busy road, with lots of people and cars passing – it's going to be difficult.'

'Well, we need to search him and his car, now. We need to see if he has the map with him as soon as possible, as a matter of urgency. There is nothing else to do.' After a slight pause Henri Lafarge changed his mind. 'Just wait and see what he does when he leaves the restaurant. Call me back. We won't be leaving for a while yet.' And then he changed his mind yet again. 'Actually, Renard, find the right time soon and just fucking do it. Perhaps on this busy road get one of the cars to run him off the carriageway, knock him down, get him unconscious and go through what he has on him, get him to hospital and keep the cops away from his car and go through that tonight if you don't find it on him.'

'Yes sir, *bon idée*. I will implement that now. One of the team is still out there walking the route he did off the road, as you suggested. I will recall them and make the plan.'

'Do it. Ah, I think we are actually going to take off now. It has suddenly cleared. So, I will be back in Marseille within a couple of hours; phone me then. Get this map, Renard. Whatever it takes. If you have to snuff him so be it, just do it.'

'Will do, sir, I will. Safe journey.' He hung up and immediately auto-dialled another number. 'Pierre? It's Reynard.'

'*Oui, monsieur.*'

'Get back to your car now. As quickly as possible. I am going to get you to meet up with Philippe and Jean near Roque de Thau and you are going to knock the rabbit down on the last stretch of road and search him. This is what the boss wants. They are now finding a good place on the route to execute this. So liaise with them now. It's the map we are after, nothing more. Good luck.'

'Yes sir. What about the dog?'

'*Encouler le chien*. Fuck the dog. Kill the fucking thing if you have to. Kill the rabbit too, if you have to. I have stressed the importance of this map to you. Do your job.' Reynard had viciously barked the order in his hotel room in Bordeaux and now, psyched-up, he looked around the empty space furtively hoping no one had heard his holler through the wafer-thin walls.

'Sorry, sir, yes of course. I am onto it now,' Reynard's junior, the Mediterranean mobster, had mumbled to his superior, slipping in the mud in his Gucci loafers out in a misty creek completely out of his comfort zone and in completely unsuitable clothing.

Having fumbled through the phone book and managed to find the two local cabbies and established they were both busy and unable to come out, Will huffed and puffed and cursed the world at large out loud. But as luck would have it a rotund jolly fellow, the manager, appeared from a back room and said he would give Will a lift. No worries. Well, well, well how nice was that? Certainly an offer he couldn't refuse. It was amazing who was there in life when you needed them.

Within fifteen minutes Will and Nelson were back beside their own car in Blaye. It wasn't even one o'clock and Will was no longer dog-tired but he was certainly weary, achy and sore, so he decided to drive the car for a few hours at least and either stop somewhere between here and where he was heading - St Malo, which was six hours away - or go the whole way and have a decent fish dinner there; he'd see how he got on. While he warmed the car up and changed his shoes he gave Sophie a call.

'Sophie, hi hon it's me. How's it going?'

'Fine, me dear, ploughing through the marking, and you? You sound well.'

'Well, I'm done. I've done it, yee ha; well, all except the last two hours where we would have been walking alongside a busy road which would have been depressing and frankly dangerous too. It's misty as hell here,' Will exclaimed happily.

'Well done, my love, excellent news. Quite an achievement. Can't wait to hear all about it. How's our little boy?'

'He's absolutely fine. He looks as if he'd like to do it all again, the little mucker.'

'Ah, bless. Where are you off to now?'

'Well, I'm just going to boot off and see where I get to but I'd really like to get up to St Malo this evening if poss. The ferry doesn't leave until 10am tomorrow so I can do a few more hours driving in the morning if I have to stop somewhere. Anyway, I'll phone you later and let you know where I am.' BASH. They were rudely interrupted by an incredibly loud bang. Nelson let out a fearful yelp. 'Bloody hell, sorry Soph, some fucker's just hit me.'

'Are you okay?'

'Yeah, we're fine. They just hit the wing mirror. Bloody moron. And they've driven off. Look, hon, I better get on. I'll buzz you in a bit.'

'Take care,' Sophie managed to say before Will clicked off.

It was that wretched black 4x4 with the two ugly hoodlums in it that seemed to have been following me since I got here, he said to himself, *I'm sure it was. I'm going to get going, I'm feeling a bit freaked out.*

With that Will had a quick peep at the road map to check his route back to the motorway and headed straight out of his parking space as quickly as possible. With his wing mirror dangling off and Nelson riding shotgun, two paws perched on the central arm rest between the two front seats and his two feet on the rear seats, Will roared off. He negotiated Blaye's town centre well, swinging his car through the one-way system, and was soon out on a long straight road that led up to the A10 motorway which in turn headed up towards La Rochelle. He went at some speed now, making slightly hairy overtaking manoeuvres, regularly keeping an eye in his rear-view mirror to see if someone else was doing the same moves to keep up. Just before he stopped at the barrier to get his ticket to enter the paying motorway all seemed quiet behind him. He had a wave of anxiety at this point as, being in a right-hand drive car in a left- hand drive country, he had to get out, go right around the outside of the car and get the ticket rather than just lean out of the window. This he did as fast as he could and then jumped back in and sped off up the empty motorway. As most of the houses in rural France were empty for such a long period of the year so the motorways were virtually empty, too. It was ghostlike. He was the only car on the road.

'What? Repeat that for me, Philippe,' Reynard hissed venomously into his phone, getting up rapidly off his bed. He strode across to the window, wiping his forehead with his free hand.

'He suddenly appeared out of the restaurant with someone, sir, got into his car and drove back to Blaye,' his lieutenant was saying in mock amazement. 'He then got into his own car and drove off before we could get back. The brothers, though, did get back and tried to smash into his car to get him out but they only hit his wing mirror and all that did was make him just drive off - he didn't even get out. We are following him with the tracker. The brothers too. He is going out towards the motorway.'

'*Zut alors*, get after him. Ram him off the road if you have to. Do whatever it takes. Just stop him,' Reynard demanded.

'Yes, sir, of course,' the underling replied professionally, though with the slight ring of doubt in his voice. He wondered privately what on earth they were all doing taking this muddy boffin on a walk with his dog so seriously for.

CHAPTER 13
RUN RABBIT RUN

Will put his foot right to the floor, booting his old Audi aggressively onwards. He was clocking ninety miles an hour, hammering along the empty auto-route and thoroughly enjoying the sensation of being chased. He clenched the steering-wheel as it began to judder. The urgency of being stalked by a predator impelled him forward regardless; keeping him wide-eyed and fully alert. His eyes flashed from rear-view mirror to side left, side right and dead ahead. And then, as the adrenalin eased, and the monotony of tarmac took its toll, Will began to tire. He forced himself to concentrate on his breathing, to regulate his body's motions into some sort of order, to calm down and reign himself in. And as he eased, a deflated Will rationalised that it must have just been his imagination running away with him. He asked himself truthfully, how and why there could be anyone chasing him: it was too preposterous. It must have been a different black 4x4, surely? And even if it was the same one he must have looked a bit odd out on the lanes, after all. A stranger out walking in mid- winter, in freezing conditions, caked in mud? It'd be perfectly natural for the locals to think he was up to no good and to begin snooping around keeping an eye on him. With all the empty houses he could easily have been seen as a scouting burglar.

With that in mind Will put some music on, eased up to top legal speed limits and concentrated on the dull road ahead.

For some odd reason, superstition perhaps or just another cathartic gesture, Will reached across to the passenger seat with his left hand and scrunched up the local map onto which he had carefully copied the markings onto from his father's original, stashed back at home. And, having checked that the road ahead and behind were clear, Will unwound his window halfway, let the map flap loudly beside his ear and then released it. He saw it flutter down the road in the rear-view mirror and then it flared up into the air on an updraft one last time before finally settling on the verge. He sped on and disappeared over a rise in the road. *That's that over with*, he said to himself.

After an hour Will swung into a service station and filled up the tank. He paid, grabbing a sandwich and Coke on the way to the counter, went to the toilet, splashed his face with cold water and was back out on the road in no time. On the slipway leading to the carriageway there was no possible way he could have noticed a small red hatchback and a black 4x4 Mercedes pull into the services behind him.

Will had soon passed La Rochelle and then he swung around the Nantes ring-road where he thought he might stop for the night, as he was feeling a bit weary. But it was only three o'clock and he forced himself to keep going. Then he thought that perhaps he'd stop at Rennes, but by the time he got there, an hour and a half later, he decided, sod it, he would just do the last hour or so up to St Malo and get up to the sea. So having stopped one last time for fuel and a sugar-laden double espresso Will was soon pulling into the ancient French coastal stronghold at six o'clock that evening, chuffed that he'd made such good time.

The old city of St Malo sits on a promontory, a jagged edge, jutting into the English Channel. It is completely walled-in, safe against any invasion and the crashing waves which thrash against the high city walls on three sides. However charming it may look on a sunny day, the city which greeted Will on this bleak winter's one had an incredibly austere and imposing atmosphere. He could see dirt-grey ten-storey tenement buildings rising up over the wave-battered stone battlements with a few church spires reaching out into the low-clouded sky. St Malo had been built as a huge military fortress, a stronghold against attack from the sea, its origins far removed from the popular tourist destination it is today. If there was an image for the perfect setting for the French Revolution, Will thought as he neared, it had to be St Malo. He pictured ragged peasants waving flags furiously on the ramparts as they shouted '*Vive la Revolution*' or banner-wielding crowds charging through the network of alleys within, yelling '*Liberty, Equality, Brotherhood*'.

The sky had darkened when Will drove through one of the ancient arches into the cobbled warren of narrow streets within the citadel. It must have been quite a metropolis back in the day, teeming with people in its tall tenement homes. In its heyday the buildings must have been the high-rise, hi-tech, chi-chi tower blocks of the eighteenth century. Its clean and up-together feel today, full of hotels, restaurants, shops and bars, quaintly disguised that St Malo was also a pirate haven.

Will parked up on a meter as soon as he could and, having grabbed the bundle of cash from his bag in the boot, he and Nelson set off on foot to find a decent place to stay for the night. The first hotel they came to did have a free room but they had only one left and Will felt it was a bit too expensive for him. Having told the receptionist to hold it for half an hour he set off again to see what else he could find. He soon discovered there was a conference going on in the Salle des Expositions so the town, for this time of year, was incredibly busy. Having wandered into a few other hotels to find out they were all fully booked he went back to the original hotel thinking to hell with it… he'd treat himself… and Nelson, too, to a comfortable night. The hotel had its own covered car-park opposite, which was a large barn, originally a stable-block or sail-loft jam-packed with cars. Having negotiated his car carefully inside, removed his bags, squeezed out, and left the car safely locked in the garage, he went up to his room right at the top of the building, five storeys up. It was more of a small suite with an internal corridor and a separate bathroom.

As he was settling in, unpacking and running a bath, the black Mercedes 4x4 and small hatchback were pulling into the town walls beneath him and, having cruised around, they'd honed right in on Will and were now parked up on the street below; one of the cars even took the bay Will had left a few minutes before.

'Sir, *c'est moi*, Philippe.'

'Yes, where are you now?' Reynard wearily said into his mobile phone, having realised an hour ago, as it started to get dark, that there was no chance of being able to take Will off the motorway. The 4x4 could easily have got ahead of Will and slowed him down but in order to execute the manoeuvre safely, so as to make the car stop and not spin off into a potential fireball, they would have needed both cars, and the little hatchback just wasn't up to it. Reynard was still in his socks in the hotel room in Bordeaux having only been out once since he'd got back from Bourg that morning. He'd had a quick stroll and picked up a croque monsieur from a local bakery.

'We are in St Malo, sir; we are all together, both cars parked up.'

'Christ almighty, in that old citadel? Right up there? Where is the rabbit? Quickly.'

'Yes, sir, in the walls. His car is very nearby, we can tell, but it is not on the street. We think he has checked into the hotel we are outside of and put his car in their garage. What do you want us to do?'

'What is the name of the hotel? I'll find out if he is there.'

'The Ajoncs d'Or, sir.'

'Spell that for me. Okay. Now get out and look around and see if you can locate his car, but don't go doing anything stupid – do you hear me?'

'Yes, sir.'

'Good, I'll call you back in a minute.'

Reynard rushed to get the phone number of the hotel through directory enquiries and immediately called the reception. His voice was the epitome of reptilian charm. 'Bon soir, monsieur, how are we this splendid evening?' he said. 'That's fantastic. Super. I am just wondering if, by any chance, you have a William Marshall staying with you this evening? I am an old friend of his.'

'*Oui, monsieur*, we do,' the proprietor replied. 'Can I put you though to his room?'

'No, no thank you. That is kind. I don't want to disturb him; he has had a very long drive today. I was simply checking to see that he'd arrived safely. We are meeting later,' Reynard said. 'There is no need to leave him a message. Many thanks. Oh, one last thing; what room is he in? I may pop over and pick him up.'

'He is in Room 508, sir.'

'Ah super, thank you. You are so kind. Oh, and, do you by any chance have any available rooms tonight? No? Oh, *quel dommage*. Very well, have a good night.' As he was making the call to the hotel Reynard could see, on his mobile screen, his boss trying to call him. He had avoided calling Henri

Lafarge for the past few hours as he had nothing concrete to tell him. This wasn't going to be an easy call. Not only was his employer a man who expected immediate results but he seemed completely on edge over this spurious affair, as if his life depended on it. Henri Lafarge had never sworn at his lieutenant before, as he had done earlier. Reynard was still utterly bemused about the story he'd heard the night before and hadn't been able to fully assimilate it yet. He'd been thinking about it all day. The overwhelming impression he'd been left with was the Lafarge magic aura had dimmed. The respect and high regard he'd had for his boss was fading. This was not going to be an easy call; he had to turn it around.

'Sir, good evening, Reynard here.'

'Good evening, Renard,' Henri Lafarge said gruffly. 'Give me the good news then?' he asked, somewhat sarcastically.

'The guys couldn't do anything on the motorway, I'm afraid to report, sir. The smaller car with the tracker could barely keep up; we didn't know where and when he was going to stop and he just kept going. No stops to speak of at all, only fuel. He is now in a hotel in St Malo. Both cars and all four men are up there too,' Reynard said, calmly but without taking breath, thinking it best just to keep talking facts, to sound calm and in control and just try to keep his volatile boss from exploding.

'Oh, *mon Dieu*, in St Malo – Brittany! What the hell is he up to now?' the older man exclaimed.

'Well, I assume he is aiming to get the ferry back to England tomorrow, sir.'

'Oh yes, of course he is. Yes, yes. Okay, what do we do now?' Henri Lafarge replied, thinking out loud. Then he continued, positively. 'We must search his stuff tonight, Renard. It has to be tonight.'

'We will, sir, we will execute your order as soon as we can, do not worry. Also we will not receive the tracking signal in the UK, you are aware of that? The frequencies are different. However, we know where he lives in the UK. And for now we know what room he is in but there are no other available rooms for us, so it may be impossible to get into the room tonight. We will try and search the car too but we think it is locked in a garage. Alternatively, I thought we could try something on the ferry; that may well be easier. So, I will book one of the cars to go over, sir, just in case. We may, I am sorry to say, sir, have to get the English guys on the case too. Shall I prime them? Also he may just not have anything on him. And what we don't want is Pierre and the other mutt-heads killing him, getting arrested or doing something stupid. We need him alive for now, don't we? What do you think, sir?'

After a moments silence Henri Lafarge sighed, acquiesced and agreed with his right-hand man. 'Yes, okay, you are right. Quite correct. Get the boys to do what they can tonight but, as you say, tell them not to do anything stupid. We don't want to scare him either so just tell them to take it easy now. No rush. You're right, the cowboy, this Marshall, is the key. If we just stay near him he will lead us to what we want sooner or later. So yes, book one of the cars, the one with the receiver, on the ferry and tell the other two to come back here to Marseille when the boat leaves. In fact, send them home now. I will call the UK guys now and get them prepared. Leave that to me. But tell me, Renard, how long does the battery on the tracker last and what sort of range does it cover?' Henri's mind had engaged. This is what he was good at, strategic thinking and organisational capability.

'I am not too sure. We only use them for a week or two usually. I will find out and let you know.'

'I want to know that the moment he sets foot in France again we will be onto him. Look, I am entertaining tonight. Call me if there is anything major to report, otherwise phone me first thing tomorrow, okay?'

'Yes sir, thank you, I will. Good night.'

Reynard was pleased with the call, and amazed that Henri Lafarge had mellowed somewhat and was not putting him and his men under unnecessary pressure. He seemed to have resumed his composure.

Henri Lafarge had spoken standing, staring out through a tall set of French doors in the first-floor lounge of his palatial family home, a huge sprawling Belle Époque villa perched high above the Mediterranean. Dressed for dinner, he'd watched the sun melt into the sea as he talked to Reynard and only turned back to the room when the strawberry-coloured orb had dissolved completely beneath the broken line of waves on the horizon. He walked slowly across the intricate parquet floor, slipping his mobile phone into his dinner jacket pocket as he went; snatching up the satchel from an armchair, he stopped for a moment to gaze at the wonderful objets d'art around him - all reminders of his father. The dated splendour of the room never ceased to fill him with awe; it had been designed to do just this. The room was a catalogue of rare materials: precious woods, metals, stuffs and stones. It'd be hard to picture anything more ornate. Hard to dream of so much glass and glitz, so much velvet and plush, so much rosewood, marble and malachite. But what truly wowed the rare guest permitted to enter this room was the misguided cost of everything, the lack of respect for morals and money. The room was more of a shrine to his father's generation than anything else.

At that moment, as his head turned, Henri pictured himself scampering around this room as a young boy; and the memory triggered reminders that the quest for Bousquet's wines had been lifelong. It was now, aged nearly seventy, that Henri realised it was right here in this room where it had all begun. He was absolutely positive he was finally close to making his oldest childhood dream become a reality.

There's no need to rush now, he said to himself. And saying that immediately invoked a reminder of one of his father's oldest sayings which he had not thought of for many years: 'Act in haste, my son, repent at your leisure.' This made Henri stop, stand still and, rather than simply look around, he began to gaze about with a deeper regard. His vain consciousness actually caressed the dated antiques and furniture in this grand room which he had, only two weeks before, contemplated selling. His eyes settled on the blue and silver Sevres porcelain urns his father had collected, lit up brilliantly in floor-to-ceiling glass cabinets on either side of the marble fireplace. He was under the deluded impression that they contrasted beautifully with the fake Blue period Picasso hanging between them. I am a lucky man, he thought. And then a breath of sadness wafted over him: he didn't have a son to pass all this onto. He did though have three beautiful daughters, and he could hear them downstairs, waiting excitedly to greet their father's return.

Before he left the salon to join them he locked the door as quietly as he could, coughing to mask the bolt clicking shut and pulled a key from around his neck. Nimbly he went across to a beautifully lacquered Louis XIV armoire at the far end of the room. The key released a secret compartment into which he placed the thirty-nine new maps he had just acquired. He placed the new pile alongside the other eighty identical ones which were neatly stacked in their two original piles. All three were tied up with matching straps; he touched the red ribbons lovingly, each in turn, amazed they had all remained intact, holding together their original contents for so long. He breathed in the maps' musty aroma deeply. Then, sighing reverently, he re-locked the armoire, unlocked the door with another cough and skipped down the staircase debating with himself about which one of the very last depleted war-chest wines he should open tonight.

Meanwhile, at completely diametrically opposite ends of the country, Will was having a thoroughly enjoyable soak in his hotel's generously long bath, lying back listening to the sea gulls squawking ferociously outside and feeling very pleased with himself. He had not only completed what he'd set out to achieve - the walk - but he also felt that the trip had genuinely reconciled some part of him with his recently deceased father. Or, more to the point, he felt he had come to terms with himself a little more. He felt a deeper peace. As he soaked and felt the warmth penetrate and melt his marrow he thought perhaps he did have too high expectations of what a normal relationship to have with your parents should be, and therefore it might have been him who put too much pressure on the whole situation. The negatives had obsessed him for a decade; he'd allowed those negatives to eat into him and fester. And that was his fault and no one else's. And as he topped up with hot water, using his toes to turn on the tap, he determined to concentrate on the positives from now on. That was vital. And the positives, he concluded, were that he'd been given a good education and, up until his parents' divorce, he had had an enviable childhood. His first seven years, his foundation years, were solid. Also his father, having not been around, had actually allowed him to develop himself as he saw fit, and he hadn't been unduly swayed or influenced by overt paternal pressure, unlike a host of his friends. All this had given him the opportunity to grow up to be an individual rather than the product of someone else's desires. To have the perfect relationship with your parents would be nice but it wasn't always possible for all sorts of reasons. In many ways he was actually proud that his father had left him to grow up independently, and, as he'd concluded earlier, perhaps he was from a family of loners anyway. It might well be in his and his father's genetic make-up to be just that. Deep down he knew that was so. Some people just are. We inherit DNA. Even being in a tight-knit group of friends could halt one's ability to grow autonomously.

Anyway, who gives a monkey's, Will thought as he dried his hair vigorously; he was feeling good right now, and that was the main thing. That was all that really mattered in life. Feeling good right now: that was the goal.

Lying back on the bed a few moments later, cooling down, with his wet hair on a big square pillow he called Sophie to let her know where he, and of course Nelson, had ended up that evening.

'Hey, hon, *c'est moi.*'

'Hey darling, where are you?'

'I'm in St Malo. We made it. Just had a lovely bath and am about to head out for a decent platter of *fruits-de-mer* in a minute. And you, hon, what are you up to?'

'Lucky you, very nice. Well, I'm still wading through all these papers, I'm virtually going googly-eyed, and my brain is starting to scramble but I'm nearly there, and think I'll be done in an hour or so. I'll then be cracking open a decent bottle of wine myself.'

'Ah, good for you, well done, babe. On the wine front I've got an hour or so in the morning to stock up on some goodies. Anything you particularly want me to get?'

'No, not really, darling, thanks. Well, on second thoughts if you can get a crate of oysters, that'd be great - otherwise a bottle of Armagnac, I'll do one of my festive trifles for Christmas, but no worries, we can get everything here now, can't we?'

'Yeah, yeah, of course we can. I'll have a sniff around and see what's here. Okay hon, I'll call in the morning when I am getting on board. If you think of anything overnight let me know.'

'Yes, I will. But hey, I've been worried about you all day. That bang, that crash.'

'Oh, it was just the wing mirror, hon. It sounded worse than it was.'

'No more ghosts in the machine then, eh Bond?!'

'Ha, ha, Mish Monaypenney,' Will said in a Sean Connery accent, 'all cool. It was just some idiot, and probably just my imagination running away with me.'

Within minutes of hanging up Will had booted and spurred and headed out for a huge Breton fish feast leaving Nelson happily sprawled out on his back in the middle of the bed. An immovable object.

CHAPTER 14
MISSING THE BEAT

As Will hopped out of the lift and handed his key to the receptionist, the proprietor caught him, saying, '*Bon soir, monsieur*, have a good evening. I hope you meet up with your friend.'

Will stopped in his tracks. 'I'm sorry - friend?' he said quickly, before even turning back.

'Yes, the gentleman who phoned to check you had arrived safely and whom you are going to meet later for a dinner.'

Will turned full around to face him. 'You must be mistaken, monsieur.'

'Non – William Marshall, yes? He asked for you.'

'That's right, ungh,' Will muttered. 'Very interesting… oh well, *merci beaucoup*.'

He left the hotel naturally bemused. The spring had left his step. As he walked he started to get annoyed. *That's just twisted my melon man, I've just had my joie de vivre, my bubble burst*, he muttered to himself. After ten metres he realised he was actually pissed off, so he turned and went back to the hotel.

Having confirmed that the proprietor had definitely received a call about him he said openly and matter-of-factly to him: 'Look, monsieur, I am not expecting anyone. I am here in St Malo on my own. I am getting the ferry back to Portsmouth tomorrow morning. I want you to assure me that my room is completely safe from intruders, and that my dog and car are safe, too? Please be honest with me.'

'*Mais bien sur*,' he insisted. 'We have never had any problems before.' He spoke defiantly, his feathers ruffled.

'Okay fine, I'm so sorry. I didn't mean to offend you,' Will said quickly. 'Is the lad who let me into the garage around, please?'

'*Oui*, my son, I will get him.'

'Please, that'd be great, super, many thanks.'

Ruddy French, he thought, *they're so darn touchy*. Within moments the fifteen-year-old, or thereabouts, teenager appeared in the foyer looking slightly sheepish.

'Sorry, but I would like a quick look at something in my car,' Will said.

'Yes, of course, monsieur.'

Will and the young man went outside onto the street and around the corner to the full-of-cars garage. He un-padlocked the door and opened up for Will, switching on some low neon strips. It was a tight squeeze to wander around to the Audi. Will fiddled half-heartedly with the wing mirror.

'The car is fine, thank you,' he said, approaching the lad. 'Look, I want you to keep a close eye on it and my room while I am out for the next couple of hours, can I trust you to do that for me?' He looked intently into the lad's eyes as he purposefully took out his big wad of cash.

'Yes, of course, sir,' the younger man replied, his eyes lighting up. It was the teenager's steady gaze, looking straight back at him, that reassured Will this was a serious individual who could be trusted. Will peeled off two twenty- euro notes, handed them to him with one hand and with the other gave him a paternal pat on the shoulder. Once the young man took the notes Will shook his hand and finally put two fingers up towards his own eyes and with a flicking gesture said, for some reason, 'Like a dog, my friend, like a dog.' He had meant to say 'Keep your eyes peeled like an eagle', but he didn't know the word for that bird in French. The word dog just slipped out. However, the intended message was registered, he was sure of that: act like a guard dog; that's what the gesture said. 'Good man. See you later. Call the police if you have any concerns, okay,' Will called back as he left the shed, a hundred percent confident that his new accomplice was suitably empowered.

As he turned up the cobbles and headed towards the central squares of the old pirate fortress, reassured that his pet and belongings were completely safe, he didn't notice four men, in two cars, parked in view some way up the street behind. One pair got out, stretched lazily and then fell in behind Will as he strode up an empty, orange-lit lane beneath the ramparts.

It was far too cold to sit outside a café, even with the Californian lamps on, he realised as he reached the main square. So he headed into the smartest bar he could find. He ordered an Americano cocktail, which always gave a zing, and established with the waiter (more of a 'mince-you're' than a monsieur, sporting a neat little moustache that was hiding rather a nasty flaky skin condition) where the best restaurant in St Malo was. The very best ones, he was informed, were in fact outside the city walls in the surrounding area like Dinard across the bay or Cancale up the coast. Okay, but what about here, now? He was directed to a restaurant on the opposite corner. Within half an hour Will was plonked in front of a small mountain of oysters, langoustines and jumbo prawns, a lobster, half a crab and a host of crustaceans, all piled up on a silver platter raised off the table-top on a little metal dais.

He sat forward with a bib tucked in his collar, elbows on the table, crunching shells, gnawing on delicate white flesh and slurping juicy oysters, quaffing it all down with a bottle of white Pessac-Leognan.

As Will attacked the seafood he began to compute that he hadn't really got anywhere with the riddle of the map. He hadn't got what the symbols meant. And right then he was perfectly happy to disregard its' real purpose in favour of the fact that the map had led, in a roundabout way, to him coming to terms with and forgiving his shitty father. And that was it. Result.

But the points he was missing; all the little coincidences and incidents, facts and feelings, were fast flying over his head. The long list of little things, pushed together, should have accumulated into one big unavoidable reality. On their own they could easily be dismissed but concertinaed as they were - well, it was odd to say the least.

He guzzled the bottle dry, completely forgetting that the maps had triggered something. He should have felt they were more than just his: that they had a history of their own. He should have been more determined to discover exactly what their provenance was - not gloated about personal reconciliations. He should have been kicking himself for not asking Degas a few more questions. No excuses that his French was rusty, or that he was still woozy from the ferry journey, or that he was so bamboozled by the value of the maps that he'd just wanted to get out of the shop with the dosh as quickly as he could.

An hour later he was tottering back along the busy cobbled streets, oblivious to danger, doing a long weaving walk back to the hotel. He dived into one bar en route and had a swift coffee and Armagnac and then, fully refreshed, headed off again, swaying his jolly inebriated way back to the Ajoncs d'Or. He didn't even ask at reception if all was quiet, he really didn't care; he just rolled into the lift, wafted up to his room and flopped down on the bed. Nelson would be forced to have an uncomfortable night without a stroll to relieve himself. It had been an incredibly long day for them both, waking up in Bourg very early that day in the fog, the walk, the fall and then the epic six-hour drive up to St Malo. *It feels like a week ago*, Will thought - briefly, before his fuzzing head spun him off into oblivion.

'Sir, it's Pierre,' the weary foot soldier said to his lieutenant, standing outside on the phone, beneath the window of the snoring Will.

'What's new?' Reynard replied sharply, still lying on the Bordeaux hotel room bed, fully dressed, socks on, the television blurting away in the background.

'Well, sir, Maurice and I followed him and all he did was eat a massive *Fruits de Mer* and then walk back to the hotel, nothing more – he was pretty drunk by the look of things.'

'Typical Englishman! What about the room and the car?'

'Philippe and Jean went into the hotel but the foyer is so confined, they couldn't even see a staircase, and there are no available rooms. The whole place is full; there's a conference of some sort going on here. They had a look in the garage, too; it was locked but they did peer in. The cars are rammed in like sardines. To neutralise the alarm we needed to get under the dashboard with the doors wide open, and this just isn't going to be possible. I don't know what to say. Searching his car and room are, frankly, not going to happen tonight. What do you want us to do, sir?'

'Tell Philippe and Jean to leave now, to head back to Marseille, they can stay at a travel lodge en route. You two just do nothing tonight, nothing I say but be onto him in the morning. I have booked you and Maurice on the ferry to England tomorrow, which should be amusing for you. All that soggy roast beef and fish 'n' chips to look forward to, hungh?' Reynard informed him. They both enjoyed the cliché Gallic humour.

'*Oh mon Dieu*, how disgusting. Please, sir, no!' Pierre pleaded mockingly, making even the reserved Reynard release a snigger into his hand-set.

'Get some sleep if you can but just make sure you are onto him first thing in the morning.'

'Yes, sir, we will.'

'Okay, *bon nuit* then, phone me as soon as you see him appear.'

'Of course, good night, sir.'

The next morning Will was awake at six thirty, having zonked out at ten the previous evening. He had a quick wash and tidy up and, having being made to feel horrendously guilty by his glaring pet, he took Nelson for the desired walk. It was not yet light and incredibly windy when they stepped out. Great billowy gusts of moist, sea-weed-scented air, smelling more like big wet dogs, engulfed the empty cobbled streets. Will battled his way to the city's protective fortress walls; he could sense the angry sea pounding the fortifications just two metres away on the other side. He ascended a set of steep stairs carved into the walls with Nelson in tow, now off the lead, sniffing around. They emerged onto the open ramparts to the full force of the English Channel which began to flay Will around like a drunk in the hazy, navy blues of first light. His head cleared instantly, his hangover vaporised. At a corner, where the rampart turned right - to fully pierce the ocean, fifty metres further on, there were some more stairs leading back down to the relative calm of the streets below which Will and Nelson descended carefully and then, doing a rough circuit, came back around towards the hotel. *It's going to be another rough crossing, my boy*, he said to Nelson without words.

As he approached the entrance he passed a small red hatchback car where someone was getting out and stretching, obviously having just woken up, completely dishevelled.

'*Bonjour monsieur*, *ça va* – you okay?' Will enquired pleasantly, as he passed.

'Ungh, *oui* – merci,' the man replied gruffly, making Will laugh to himself at the thought of what an uncomfortable night this thickset man must have had squashed into the little car, being tossed about by the weather. He didn't notice another man scrunched up in the back. *At least it was free!* said another voice in his head, further amusing him as he turned into his overpriced hotel. He didn't hear the Frenchman behind him swearing and cursing at having met and missed his 'mark', *le lapin*, the rabbit.

Will went straight down to a cellar breakfast room for a coffee and croissant with Nelson in tow. The room was already full of life with buzzing-around delegates gearing-up for their conference. He then deposited Nelson back in the room and went out to do a bit of shopping as dawn's soft blue hues had transformed into the fully switched-on bright light of day. He found an open-early, dressed-for-Christmas off-license and bought the Armagnac Sophie wanted and a decent bottle of aged rum for himself, which he pictured himself sipping by the fireside over the festive period. He also found and bought some quality local toiletries for Sophie and his sister and then headed back to the hotel where he loaded up the car and, having negotiated it out of the tight garage, headed straight over to the ferry port, a quarter of a mile outside the city walls.

Boarding was incredibly straightforward. Will never had to leave his car. He literally just handed his and Nelson's passports out the car window to a person in a booth, Nelson's chip was scanned, and then they moved to a queue of cars and waited to be directed on board. A group of police men and women appeared to be conducting a vague effort to wander around, security checking but, because of the foul weather, no real interest was taken and they soon disappeared. Before long his vehicle was rattling over the metal drawbridge and ramps into the creaking hulk. It was all loud clanking noises within, metal on metal, echoing around the groaning ferry's belly in a cacophony of abrasion. As soon as Will had negotiated the sinews of the massive car and lorry parking chambers and pulled up in his allotted space, a friendly crew member informed him that it was acceptable for Nelson to stay in the car as opposed to a kennel, if Will preferred. He naturally did as he was sure Nelson would feel a whole lot safer and more comfortable in the car than in a cage. So, having disengaged the alarm and left some water in a bowl and a few doggy snacks dotted around, he grabbed his overnight bag and headed up to his cabin. He thought he'd get a proper berth to have somewhere pukka to relax: sod the money.

A few minutes before, out in the ferry's car queue behind him. Pierre had telephoned his immediate superior in Bordeaux which was, scenically, a bit of a déjà-vu with Reynard standing in his socks by the same window of the same hotel room, in the same clothes, looking out at the same view: Bordeaux's Chartrons district.

'Good morning, sir, it's Pierre here. We are in the queue about to board. Nothing's happened overnight, *le lapin etait comme un souris dans l'eglise*, the rabbit's been like a mouse in the church,' he said, confidently omitting to mention the embarrassing encounter he'd had with Will on the street a couple of hours earlier.

'Okay. What one of you is going to do now is this - I don't care which of you it is, toss for it – and that is to hide in the car when you get on board and then when the car decks are locked, whichever of you it is, will find the rabbit's car and search it. The dog must be kept in a locked kennel so there will be nothing to disturb you. Do you see?' Reynard said, pleased with the plan he'd researched.

'No passengers are allowed in the car holds during the journey then?'

'That's right; once the cars have been unloaded no passenger is allowed back to their cars until half an hour before you all disembark; that is what I have been informed. It's a short straw I know for whichever of you has to do it but this is our last chance to get this map.'

'Yes, sir, I understand fully – leave it to us. I will phone again in twelve hours when we disembark.'

'Oh, and get our tracking device back off the car. That is vital too. Good luck, *bon courage*.'

With that Reynard hung up and immediately called his boss in Marseille who sounded in good cheer.

'Good morning, sir.'

'*Salut, mon brave*, what's new?' Henri enquired.

'Well, sir, I sent Philippe and Jean back to Marseille last night as you ordered and Maurice and Pierre are about to board the ferry. One of them will stay in the car and search le lapin's car during the crossing.'

'Okay, fine, that is good but get them to come back to France immediately as I have got our English friends on the case and those two will be absolutely useless in England, can you imagine? Not a word of English between them - they'll stand out like sore thumbs. Our British friends have organised someone to follow him from Portsmouth and take over from there; that's all in hand. I want you to fly over to England to supervise the operation though. I want you to get there as soon as possible today.'

'But, sir, we have a shipment coming in today from Nicosia. I am heading down to Marseille to supervise the unloading of that now.' There was a brief silence. Reynard broke first. He spoke with resignation. 'I suppose I can get a flight over to England later today, though? Perhaps this evening.'

'Exactly, Renard. Do that. I will get Laura at the office to organise your ticket. Unless of course the mutt-heads discover what we are looking for on the crossing,' Henri said, offering a conciliatory gesture, having read Reynard's tone. 'How long is the ferry journey?'

'Twelve hours, sir.'

'Okay, good, I will meet you down at the office at two o'clock, after lunch, when our ship's due in, and then prepare to get over to England this evening; there's time. I can't imagine them finding anything. So, work on Plan B.'

'Yes, sir, see you after lunch. I am on my way now. We may know more then.'

Reynard hung up, zipped up his patent ankle boots over his knife, snatched his flimsy old valise and headed out to the airport. The relief of having left the sterile confines of his hotel room were palpable. He had been static for nearly twenty-four hours, and now it was all go. He wound down the taxi's window and sat back to allow the biting air to rush in and revitalise him. The arctic blast woke him with a start and alerted him to the reality that it was actually going to be him that had to go to England and eat their dreadful food. He grimaced and shook his head.

It was always him, Reynard the silent one, who supervised the unloading of goods onto the Lafarge family quay. He hadn't missed one delivery since he replaced his predecessor ten years previously. He'd never been ill.

Lafarge's sole business operation was a monthly shipment of heroin hidden within a huge consignment of citrus fruit sent from Turkey through Cyprus. Oranges, lemons and grapefruit, in the main. The fruit's quality was high but there was no real profit in it any more, supermarkets had seen to that.

It was vitally important to isolate the correct crates and secure them immediately. Although he never came into direct contact with the sordid end of addiction, Reynard was, and more so as he was getting older, becoming increasingly despondent about the grubby business he had got into. He'd stand in the same spot on the harbour wall staring intently at each vessel entering harbour, awaiting his harbinger of death and misery to churn and moor up beside him. There was never any concern about customs; his boss dealt with that. Generally, within three hours of docking, he'd watch cargo-laden lorries depart the yard and disperse across Europe to wreak havoc with individuals, families and everyone and everything the drugs they contained met. He was fully aware of that. Like the Black Death, innocently enough, arriving from China one lovely day centuries before and scuttling ashore, this powdery, brown death they traded in, arrived like clockwork to keep this particular plague fed. His boss justified it by saying that if they didn't do the business, quite simply, someone else would. The sooner Henri could get hold of Bousquet's wine stash the better. The fortune it hinted at would free Reynard, as well as his boss, from this life of gilt-edged grime and enable him to finally legitimise himself too. Right then, in the taxi, it seemed to Reynard that this spurious quest he was on might well be his last chance to escape this dead-end career.

Back in Brittany Will's car ferry was setting off and beginning its laboured journey across the heaving English Channel. Will found his cabin, deposited his bag and then went to stand at the bar to sup coffee, watching the assortment of fellow travellers milling around trying to keep steady. He then tottered up on deck himself to see the French coastline disappear behind him, all grey and weather-beaten, broken-up in the stormy morning. He stood on the aft deck looking at the walled city fade slowly into the gloom as the ship forged its way stoically through turbulent waters. Will thought the fast fading citadel city of St Malo looked like an Avalon crumbling into the mists of time as he turned and headed towards another world entirely.

He made his way down to the Information desk and found out that he could check on his dog in one hour's time, supervised by a member of the crew. He swayed around the Duty Free shop aimlessly picking up bottles of wine and some pate and, having paid and put them in his cabin, went back to Reception and waited for a member of the cabin crew to take him and another couple of other pet-owning passengers down to the car decks to check all was fine. The ship continued to list and roll on huge ocean swells.

Meanwhile, across the other side of the ferry, Pierre was fast asleep, snoring on one of the recliner seats while his partner in crime, Maurice, was surreptitiously moving awkwardly about the car decks beneath him. Having managed to locate Will's Audi, Maurice now peered into the front window with a metal rod in one hand, poised to smash the glass. As he couldn't stand up straight, with the ship's rolling, he held onto one of the door handles to balance himself, ready for impact. The groaning of the ship's superstructure, added to by occasional incredibly loud banging noises, which were waves breaking onto the hull, made the atmosphere in the hold ominous to say the least. More like hideous indigestion within the belly of a vast metal beast. Maurice suddenly recoiled back in shock as a snarling Nelson appeared at the window he was about to smash. In a flash the dog had leapt up from his sanctuary under the passenger seat and was growling ferociously at the mobster about to break in. He was only held back by the clear glass of the closed window, his teeth barred menacingly on the fast steaming division which separated them.

'Oh *merde*,' Maurice cried out loud.

At that same moment the car deck access door slid open and Will and the few other passengers followed the uniformed crew member into the hold. As the passengers fanned-out and milled through the vehicles Maurice immediately ducked and crouched down. He began to scuttle off as quickly as he could, low down, crawling around the cars like a crab. Even that was difficult with the ship's erratic motions. Will soon reached his car and clicked it open to the delight of Nelson who immediately leapt out and began his terrier motions of scouring the ground in front of him, snorting frantically and quickly disappeared off into the maze of vehicles, on the hunt.

'Oi you, Nelson, get here,' Will shouted out, as he went after his pet, alerting the crew member who began to step towards him.

The next thing Will knew he found Nelson barking menacingly over a prostrate man lying on the deck floor a few cars away cowering beneath the vicious canine.

'Get here, now, good boy,' Will demanded harshly, as he approached the shenanigans.

The alert sailor arrived at the scene at the same time. Will got hold of Nelson tightly by the collar. The dog was in no mood to stop his offensive and harness his acute desire to lay his fangs into the whimpering man on the ground. The racket was insane: creaks and clanks and booms and crashes combined with the furious dog's barking, all as the vessel rolled and heaved through the angry waves, made it one hell of a scene.

'What are you doing here?' the uniformed sailor said loudly in French to Maurice, now up on his knees.

'I... I was asleep in the car and got locked in and was just trying to find my way out, monsieur,' Maurice mumbled.

'What is your name?'

'Maurice Duboef, monsieur.'

'Okay, go through that open door there onto the passenger decks, please, now. *Tout suite.*'

'Yes, monsieur, *merci beaucoup,*' Maurice whimpered appreciatively.

As the relieved Maurice sidled away he turned and scowled, unprofessionally at Will as he went. He had slid his rod under one of the cars as he'd scuttled off on all fours.

Oh shit, Will thought as he looked at him upright, *that's the fuckwit I saw this morning outside the hotel.*

The rest of the journey passed off without event and, having had a couple of beers, Will spent the remainder of the journey on his bunk in his cabin finishing his Cockleshell Hero book and a Sunday newspaper he'd found up at the bar. It was easier to lie down than stand up on this journey and he knew that whenever he closed his eyes for the next couple of days, he'd still be on board the Pride of Roscoff.

Chapter 15

HOMING IN...

By eleven o'clock that night Sophie and Will were lying side-by-side on their generous three-seater sofa, prostrate in front of the throbbing wood burner with Nelson sprawled on the carpet below. Independently they wallowed in their weekend's achievements.

Although he'd only been away four nights it felt more like ten, for both of them. Will had decided to keep shtum about the possibility he had been trailed during his visit to Bordeaux, Bourg and Blaye as well as up to St Malo and on the ferry too. He didn't want to upset Sophie in any way and, importantly, he really didn't want to believe it himself. He was trying to keep any notions of danger bottled-up in the hope they'd simply fade away. Yet there were recurring suspicions, accompanied by waves of anxiety, which swept over him whenever he thought of the map.

'D'you think the trip helped in any way, Will?' Sophie asked casually, as she sat up and poured the dregs of a bottle of red into two glasses.

Will stared numbly down, gazing at their adored pet and into the glowing clear-screened wood burner blazing in front of him. 'I do actually, love, it was empowering,' he replied dreamily. 'At the start of the walk I really felt I wanted James there walking with me and how sad it all was we couldn't have done more together but by the end… actually, he was the last person I wanted around – funny, eh?'

'Mmm, yes interesting. I'll think about that one.' She passed him his glass.

'Thanks, hon. I do feel I have achieved *something* though, but it's all just sinking in, really; it's been a hectic few days. The main conclusion I've reached is to keep positive about my memories of him. That was the main thing. Not a big life changer I know, it's subtle but…'

'Important,' she added.

'Yes, definitely. Again, it's simply a case of either looking at your glass as being half full or half empty, isn't it? It's a choice. Either to be positive or negative. And I'm going to make my memories of him positive from now on and not dwell on the negatives.'

'Well, that's great. All I can say is keep a PMA at all times, a positive mental attitude, and you can't go wrong. You've certainly done a lot.'

'Absolutely. And the trip really was a win, win one. It was all worthwhile. We got the fifteen hundred Euros, don't forget, which paid for the trip and I really look forward giving half to Lou. It'll come in handy for her Christmas, I'm sure, and hopefully ease her up a tiny bit on the dad thing too. There's an article there. And I really did plumb some personal depths.'

'Lou sounded delighted when I told her. And I hope you don't mind but I invited her down - either for Christmas or New Year? I thought it'd be nice to have some family around.'

'No, not at all, that's great. Well done. Can't wait to see her. When's she going to let us know?'

'She said she'd phone this week.'

'Excellent. I can't believe Christmas is only two weeks away now. It's been one of those years where it's just sprung up, no long drawn-out run-up. I guess we better get planning for it.'

'Definitely, let's send our cards out this week, and go through the diary of what we are doing and when, and get the decorations up. Sound like a plan?'

With that they both pulled themselves off the sofa lazily and began to switch off for the night.

Will eyed Sophie's posterior as she leant to shut the burner down. 'Let's hit the hay - hey, hay. Better brace yourself!' he said naughtily as he held his hand out and pulled Sophie towards him warmly.

'Oo, you naughty boy, you. I'm quivering at the prospect...' Sophie chuckled as she drew close to her intrepid adventurer.

Whilst they were jumping through the hoops together upstairs minutes later, by candlelight, no one, not even Nelson, detected a 4x4 pull up in the heavy rain on the lane outside. The driver, dressed entirely in black, hopped out, crept up behind the cars parked beneath their window and put two small magnetic tracking devices in place, one underneath each boot; then he slipped back into the vehicle and purred silently into the night, up towards the village.

Earlier that evening a low-cost carrier, which had departed from Marseille at 17:05, touched down at a bleary Heathrow with Reynard on board. After a slow shuffle through passport control and baggage claim he was met by one of the Lafarge enterprise's English associates at Arrivals. They were soon out on the M3 motorway heading down to the West Country on the rain-sodden carriageway in virtual silence.

Frank, the bald driver, dressed entirely in black, sat beside Reynard. A phone rang. He put the mobile to his ear. 'Kamal, how's it going?' he said. Frank listened to the reply. 'That's great, mate. See you round.' He hung up and turned to Reynard. 'Our man's back, he's at the address we are heading to.'

'Okay, good, 'ave you got the tracking devices?' Reynard said in his rusty English.

'Yes, sir, I have,' the bulldog beside him replied.

'We can follow them from the hotel you 'ave booked?' Poor Reynard was struggling; his English was slow and broken. He really didn't want to be there.

'Yes, we should do, they have a range of twenty miles and the hotel is fifteen miles away from where he lives. It'll be fine. We're going to his house now to place the transmitters. We've got plenty of time to stop for something to eat, though, so I am going to pull off soon. Better wait for them to go to bed.'

'Ungh. Eat!' Reynard exclaimed. 'Okay, ça va.' In his mind he saw a plate of overcooked meat, drowned in gravy, being shoved in front of him and a tankard of warm, brown frothy ale being slammed down. He heaved slightly.

Reynard was oblivious to recent culinary advances that had occurred in the British Isles, as he hadn't been there for six or seven years. The only connection he had with these English partners was overseeing the consignments of fruit onto their lorries in Marseille. They were obviously good payers, these Englishmen; he never had to visit them.

Earlier in the day he'd got down to Marseille from Bordeaux in good time for lunch and was by the docks to see the Panamanian registered container ship heave to and the hundreds of crates of oranges, lemons and grapefruit cradled onto the quay and fork-lifted straight into the Lafarge warehouse. He'd then located the dozen specifically marked crates which contained the hidden narcotics and closely supervised their transfer to the locked cold store. From there he ensured that the loading-up of four lorries with the rest of the fruit was done as quickly as possible before personally placing three of the highly valuable marked crates in amongst each vehicle. He finally secured each lorry himself with a seal and sent them on their way. The sooner the contraband was out of the warehouse the better. It was a two-hour operation from ship mooring to lorries leaving.

Lafarge dealt with four territories around Europe, each receiving ten kilos of heroin, the highest grade available through the kingpin families in Turkey, each month. It was a well-oiled machine that had been in operation for fifteen years now. The English shipments were sent to New Covent Garden fruit and vegetable market in South London where there was another Reynard type who would extract the three crates from their order and then cut and distribute the drugs from there. During the whole Marseille operation Reynard could see his boss where he always was, first standing high above the dock in his office anxiously looking down at the cranes hoisting the fruit-laden crates out of his ship's hold below and then, once that'd been done, he'd move down to a glass window within the actual warehouse where he could get a closer look at Reynard at work. He always stood smoking endless cigarettes at the two windows until he saw the last lorry leave. Reynard would then join him to say what he already knew. All done. Today, though, Henri Lafarge was in a surprisingly good mood; he even pressed a big wad of Euros into Reynard's hand and wished him a good trip. He was back at the airport in twenty-five minutes.

An hour from Heathrow the Range Rover pulled off the busy, spray-covered motorway and joined the dual-lane A303, windscreen wipers going full tilt in the lashing rain. The mesmeric action combined with the comfort of the plush interior had momentarily enabled Reynard drop off and he came to as the car pulled off onto a smaller, B-road. Minutes later they swung into a welcoming country pub's car-park with the illuminated pub sign flapping in the wind. The Black Horse was a quintessential old coaching inn with a fabulous ancient knotted wisteria hugging the outside. As the two men headed quickly inside, out of the deluge, they were greeted by a warm blast, a packed cheerful crowd chatting and laughing in the golden glow of a big open fire, emanating warmth throughout the bar. Reynard felt instantly awkward in this convivial, alien atmosphere and felt utterly uncomfortable with this dramatic contrast to his reason for being in the country. As they stood at the bar his associate took control and asked for some menus. From the corner of his eye Reynard could see platters of food coming out from the kitchen and he couldn't believe that it actually looked and smelt delicious. The whole experience was completely unexpected; he was taking time to adjust. He struggled to admit it but everything on the menu sounded fabulous too. The thought of local trout, home-reared buffalo, partridge and lamb dishes made his mouth water. *Mon Dieu, this is incredible*, a voice inside yelled as he scanned the superb wine list on the back of the card.

'Have you decided, sir?' his accomplice enquired, over the hubbub.

'Ungh, yes, actually I have, Frank. I am going to have the local lamb, and let's get a bottle of this Côtes-du-Rhône,' he said, pointing a finger at his choice of wine.

After paying, they were showed across by the jovial landlord to an empty table at the back of the bar near the roaring fire. There was little chance of feeling out of place or unwelcome in this hearty comfortable atmosphere.

Early the following morning Will was disturbed by a dream where he was stopped at a desert check-point, driving an old army lorry. He was just about to be pistol-whipped when he woke up, gasping, and slid straight out of bed without disturbing Sophie. It was still dark when he crept downstairs. As always he was greeted at the bottom by the ever cheerful Nelson wagging his tail ferociously, eagerly waiting to get out and reassert his territorial rights over the garden.

Having released Nelson Will opened the curtains as the sun began to, just, make its presence felt. He then went straight to the corner of the sitting-room; he couldn't help himself. Crouching down, he released a secret compartment within a fragile, heavy old Arabic Bedouin chest which one of his uncles had given him. He'd been itching to do this ever since he'd got in the previous evening, and now he carefully took out the original map hidden within and placed it reverently on the dining table at the far end of the room, in front of the window, and went to make himself a cup of tea. When he returned and sat down in front of the map he could see that the sunrise had turned the sky into the most incredible vermilion colour that covered the whole vista before him in a blanket of tight red cotton wool balls. The ruby-coloured light filtered into the room and refracted on every object. There's an old British country saying: 'Red sky at night shepherd's delight, and red sky in the morning, shepherd's warning', which means that a red dawn, in the Northern Hemisphere, indicates a foul day ahead. But at that moment it was hard to imagine; it just looked majestic outside. Will's eyes dropped to the cover of the map in front of him and immediately, bathed in this peculiar blood-red colour, it reignited wonder in him as to what on earth his map meant, and what it could possibly be hiding - this flimsy object that was dominating his life. The now familiar musty aroma that the map emitted combined with such strange light, spilling through the window onto the map's cover, made him concentrate and stare deeply within its folds and creases. As he gazed, mesmerised by the ancient rectangle changing colour, Will invoked the map to come to life and reveal its truth. One eye focused on the map's surface and the other eye went through the paper into infinity as his senses took over and closely scanned every millimetre of its face. He stroked the surface ever so gently and then his forefinger returned to a particular spot. It was as if Will was temporarily blinded and his only sense was touch. It was like Braille. *What's this*? he whispered to himself, coming to. He'd discovered, perhaps due to the peculiar light, vague scratches etched into the coarse paper in the cover's right-hand corner. Will had an idea. He crouched down low to get a different angle and he was sure he could just see the flickering of an ordered imprint emerge and then disappear. Suddenly the surface of the map which he was holding close to his face changed colour again, flaring to become brilliantly illuminated by this alien glow, and then, before his eyes, the light turned the map orange as the sunrise progressed through this magic-hour phase. *There's something here*, he said to himself. *Jesus*. He sat back very slowly.

He then proceeded, as gently as he could, to rub his right index finger ever so delicately over the faintest of suggestions he'd found on the surface. He was positive he could feel something abnormal on the surface. He glanced up as the fantastic dawn was turning a soft peachy colour in its final display. And, as a curtain of grey cloud closed in fast, Will felt a surge of excitement rise up within him. He rushed across to his stationery cupboard, fumbled around, snatched up a magnifying glass and then scooted back and held it up to the map's face. He worked fast, shifting the map to various angles under the brightest lamp in the room. *I can see, yes, there, there. No, no, go back, there, there. Yes, right, bloody there*. He was talking to himself. Definite scratches, which might well be words, he thought, were etched onto the surface ever so lightly: probably pencil marks that had been erased.

Within moments the sky had returned to the grey characterless dirty whitewash shroud that is the ever-present canopy which perpetually looms over British winters. Sophie was stirring upstairs so Will hurriedly replaced the map within its hidden chamber in the ancient chest and was standing innocently at the sink when Sophie came down in her dressing gown moments later, trailed by Nelson who had joined her on the bed for a morning cuddle.

'There's my rover back from his voyage tucked up by the sink where he should be,' Sophie said, chuckling as she came into the kitchen.

'Someone's in a good mood this morning,' was Will's nonchalant reply.

'Only three more days to go, three more days of this old term and I'll be home tomorrow… fa, la-la…' she began singing.

'Crikey yes, it's your last day on Thursday. Three more days and then three weeks off. Lucky you,' Will said, as he filled the kettle.

'What are you doing today, hon?' she enquired, opening a box of muesli.

'Well, I'm going to take the car to the garage and get that broken wing mirror mended and I've got to write up my yearly crop reports for the Journal and… while it's fresh I may well start to write down the trip I've just done, you know the walk, and talk about the Gironde and fluff up the wine element and see if any of the mags want it,' he replied.

'Okay me dear, good for you, get some stuff for supper too would you, oh and thirty odd stamps for the cards?'

'Yes, boss,' he said, saluting with a dripping hand. 'Sophie, I'm going to try and coordinate you picking me up at Mick's garage at four o'clock when you finish. I'll text you and let you know…' His voice trailed off as he rushed to disappear upstairs before another barrage of orders came his way.

Fifteen miles away Reynard and Frank, the English foot soldier assigned to the Frenchman, were huddled over a laptop computer at the desk in Reynard's hotel room. Reynard was dressed but shoeless. He had a thing about socks and always travelled with a huge pack of new ones that he religiously bought at airport departure lounges; he would invariably put on a brand-new pair every day and bin the ones he'd worn the previous day. It was a luxury for Reynard. A subtle acknowledgement to himself that he'd made it in life. Frank was wearing his standard attire, black jeans with a white t-shirt, his black leather jacket behind the seat. The hotel was a half-decent big commercial establishment on the edge Salisbury which would give them a little anonymity but the rooms had no individual character and could have been anywhere in the world.

'Great, here we go, we are receiving the trackers. Marshall's car gives off a blue signal and the other car a red one. Can you see on the map here, sir?' Frank said, pointing at the screen, somewhat relieved that the programme was up and running.

'Oui, yes.'

'The software records the data so let's go down for breakfast and then see who does what when we get back, particularly what he does for the next hour or so and then go from there. Sound okay?'

'Oui.'

'Are you up for the full English?'

'Le full English. D'accord, pourquoi pas?' Reynard replied morosely, dreading the gargantuan stodgy start to the day he was about to be served.

Within the hour Will and Sophie were standing outside their cottage kissing goodbye before getting into their respective vehicles.

'Have a good day, hon. Oh, and I spoke to Mick and he says it's okay to drop the car off at four, so will you pick me up from there?'

'Sure; if I'm going to be late for any reason I'll text. Oh, and darling, if you can get some wrapping paper and Sellotape that'd be great.'

'Yes dear,' he droned.

Will then jumped in the car as quick as he could, starting the engine, revving loudly and shooting off before his day could be taken up running around doing endless errands for Sophie.

Parked up in Salisbury twenty minutes later Wil went straight to the art shop he knew near the Cathedral Close. He and Sophie had spent one Saturday six months ago in the Cathedral doing brass rubbings so Will knew the place to get professional kit which would give him the best chance of extracting the possible wording he saw earlier. He was excited. The shopkeeper said the sort of task Will wanted to achieve was best done with tracing paper and fine pencils, and he kindly demonstrated to Will the technique required.

'Excellent, thank you very much indeed, much appreciated,' Will said, as he pocketed his change and took the paper bag of tools out into the busy street. He popped in to the offices of the Salisbury Journal and had a quick chat with his editor, grabbing the research periodicals he needed for his article on the latest crop reports; the annual summary of the local harvest just in.

'I know it's a tall ask: five thousand words by Thursday, Will; midday at the latest. Comprondo?' his editor called out, as Will hurried out.

'Yes, boss. No problemo.'

He flew around WH Smith and bought wrapping paper, a few packs of Christmas cards and two dozen stamps at the till on the way out and then rushed back to his car.

Seated back at the dining table with the map laid out in front of him and a lamp close by, Will began the process of gently rubbing over the scratches he'd found onto tracing paper. It was immediate. Letters began to clearly and magically reveal themselves. When that part of the process was completed Will turned the tracing paper over and repeated the rubbing process on the reverse side, onto a clean piece of white paper, and, hey presto, legible words became visible. He stood up, took a deep breath and went to make a coffee, to take five, to take stock.

When he came back, mug in hand, he stared at the three words etched one on top of the other. The top word said 'Bousquet', the one below 'Bourg', and the bottom one 'Coiffeur'. Will lunged for his laptop, fired it up and Googled the word Bousquet; straightaway he clicked open a Wikipedia entry for a Maurice Bousquet and quickly scanned the profile. This Bousquet was Chief of Police in Bordeaux and Paris and was an infamous Nazi collaborator during the Second World War. Will read he was born in Bourg and died in Paris in 1944. The correlation for Will that his father had been a Chief of Police, too – okay, with the United Nations, was immediate; he sensed that was the link. Was this how his father had got the maps in the first place somehow? The Wikipedia page was quite brief but it was evident that the guy was an absolute bastard, his name going down in history with numerous crimes against humanity pinned to it: crimes such as torturing numerous prisoners and participating in deporting thousands of Jews to concentration camps. Will also read that Bousquet was assassinated as he tried to flee Paris when the Allies arrived and the Germans left in August 1944.

'What a devil,' Will sighed out loud.

His mind continued to race, and the excitement of discovery made his pulse gallop uncontrollably. *You're getting somewhere*, a voice rang inside. He fumbled to replace the map and the sheet of paper with the three names back into the compartment within the chest.

He simply had to make a start on going through the local harvest data and write his report. He had to focus on what he had to do and not get carried away at all. The deadline for submitting the article was looming, and to write five thousand words in two and a half days was going to be an almighty challenge. However this was the third year he had written the two-page main spread in the newspaper so he was pretty clear on the format it should take and the information he had to gather - but his mind kept going back to the names, to the words. He just couldn't believe it and he kicked himself for not having discovered the impregnated words before he'd done the trip.

He knew 'Coiffeur' meant 'hairdresser' but what was that all about? Bourg was where his father had written 'START'. With great difficulty Will forced himself to concentrate, to get going on the article at least, and he did manage to write a thousand words before lunch. He'd justified getting back to the map affair as soon as he'd reached that benchmark number of words. He revisited the Wikipedia entry for Bousquet and began to jot down some of the key points in his notebook. Bousquet was born in 1899 in Bourg, the only son of a long line of butchers from that town. His father died when he was young and he was educated at a minor boarding school in the area and then entered a local military academy from where he went and fought in the last year of the First World War, receiving recognition and two mentions in dispatches for bravery. This enabled him to join a police academy in Lyons as an officer and then he rapidly progressed up the ranks back in his home city of Bordeaux, becoming chief of police in 1937. There was then a section on his Second World War career where it said that he was renowned for 'dejudaising'- asset-stripping hundreds of Jewish businesses and disposing of their assets. He was a great friend and advisor to Hitler's right-hand man, Hermann Göring, the notorious art thief and bon vivant, during his tenure in the prefecture in Paris later in the war. Apparently Bousquet assisted in the theft of vast amounts of rare wines both in Paris and Bordeaux from Jewish chateau owners and their properties in Paris as well as many restaurants and institutions. Finally Will read that Bousquet's body was found in an official car in August 1944; presumably killed by French partisans or German soldiers. Verdict: open.

CHAPTER 16

THE CAT'S OUT OF THE...

Across the valley in Wiltshire, at their hotel, Reynard and Frank were back at the desk, hovering over the computer, rewinding Will and Sophie's recent movements. They could see that Sophie had driven directly to a school on the other side of Salisbury from where they lived, arriving just before 08:45. Frank pointed out that her car had actually passed the hotel they were in. It was evident on the screen's detailed map that her car was parked within a school compound and had not moved since it arrived.

'Well, I reckon whoever lives with him works at the school. We'll just have to keep an eye on the car throughout the day and see what it does,' said Frank.

'Forget that. What about the rabbit, Marshall? What has he been doing?' Reynard asked abruptly.

'Right, here we are,' Frank said, as he clicked onto Will's Audi tracker history on the screen. 'Okay, we can see he left his house at the same time as the driver of other car and came into Salisbury town centre, parking in a public car-park here. The car stayed for, let me see, one hour and ten minutes and then he went straight home, which is where he is now. So, what do you want me to do, sir?'

'Um, nothing for now,' Reynard replied, 'but we must get into the house as soon as possible, to search it. I am going to go and buy some gloves: do you need some too? I want you to go and get a crowbar, two powerful torches, and some liquid rat poison and I will meet you back here in one hour.'

'Okay, will do, sir,' Frank mumbled. 'Don't worry about the gloves - I have some in the motor,' he continued somewhat hesitantly, trying not to show his concern at what this venomous individual he'd been assigned to was planning. He decided it best not to ask any questions; he really didn't want to hear the answers.

Like Degas, the antique dealer in Bordeaux, Frank found it incredibly hard to look at Reynard straight on; his inward-looking dark eyes had not one inkling of warmth in them, they were blanks, black holes that exuded nothing but coldness; he even put the willies up a semi-hardened criminal like Frank, who shut down the programme, picked up the laptop and his leather jacket and left Reynard's room.

Reynard wasn't a hundred percent sure what his next move was going to be but what he was clear on was that he wanted to get this business done and dusted, tout suite, and get back home as soon as possible. He was well aware that the wines they were searching for supposedly had a value of two hundred million Euros but, right then, he really didn't care; he just wanted to get back to France fast. If he could make the right noises to his boss that he had done all he could there would be no point in him continuing to be here in England.

Will made himself a cheese and chutney sandwich and, as he sat back at the table tearing through the farmhouse loaf wedge, he downloaded the photos he had taken in France. And then, sitting back while he chomped, he began to view the photos in slide-show mode. A single photo held the screen for a few moments before fading away and being replaced with the next one. He viewed rainy images of the grim road out of Blaye on the first morning, only three days previously, and then the slimy piles of boulders by the road re-appeared, which made him shudder. These images were followed by a series of atmospheric river shots. Then roadside shrines of the dead drivers were resurrected, then the hulk of the stranded MJ Fujiyama. Will paused, mid-mouthful, as the photograph reminded him of his epiphany moment, where he'd shed his skin and let it float away as simply as water moving under a bridge. Then stark-naked vineyards faded up and the ominous chateau that made the hairs on his arms prickle and, finally, the series of shots he'd taken in Bourg's town centre. The market square and all the derelict shops and buildings came to life through the mist and then melted away before the next image softly appeared. The photographs looked eerie, like from another time. The old-fashioned street lamps, with their golden light, mingled with the fine fog to form a series of rings around the square like buttery halos. *This was my photographic highlight of the trip. The shops, the square, everything about this place looks so ancient and mysterious.* Will struggled to fathom that the photographs had been taken so recently.

When he'd completed viewing the whole series of shots he clicked back to review the individual ones of Bourg more intently; he wanted to look at them in a bit more detail. He honed in. One of the words that had appeared through the tracing was 'Bourg'. This was surely where the map's hidden secret lay. And now he had a more specific clue: the third word said 'Coiffeur'. The mist and the blue light of dawn gave the images an ethereal quality which enhanced the urban neglect perfectly. His eyes were drawn-in to inspect the empty buildings surrounding the square, due to their mesmeric quality. Like haunted houses. He wanted to go in. He enlarged the images and scrolled and scanned each building's façade closely. As he studied one shot he could clearly see, emerging in very faded, floral cream sign-writing above one of the old shop fronts, the word 'Coiffeur'. *Hello.* Will's face moved closer to the screen and there, quite definitely, written into a fading arc, onto a panel above the windows was that word. He clicked the macro button a few more times, to enlarge the photo further, and there it was, quite definitely: Coiffeur, indelibly written above the frontage. He shook his head.

'Bloody hell!' Will whispered out loud. He stood up, paced around the room, and then sat down again. *Will coincidences never cease?* he said to himself.

The old salon dominated a large plot on the south side of the market square. To its right, a block away, a narrow road dropped down towards the river. Will could just see, from one angle, a lane that cut left to the rear of the building. At its front, the old hairdressing salon had two large ornate bay windows, divided by a front door, which was set back in a recess. The neglected building had obviously not been occupied for many years. The glass was incredibly dirty and, by enlarging the image further, Will could see mounds of white cobwebs clouding each corner of the windows. It was one of the buildings he'd seen that had some windows bricked up on the first and second floors. It was a sad sight, a crying shame to see the neglect of such a fine, solid structure, built in the wonderful Bourg stone, now filthy through previous decades of coal and wood smoke having stained its exterior. It made the grand old building look terrifically un-loved, in desperate need of restoration: a re-birth.

Okay, he said to himself, perking up, *let's be rational about this. How do I find the history of this building?*

He had used British online national public access records countless times, to research articles about the history of certain country houses and individuals. In the UK the official body that collated this information on behalf of the government was called the Land Registry, and anyone could access, quickly and simply through their website, a full history of the ownership of any property. You simply paid three pounds per record you wanted to access. Not only did it give you information on the current owner of a particular property but also on all previous owners.

That's the starting point, he said to himself. *I'll give myself half an hour more on this and then get back to the article.*

He Googled 'French Land Registry' and bingo, up came the address for the French website equivalent, called 'cadestre. fr'. Will began to fill in their online form, jumped back to the photo of the shop, scanned closely over the whole image and soon found alongside the coiffeur sign writing the number '23' painted perfectly clearly onto the frontage. He then looked at another photo which showed another corner of the square which he zoomed in on and he could see a navy-blue street sign saying 'Place du Marché', or Market Square. His heart began to beat rapidly as he now knew he had the complete address so he typed all the information into the appropriate boxes, found his credit card, paid the few Euros required, pressed the Submit button and within seconds the file relating to the property appeared on his screen. He could also press a button through Google that translated the copy into English.

Jeepers, that was easy, he said to himself. *Okay, let's have a look.*

He scanned down and could see that the property was now owned by a certain Mme Estournel who had owned it for nearly seventy years, and prior to her, the property had been owned by various members of the Bousquet family since records began. An ethereal weight seemed to descend and crunch Will, making him hunch in his seat. He went more slowly now. Time altered to slow-motion as he simultaneously read and absorbed the facts.

Holy mother, he said to himself, *I wonder if this was the Bousquet family's old butchers shop*? He added Mrs Estournel's name to the sheet of paper onto which he'd traced the three words from the map.

He snapped himself up and looked at the clock on the mantelpiece. *Oh shit, I've run out of time*, he said to himself. He then diligently and ever so carefully replaced the map and the piece of paper back in the secret compartment in his chest and got straight back to the article he had to write. The discipline really helped. It was something concrete to concentrate on. Something real. Something tangible. He needed that, as he felt he was being sucked rapidly into the realms of fantasy fiction.

Will focussed on the crop reports, analysed documents and compared them to last year's, shoving all thoughts of the map to one side. The article demanded all his attention. He looked up current prices that farmers were receiving for wheat, barley, rapeseed and other crops. He calculated incomes compared to previous years and made assumptions on how good a harvest this year actually was, comparatively, writing it all down furiously. Importantly, he was forcing himself to keep aside all thoughts of the map and his fluttering new discoveries.

The relief of finally starting to make sense of the map, surprisingly, allowed him to focus his mind on the article much more clearly. Questions were finally being answered. So before he knew it, he was looking up at the clock and saying to himself, again, *Oh shit! I better get going, I've only got half an hour to get up to the garage.*

He quickly looked up the properties of the document he was laying out his article onto and saw that he had completed 2,500 words. *Halfway house, not too shabby*, he thought, congratulating himself. He was now fully engaged in the article and could see that the end was in sight, so he left the house with Nelson in tow feeling pretty good about himself: even slightly smug. He was energised, a man on top of his game.

He soon pulled up at Mick's garage which was simply a big dirty old barn beside a main road that Mick and his family had earned their living from for generations, going back to horse-drawn days. As he bumped onto the pitted, puddled forecourt Will could see hundreds of old tyres piled all down the shed's sides and a chained-up Alsatian dog straining madly on its tether, barking ferociously. He got out. Mick appeared at the corner of the open barn doors. He was a tall, dark-skinned, angular individual, surprisingly elegant and refined with piercing green eyes. He was obviously gypsy stock. Mick was always covered in oil during the day but whenever Will saw him in the pub of an evening he glowed like well-polished brass and he always put jewellery on when he went out: sparkling rings on his fingers and heavy gold chains round his neck, which made his eyes twinkle all the more.

'Aright, Will, what's up mate?' he said loudly above the barking, as Will approached, and then, before Will could answer, he'd twisted his head around the side of the shed and shouted, 'Shut up, King!', making his guard dog do just that, immediately.

'That's better,' Will said. 'You alright Mick?'

'Yes, fine, mister Marshall, can't complain. What's the problem?'

'I got the wing mirror knocked off in France a couple of days ago, some prat careered into me. It needs replacing and I want you to give the car a service. Give it a thorough check over, would you? It's feeling a little sluggish after the long journey.'

'Yeah no worries, leave it with me. I'll have a look now and order the wing mirror straight away. It should be in tomorrow. Better be safe than sorry, though, and let's say it'll be ready for you by Thursday lunchtime; anything different and I'll let you know. Sound alright?'

'Yeah great, no problem.'

'Do you want a lift home? We could stop off at the Black Horse for a cheeky one.'

'No, cheers, Mick, Sophie should be here in a minute. She's picking me up on her way back from school. Thanks though, nice idea. We'll probably be up there later though.'

Back across the valley, in the Salisbury hotel room, the bruiser Frank sat hunched over his computer. The snake-like Reynard lay, supine on the bed, his socked feet crossed.

'Hey boss, have a look at this,' Frank exclaimed.

'What is it?' Reynard replied dozily, without moving.

'Well, Marshall has driven up somewhere and is parked on the side of a main road less than ten miles from here. I'm not sure what exactly it is and the other car is on the move too. Schools have just closed for the day so I reckon whoever's car that is does work there.'

'Forget that car. How long has his car stopped for? Could it be a petrol station?' Reynard snapped, slowly getting up from the bed and padding over to the computer.

'Let me see,' Frank began. 'Well, he's been there for five minutes, and, hold on, the other car has joined him, it's pulling up there now.' Both men stared at the map on the screen looking at the red and blue flashing dots converge and pulse together outside Mick's garage.

'Right, the other car's off now, and he's staying there,' Frank continued, a minute later.

'Mmm, okay, wait a few minutes, and let us see.'

Reynard went back to the bed and sat on the side with his head bowed psyching himself up for action. He galvanised himself to get this business over and done with and get back to the bright familiarity of Marseille with its bustling ports, its busy markets, his regular eateries and, really, to just get away from this dreary alien land as quickly as he could. He had made noises to that effect to his boss earlier in the day and was told that as soon as he'd searched the car and the house he could return to France. And, in fact, Henri Lafarge wanted him to go to Brussels as soon as possible and have a conversation with a customer who hadn't paid up on time. Frank wasn't able to get liquid rat or vermin poison, only pellets. Reynard had bought a steak when he'd gone out earlier. It looked marvellous, beautifully marbled, he thought as he began to crush a big handful of the pellets in a plastic bag with his foot. He then put the steak into the bag, shook it vigorously and finally sealed it with a knot. Satisfied, he looked up. 'What now, Frank?' he demanded.

'Okay, the other car has gone back to Marshall's home, sir, and his car is still at that same position by the road,' Frank replied.

'Come on, let's go.'

The two men hopped into the gleaming black Range Rover and headed out of town towards the flashing blue light, pulsing on the laptop screen sitting on Reynard's lap. It was dusk when Frank pulled slowly onto the garage's open forecourt and came to a halt just off the road facing the large shed just as Mick was pulling the heavy sliding doors shut for the day.

'It's a mechanic's workshop, a garage,' Frank said.

'I see, a garage,' Reynard echoed. 'One of my men scraped his car the other day. It is that one, the Audi parked on the side, he must be getting it fixed.' He pointed a claw at Will's estate car, parked beside the shed on the same side as the dog, King, which they couldn't quite see from the angle they were parked at or even hear any barking from within the hermetic seal of their executive vehicle.

'Let's go. This will be easy. We will come back later,' Reynard said, as he saw Mick peer around at them as he locked up.

CHAPTER 17
WAKEY, WAKEY...

'Sorry, Soph, I forgot to get supper,' Will said, as they walked into the house. 'Let's just go up to Nick and Elaine's. It's steak night, two for one, how about that?'

'Yes, it's just what I feel like. Good idea. What are you up to now, fancy a quick walk?'

'Sorry, hon, you go. I'm going to write a tad more of the annual crop report article and try and get that buttoned up as soon as poss, they want in by Thursday morning.'

'Okay, love, I'll take his nibs straight out now while I've got my coat on and get out of your hair for a bit, I could do with a bit of fresh air.' Nelson's ears were pricked. He'd heard the magic 'W' word.

'Cheers me dear, how was your day, by the way?'

'Fine, all just winding down really, obviously the kids are fully excited about Christmas. Oh, by the way, it's the carol service tomorrow evening at six o'clock in the cathedral if you want to come.'

'Sounds good, but I better just see how I'm getting on with this article. Got to get that done.'

'Did you get cards? We better get one off to your mum as soon as poss, otherwise it'll never get to the States in time.'

'Yeah, I did, let's try and do a few before we go out.'

With that Sophie began the laborious process of getting

wrapped up in more layers of clothing before heading out into the gloomy wet evening with Nelson who, given the green light, had begun to scoot around the sitting-room excitedly to their perpetual amusement. The moment thick socks appeared he knew they were the signal for action. 'Socks' - well 'sockies' to be precise - was one of the handful of words he knew. Nelson loved sockies because they were a word away from walkies.

'Take a torch, hon,' Will called out, as Sophie was yanked out of the door by their surrogate child.

Will immediately got back to work. Having made good headway on the article earlier in the day, he was now able to proceed rapidly. He completed the historical data section by writing a bulk summary of the past few year's crop reports which he'd previously written and now he outlined, he felt, an accurate assessment of this year's harvest. He even made a start of his summing up, ambitiously suggesting what the best crops to plant next year were likely to be judging on yields and prices.

Half an hour later he heard Sophie and Nelson enter the porch. Again he checked the total amount of words written as the rain-sodden pair burst back into the sitting-room. He could see he had completed just over 3500 words that day, all in five hours.

'It's amazing how much easier things become once you have done them before,' he mused to Sophie as she took off her coat. 'Last year it took me at least twice the time to do the same.' He looked up at a soaked Sophie. 'I'll pop the kettle on, hon, you look as if you could do with a brew. I'm just going to send what I've done so far to Simon at the office, so he can have a quick look.'

With that Will composed an email to his editor at the Journal and pinged it over to him, attaching the article he had drafted, and then closed his laptop for the day.

Two hours later Will stood in the sitting-room, shaved and changed. He bent to shut the wood burner down ready to go out and then stepped back to gaze around the cosy homeliness. They'd put up a few Christmas decorations, including his favourite, a set of orange illuminated glowing furry ball lights, which were now draped across the mantel piece. He basked in the glow of the whole room's radiating warmth.

'Shall we bring the dog?' he called out to Sophie, looking down at Nelson who had his head tilted to the side and was putting on his soppy-eyed look. He even had one paw raised – giving out the picture postcard image of innocence and vulnerability as if to say, poor me, you can't leave me here on my little lonesome, can you meanie? You can't be that cruel, surely?

'Mmm, what do you think?' Sophie asked, as she came into their snug lounge. She looked down at Nelson, and her heart melted immediately. 'How can we leave him, just look at him.'

'Alright, alright, you win,' Will concurred. 'Give me a hug, hon.'

'Why?'

'It's the room, it's saying hug me, it's gone all kinda' hygge,' he replied smiling, holding out a hand, urging her close and then, quite simply, he stopped and just looked at her. 'My, you look wonderful tonight. This fairy light suits you perfectly.' He leant forward and kissed her tenderly on the lips.

'Stop that, Romeo…' she murmured. 'You're smudging my lipstick.'

Having stopped at the post box on the way they were soon pulling into the car-park of the old country inn with the illuminated pub sign swaying in the wind, flaying shadows. The Black Horse was their local and just happened to be their favourite pub in the area too. As soon as Will opened the latch to let them in, they were immediately greeted by a blast of familiarity. Warmth, chatter and cheer burst from within to greet them. Although it was only a Tuesday night, and still twelve days before Christmas, the pub customers seemed to be celebrating already. A large crowd of red, healthy-faced men in tweeds were gathered at the bar whilst their womenfolk were arranging themselves at the long dining table behind.

'Must be a Christmas party,' Sophie said into Will's ear, above the din.

'Yeah, they're from the Eagleford Estate, I recognise a few of them.'

The regulars, as a whole, liked Will. Not only did he drink up at the bar and have a laugh with them on a regular basis but importantly he was always interested in what was going on locally. Whether it was being a journalist or not he always asked questions, was a good listener and had the knack of getting people talking. Will had written many articles on local issues, on rural crime and topics he'd heard right here. As a result he was always someone the locals wanted to gossip with and, over the two years he'd lived in the area, he'd had endless people coming up to him saying things like: 'Don't tell anyone I told you this, Will, but...' in quiet country accents or, 'did you hear about this, Will? I'm not sure if it's true or not but...'

It was a rare breed pub, the Black Horse. It was one of those nearly extinct traditional British democratic institutions where people actually talk to each other. The whole spectrum of society was generally represented at the bar and all communicated together freely. The only 'no-no' subjects – officially - never to be discussed in a pub are religion and politics but, more often than not, that rule's ignored; they produce the best arguments. However, on this occasion, the large group was slightly overpowering so Will and Sophie ordered their steaks and discreetly settled in a corner table over by the fire which Nelson got as near to as he could.

Various familiar locals drifted in and out and Will and Sophie constantly found themselves pleasantly interrupted as people called out welcomes or came up for a quick chat. They saw Mick from the garage slip in like the Lone Ranger, tall and lithe, fully kitted. He always stood at the bar in the same spot and was regularly called upon to remember the names of people and characters from the village long gone. He, as one of the few remaining members of a truly local family, the Pages, was a highly-respected individual as most of the pub regulars, particularly the farmers, were his customers too and they very well knew the value and importance of having well-maintained reliable vehicles. The result was Mick was always kept well-lubricated himself.

By ten thirty the pub had thinned out considerably and as Will and Sophie stood at the bar paying their bill Mick's phone suddenly rang out from his waistcoat pocket.

'Who the hell is this?' he exclaimed, fumbling to get his mobile out. 'Mick 'ere,' he said. 'Oh right, what's the damage? One car eh? Has the alarm gone off? Thanks for letting me know, officer, I'll be there in a minute.' Momentarily bemused, he then said out loud to everyone, but to no one in particular as he hung up, 'My darn workshop's been broken into, or a car or something. I better get up there.'

'Bloody hell!' Will exclaimed. 'I hope they haven't got your tools.'

'Sorry, Will, but can you give me a lift up there please, mate?' Mick asked in a bit of a daze. 'I've had one sherbet too many. I don't want the old bill nicking me for D and D.'

'Yeah sure, Sophie's driving but I'm sure we can. Is that alright, Soph?' Will enquired.

'Yes, of course, we're just off now anyway.'

Minutes later they pulled up outside Mick's garage, where they were greeted by the blue flashing lights of a police car.

Sophie stayed in the car with Nelson while the boys got out and walked across to the shed doors where the local constable was standing with Mick's nearest neighbour, who'd called the police.

'King's not barking, that's odd,' Mick mumbled to Will under his breath as they approached the other pair. 'Good evening, officer, what seems to be the problem?' he continued.

'I'm not too sure, sir, but I've had a good look around and there doesn't seem to be any break-in to your actual workshop but that one car there has been broken into,' the local bobby said, flashing his torch around at Will's Audi. 'And Mr Page, I am dreadfully very sorry to inform you but your dog seems to have been killed.'

'What? Dead,' was all Mick could say.

Will stood back as the police officer, torch in hand, and Mick went around to the side of the shed. He could clearly see by glass littering the ground in the beam of light beside the Audi that it was definitely his car that had been broken into. Anxiety and paranoia immediately engulfed him. He shuffled around to the side to get a closer look; his legs jellified immediately. He could see the two men standing over the lifeless Alsatian in the torchlight. Shards of glass from his broken window sparkled around the dead dog.

'Look, there's something frothing in his mouth,' Will could hear Mick exclaim to the policeman.

'Yes, sir, I noticed that – I am sorry to say it looks as if he's been poisoned. I have called for a police vet and, if it is okay with you, we'll take him away for a forensic autopsy.'

Will could see Mick was in shock, too; he was standing numbly, head bowed over his fallen guard dog in disbelief.

Will even noticed an illuminated tear drop roll down his cheek and fall onto the fur below. The policeman turned and shone the torch into Will's face, spotlighting him, freezing him. He then directed the beam across to fall on Will's car which was a total mess inside.

'I'm so sorry about this, Will, I'll get it all fixed up for you in the morning, don't worry,' Will could hear Mick say from the darkness.

'Shush, don't worry about that, mate,' Will replied instinctively. 'There was nothing in there anyway. Christ, I am so sorry about King. What sort of people could do that!' He turned to the policeman. 'Do you think they were scared off, officer?' he enquired, coming closer.

'I really can't tell at the moment, sir,' he replied. 'Is this your car then?' the officer asked, shining the torch at Will again. 'Oh it's you, the reporter chap.'

'That's right, officer, William Marshall from the Journal.'

'Arright. Well, I'll be getting forensics down in the morning to look at it all in a bit more detail, so don't go touching anything.' He turned as another vehicle entered the forecourt. 'Here comes the vet's van now.'

The police officer went to greet it, leaving Will and Mick standing in virtual darkness.

'You better get off, Will. I am very sorry. This has never happened before,' Mick said, shaking his head.

'Don't be silly, Mick, the car's no big deal. I'll phone up in the morning. Try and get some sleep,' Will said, clasping Mick's shoulder in a reassuring gesture. 'I'm so sorry.'

'Jesus, Sophie, it was my ruddy car they broke into,' Will said, gibbering frantically as he got in beside his girlfriend. Nelson jumped on his lap. Will began to hyperventilate slightly. 'The bastards killed Mick's dog,' he wheezed. 'By the look of things they poisoned it. Come on, let's go. Quickly'

'Oh-my-God,' was all Sophie could say, as she pulled away slowly, taking in the horrendous news.

They didn't speak at all for the short journey home. Will stroked the dog on his lap. Parking up outside their cottage they sat for a brief moment of silence and held hands, looking at the soft orange glow emanating from their sitting room window through a chink in the curtain. Will got out and opened the front door. Nelson bounded in first. All was perfectly normal in the hallway but as soon as he entered the sitting- room – boom! - Will faced a scene of total devastation. It looked as if a wild beast had run amok and gone crazy in there while they were out. Their belongings were strewn everywhere, cushions were torn open, their fluffy innards out, festooned all over the room. The bookshelves stood empty, their contents a messy cowpat on the floor. Even some of Will and Sophie's paintings were on the carpet upside down. Others dangled on their hooks, crucified. It was an absolute mess. Yet the wood burner still throbbed and Will's orange balls were still glowing on the mantelpiece.

'We've been broken into, Soph!' Will called out, turning back to Sophie as she stood in the hallway and then came forward and leant over Will's shoulder. 'Nelson, get here!' Will demanded, suddenly galvanised into action. He picked up the dog, carried him upstairs and locked him in the bathroom before coming down again. Sophie was now in tears, perched on the edge of the sofa surrounded by their precious debris.

'Our bedroom's a bloody mess too,' Will said glumly, as he took his phone out of his pocket and dialled emergency services, 999.

CHAPTER 18
REALITY CHECK

'Good morning, sir, how are we this morning?' the officer said to Will, as he took off his helmet and came straight into the house.

This was the third time in twelve hours Will had seen the same local policeman. Firstly up at Mick's garage, then shortly afterwards when he attended the crime scene at the cottage and again now, just after Sophie had left for work; he'd arrived on his motorcycle this time.

'Had a chance to find out exactly what was taken, have we?' he continued, as he entered the devastated sitting-room. He turned to look straight at Will for an answer.

'Well, not much to be honest, officer, just my laptop computer as far as we can tell. No jewellery or valuables have gone but whoever it was has trashed the house; there's been damage.'

'Laptop, interesting, insurance?' he mumbled under his breath and continued a little louder. 'It certainly looks a very professional job to me. They must have been looking for something in particular.' He began to hum annoyingly as he looked around the sitting-room in daylight. 'Forensics are up at the garage checking for prints now.' He casually flicked a painting on the floor over and then looked sharply around at Will. 'Then they'll be coming down here in about an hour; you can tidy up after they leave,' he went on, and then, turning to Will again, probed deeper. 'To be honest, Mr Marshall, I'm finding it very hard to believe it was a mere coincidence that your car and your home were broken into on the same night – don't you, sir?'

'I do, officer.' Will agreed. 'But I can't think of any reason for this at all,' he continued, trying to sound convincing whilst avoiding the probing policeman's stare.

'What exactly do you do for a living?' the policeman asked, taking his notebook out of his pocket. His little pencil poised, waiting for Will's reply. 'That's right, you're a journalist.'

'Yes, officer, as you know I'm the features writer at the Journal, and my partner is a teacher at Queen Mary's.'

'And you really can't help me at all? You can't think of any reason this may have happened? No controversial articles you've written that may have upset someone?'

'No, officer, I really can't.'

'Strange, very peculiar,' the officer mumbled.

Over at the hotel in Salisbury Reynard was packed and ready to leave when Frank knocked and came into his room.

'Okay, we go,' Reynard said straightaway, without formalities.

'Yup, I'm ready. I've paid the bill,' Frank answered.

With that the two men left the room and moments later were wafting out of town in the 4X4.

'So you removed your tracker from his car and left my French one on, is that correct?' Reynard asked, when they were on the smooth carriageway heading up to Heathrow Airport.

'Yes, sir, that's correct. We'll come back and get the other one when this has all quietened down a bit.'

'Très bien, very good.'

The night before Frank had only got out of his car once throughout the duration of the two break-ins. Firstly Reynard had gone alone and broke into Will and Sophie's cottage through the back door but Frank had seen Reynard at work up-close, when he'd briefly got out of the car up at the garage to remove the tracking device from the Audi. He saw a glove-handed Reynard gently offer the poison-laced steak to the feeble, salacious dog with the art of a whisperer. He saw Reynard jab a powerful elbow through the Audi's window effortlessly, and search Will's car in all under three minutes. They had left the hotel at half past nine and were back by a quarter to eleven; the two jobs had taken just over an hour to complete. He was only in the house for six or seven minutes. And this was all at 10pm. One thing, Frank thought as he sped up the dual carriageway away from Salisbury the following morning, was that this Frenchman, to give him his due, was one hellova an efficient operator. He had balls, this guy - in fact he had no fear whatsoever: a real pro.

'Did you find what you were looking for, sir?' Frank enquired, asking probably the first question he'd put to Reynard, apart from pleasantries, since he had arrived in the country.

'Perhaps,' Reynard answered nonchalantly, hoping the laptop he had in his suitcase held the answers his boss desired.

No further words were shared for the next hour but as soon as Reynard saw the signs for Heathrow on the motorway he loosened up. 'I thank my God I didn't have to use the steak at the house,' he said. 'I didn't know there would be a dog up at the garage too, we were lucky.'

'I suppose so,' Frank replied, trying to sound upbeat. He had a Staffordshire Bull terrier himself and loved the creature to bits. He was utterly devastated as he crouched under the Audi to remove the tracking device to see Mick's hound gobble the poisoned meat and then, with a stunned look in its eyes, keel over. Frank, transfixed, even glimpsed a foamy bile erupt from the dog's throat as it raised its head one final time in a last ditch effort to fight. But in an instant it had lain back in frothing, agonising spasms.

Frank knew there just wasn't any room for sympathy in the business he was in; it was a hard man's game, you do what you have to do and don't look back, no sentiment. It was business. He'd stood up and crept slowly back to his car, as quietly as he could. It was an image he'd never forget.

Frank didn't have a clue what William Marshall had done and didn't care either. He just wanted to get shot of Reynard as quickly as possible and be back in East London with his family for Christmas.

After the two-man forensic team, in white overalls, had finished checking for fingerprints and left, Will spent a good two hours tidying up completely, getting the house back to normal.

The police had finally departed the night before at two o'clock in the morning and Sophie was in such a state of shock she'd gone straight up to the spare room; Will had slept on the sofa. She had been silent that morning and left for work without saying a word.

While he was cleaning up he phoned his editor at the Journal.

'Morning, Simon, it's Will. Did you get the draft of the article I sent over last night? Oh, that's great, well done, that was quick. Ping it back to me, would you, and I'll finish it off by this evening? As soon as... please. Okay, mate, many thanks. Speak later, bye.'

While he waited for his article to be emailed back Will went up to the spare room and found his old laptop, untouched beneath a pile of papers, plugged it in and fired it up. He had surreptitiously checked that the contents within the secret compartment of his old chest were safe the night before and he now took out his camera. He didn't know why but he had slipped his instamatic into the hidden chamber along with his notes and what was - he was now absolutely one hundred percent convinced - one red-hot, smoking gun of a map.

The camera's software was still installed on his old computer so he was able to download the photos of his recent walk in France.

In reality nothing had been stolen in the break-in - nothing physical, anyway; all was instantly replaceable, but the fact was that the sanctity of their home had been brutally violated. They had been robbed of their privacy. It was an ugly memory and one that Will was not sure how Sophie was going to cope with. As a result he made an extra special effort to make both their bedroom and the sitting-room look cleaner and fresher than they had been before the incident and he was determined to have a decent meal ready for her when she got in later that evening; a dish that had mouth-watering fragrant aromas to make their home smell inviting and loved.

Will was determined to concentrate on finishing the article before he thought about doing anything else. His natural impulses, having been a journalist for three years, had been re-programmed. Responding to deadlines was becoming second nature and so he knuckled down and obeyed his professional instincts obediently, pushing all other thoughts to one side. However, he found completing the last fifteen hundred words of the article incredibly difficult. The contents of the box in the corner of the room were a constant distraction; the antique nomadic chest seemed to be pulsing, burning even, certainly throbbing, as if it or whatever was within was desperate to come to life again. It was as if there was a genie inside, banging on its lamp's wall, yelling to be let out. Just like the miasma in his mind.

By one o'clock Will had re-sent the completed article over to his boss for a final proofread and, having taken Nelson out for a quick walk, was back at his desk with the map laid out beside the computer and his notebook open, ready to tackle the riddle of his inheritance.

He'd lain awake on the sofa late into the previous night, amongst the debris, unable to sleep. All the bizarre little things that had happened to him ever since he first opened the cardboard boxes and arrived in France made him toss violently. All those little bangs and pops had now most definitely come to the fore and had added up to being one big, terrific mental explosion. A shocking wake-up call. This was serious now. His professional mind, fully engaged, loved the investigation; however his personal entity quaked. The culmination of the list of tiny, potentially spurious little things, which could have been brushed off, which had led to the reality of the break-ins made Will unequivocally conclude that he was in deep shit. He was under no illusions anymore and was now convinced that the map in front of him held something very special indeed. It was crystal clear that what was laid out before him was something that other people desperately wanted and were prepared to go to a great deal of effort and expense to get hold of. And if they had been prepared to kill a dog in their attempts to get hold of the map, what else would they be willing to do? The reality that he was in real and present danger finally dawned on him, shockingly. As much as it made him nervous, it excited him too. He'd never felt so alive. He visibly shook as he stared at his map.

His mind raced. *Even if I can hand over the map to these people who want it so badly I don't have a clue who they are*, he said to himself. *The only tenable link to all this must old Degas back at the antique shop in Bordeaux. He was the trigger, surely*?

But for now Will was determined to get to the bottom of all this himself, starting by finding out more about Bousquet and his relationship with Bourg.

He began to research this Maurice Bousquet in more detail.

As he scoured the internet he discovered, through one article, that Bousquet had bought himself a chateau just outside Bourg where he entertained the Third Reich during the early part of the war and where, apparently, various locals said they had been tortured. But this particular article didn't actually name the chateau so Will looked back through the marked journey he'd taken from Bourg. The only chateau he'd come across on the route was the ominous one that resembled an old institution: the Chateau Cheille. *That must be the one*, Will thought. *It certainly had the vibe; who else could have owned it?*

Will went back into the French property search website, paid his few Euros and up popped the history of the ownership of the chateau. It was now owned by a Monsieur Finkleman who had bought it nine years previously from a charity but prior to that… it had been owned by a Madame Bousquet, and prior to her by Maurice Bousquet. *Bingo.*

Wow! This was all getting confusing. *Try and think clearly, Will,* he said to himself, forcing his addled mind to focus. He got up and began to pace around the house. *Start at the beginning. The map doesn't lead to the chateau, it doesn't even mention it, it clearly says Bousquet, Bourg and the coiffeur – the hairdresser. Okay, and the hairdresser is owned by…?* He dashed to his notebook and saw the name 'Mme Estournel' that he had written down the day before. *Right, the next step is to find out who this Mme Estournel is, and whether she is still alive,* he reasoned to himself as he sat down again. *And the only way I'm going to find that out is by going into the registry of births, deaths and marriages.*

He found conversing with himself helped in the process of logical thinking. He knew that in UK it was gro.gov.uk; in France, he found out with two clicks of the mouse, it was geneaou.net. He then opened the website and filled out another short online form giving the hairdresser's address in Bourg and her name. Again he paid a few Euros on his credit card and, within moments, he had discovered that Mme Estournel was in fact born Claudette Bousquet and she had married a François Estournel in Bourg in 1932. But he had died only a few years later in 1935, and that she had lived for another sixty years, dying only ten years ago. She had reverted to her maiden name soon after her husband's death. And Will read she was buried in the same church she'd married in.

Shit, he thought to himself, *this is all happening so fast. Only a few years ago this would have taken me months to investigate, and I would have had to go down to the town hall in Bourg, sift through their records, write letters, wait for replies, and now… it's taken moments. Incredible. Encroyable!*

In the space of half an hour he had pieced together the seemingly disjointed strands of a long deceased family in another country. Henri Lafarge, two generations adrift of the new technology and caught in a web of secrecy, was left in the dark.

Will knew he had to leave it all for a moment to let the information assimilate in his mind – it had all gushed in a bit too fast.

He went to the freeze box and found some lamb steaks and took them out to defrost. He'd do a Moroccan-style dish with lots of spices; that would make the place smell nicely aromatic for Sophie's arrival home.

While working the pestle and mortar he remembered that Sophie had to attend her students' carol service in the cathedral that evening, and without a car he was housebound. So he lit the wood burner, sat down and promptly fell asleep. His mind was a mess trying to assimilate and pigeonhole all the disjointed and scary information that it had been forced to absorb over the past few days. He dreamt of old ladies writing autobiographies, bread ovens, sharp needles, sea journeys and a whole bunch of random nonsense as he slumbered in his armchair, but the moment he woke up; he felt instantly refreshed and invigorated. Having had a glass of water and opened a bottle of wine, he sat down at the table again with the map and his notes laid out in front of him, his laptop fired-up, ready to go.

Through various searches it soon became obvious to Will that the key figure to this mystery was Maurice Bousquet. And what seemed to be evident was that not only did he have a dreadful legacy as a Nazi collaborator but that he was also a thief who'd stolen stupendous wine cellars from private individuals, famous restaurants and national institutions during his tenures as police chief in Bordeaux and Paris just before and during the Second World War. The online articles he'd read were unclear as to whether these wines had been shipped out to Germany, or lost to Allied bombing, or where they were. Huge amounts of wine had been found and rescued in Germany after the war and brought back to France so people were not sure whether the wines Bousquet stole had been drunk, accounted for, stolen again, destroyed or lost in the mayhem during the last years of the war and the subsequent rebuilding of France. One article that had got Will daydreaming was the staggering value of the wines he had stolen: today's value was estimated at between one hundred and two hundred million Euros.

Will gazed at the map and then across at the misty photo of the old hairdresser shop in Bourg on his computer screen and stared at his notes. He knew that the three words he had deciphered from the cover of the map, were the key words to unlocking this secret and he kept repeating them over and over again rhythmically: Bousquet, Bourg, coiffeur – Bousquet, Bourg, coiffeur.

By the time Sophie arrived home an hour later Will had packed everything away and the moment he saw the headlights of her car outside he quickly put on a laidback CD that he knew she liked, Rickie Lee Jones's 'Cowboys', and hoped that this and the aromas of Eastern spices would combine to give her a warm welcome. He couldn't have been more wrong; when she burst in he had never seen her look more drawn and severe. She barely looked at him and when she did it was always with an evil eye. He tried.

'How was the carol service, hon?' he enquired pleasantly as she came in. No response. 'How's your day been, sweetie?' Nothing.

There was no approaching her; she was just too cold and hard, so he let her be. She disappeared upstairs with Nelson. When she did eventually come down, stomping like thunder on the stairs, she sat down opposite him with Nelson plonked on her lap.

'Now, Will, what-is-going-on?' she demanded, looking at him directly.

'What do you mean, hon?' he replied nonchalantly, stifling a fake yawn.

'Don't hon me, Will. What-is-going-on?' she snapped back alarmingly.

'I don't know, Soph, I really don't,' he implored, wide awake now, with hands up, palms towards her, on the retreat.

'Well, let me spell it out for you then. Someone broke into our house last night, okay? All they took was your wretched laptop, and they broke into your car, too, and killed a dog in the process. Hello! Can I make myself any clearer? Can't you see it could have been Nelson dead if we hadn't taken him up to the pub with us?'

'I know, I know,' he agreed feebly, and, having nothing more to add, got up awkwardly, went to the sink and started fumbling around with the washing-up. When he turned around Sophie was standing at the doorway with her hands on her hips.

'No, Will, that is not good enough. I want you to tell me now what you've been doing. I've had the police up at the school wondering what on earth this is all about too. This is serious.' As she continued she got angrier, and her voice turned gravely. 'It's all to do with those fucking maps your father gave you, isn't it?

'Maybe, maybe it is,' he stammered. 'I can't believe it though.'

'Well, what else can it be then? What else are you up to?'

'I don't know, I just don't know.'

'Wake up, Will. Have you still got the map on you?'

'Um, no, I don't think so. I haven't looked.'

'Well, look then. We are going to hand it over to the police. I told them about it and that you had been to France and there were a few small incidents.'

'You did what?' Will replied. He slowly removed his hands from the sink, shaking the bubbles off deliberately. He turned his head slowly towards her, furious now. 'What the hell do you think you were doing?'

'That's it, Will. You and your fucking father. I've had enough. Leave me alone. You sleep down here again tonight.'

With that she turned away and stomped off. Will's voice faded behind her. 'Don't be silly, hon, what about supper?' It was pointless; he was speaking to an empty room.

Half an hour later he took Sophie up her dinner on a tray and knocked on the door. 'Soph, I'm leaving your dinner out here if you want it. Come down though, hon, don't be such a sourpuss.'

'Fuck off, Will,' was all he got.

Sophie didn't appear or make any noise at all for the rest of that evening and left the house the following morning without saying a word, slamming the door as she went.

Will had lain awake again late into the night on the sofa, staring at the faint glow of the wood burner getting dimmer and dimmer. His mind was rolling over and over what he had uncovered from the map. Was it really leading anywhere? If so, where to? What would he find there? And what sort of a mess had he, or indeed his father, got him into? He gazed at the French painting of the river scene that had sparked his enthusiasm about the maps in the first place. The first inkling of a coincidence, the first seed of discovery was sown when he looked at that picture. The two men walking along the bank of the wide river with their backs to the viewer were even more symbolic now. It genuinely looked like him and his father strolling towards the horizon together, striding into the sunset in the last flickering golden rays from the fire.

After Sophie had left he'd immediately got the map and his notes out again and stared at them for a long time. He realised he had nowhere else to go, nothing else to research. He had run into a blank again. A dead end. Opening up the computer and looking at the misty photo of the Bousquet family's derelict shop in Bourg he wondered whether he had in fact stumbled across the place where Maurice Bousquet had hidden his wines. Could that be it? It was an obvious place to do it, so why hadn't anyone else discovered this? Could it simply be an oversight about Maurice Bousquet's sister's name, who'd owned the shop, which had changed to Estournel through marriage and then back again? Could it just have been overlooked, taken anyone looking off the scent? Perhaps the people of France had simply lost interest in the subject, or buried their heads in the sand on the sordid matter, or simply just given up searching for the Bousquet horde completely. French national guilt about their record of collaboration during the war is still today a very raw, embarrassing subject and one that is, although less so now, brushed under the carpet and consigned to the past; so perhaps the nation doesn't actually want to be reminded of Bousquet.

'Shit, shit, shit!' Will muttered. He realised that all led to this shop. *The map and its markings all lead to the shop, not to the chateau. Why had Dad written 'Start'? He should have written 'End'.* Looking at the photo closely again, he could see that it couldn't have been occupied for decades and it looked quite possible no one had been even in there for half a century or more. And he thought, *where do you keep wines? In a cellar. And who would even go down there? The old butchers shop had been used well before the time of electricity and freezers so they must have quite extensive cellars: underground cold stores,* he assumed.

If there is anything real that this map could lead to, then it can only be to Bousquet's unfound wines, stashed, hidden in this shop, undiscovered for decades. That's the only logical thing that this could be all about. What else could it be? As he gazed at the photo on the screen of Bourg's Place du Marché, perhaps from not having slept too well, and the excitement all this was generating, he thought the photograph actually shimmered slightly. The shroud of mist that hung over the square that morning four days ago shifted; it pulsed at Will and began to lift. It was as if the still image on the screen had turned to film and come to life.

CHAPTER 19

MAYDAY, MAYDAY...

Will phoned the Journal. Simon, his boss, was delighted with the article and didn't need Will to do any more on it. That meant work was over for another year. He wasn't required at the paper until after New Year; over two weeks away. No more features. Nothing.

Mick drove the Audi down to Will's that afternoon and Will drove him back up to the workshop. They chatted about the car's smooth running and the events two nights earlier, but rather superficially, glossing it slightly. Will was absolutely genuine in expressing how sorry he was about King, but there was a knowing look in Mick's eye as if he wanted to say 'I know you are up to something...' but Will wasn't disclosing anything, so the only stance Mick could reasonably take was a polite, deferential one. He couldn't point the finger of blame on Will without any proof, any hard evidence, and he didn't have it, all he had was his gut feeling, a strong suspicion that the break-ins at his workshop and Will's house, and the subsequent poisoning of his dog weren't coincidence, mere random acts of violence, utterly disconnected. Will handed over payment while sitting in the car.

As Mick got out, he turned before closing the door. 'I'm sorry about the break-in up here, Will. I'm sure it won't happen again. Your car's running sweetly, and all the damage is mended, so take care out there, mate,' he said. And then, staring into Will's eyes in a concerned, brotherly, unthreatening manner, he concluded, 'I mean it, Will, take care.'

'Thanks, Mick, you too.' They looked at each other, held their gaze briefly and then turned away. The door shut.

It was only three o'clock when Will got home. He took Nelson for a walk around the block. He tidied up, had a quick snack and paced around. He phoned his sister, Lou, in London.

'Hiya, it's me, how's it going?' he said.

'I'm fine, thanks, and you? Back from your epic walk, how was it?'

'Yes, it feels like ages ago now. It was really quite something. But the drama right now is that our cottage got broken into a couple of nights ago, while we were out at the pub.'

'Oh my God, how terrible,' a shocked Louise said. 'Does that go on a lot down there? What did they take?'

'No, it doesn't. They trashed the place and all they took was my laptop,' he said, and then continued thoughtfully. 'Look, Lou, I'm sure it's got something to do with those maps I got from Dad.'

Lou considered for a moment. 'Go on.'

'Well, I'd told the antiquarian bookseller in Bordeaux about the maps ten days or so before I sold them to him and I got the vibe he was expecting me and then all sorts of shite began happening, ending up with this break-in. My car was up at a local garage and it got busted into on the same night as the burglary.'

'Blimey, Will, all a bit hectic, eh,' his sister said, shocked at the information she was absorbing. 'It all goes on in the country.

I don't understand, though, I thought you simply sold the maps and got all that money for them? That's all Sophie told me.'

'Sorry, Lou, Sophie's only just realising it too. I didn't explain but there were forty maps in all and only one of them, which I kept, had these strange markings on it and Dad had even written on it, too. It seemed as if he had been there, all around this place called Bourg, just out of Bordeaux. The maps were beside his bed when he died and, so Uncle David says, he insisted they go to me.'

'What's the place called again, spell it out for me?'

'Bourg, B-O-U-R-G. Ever heard of it?'

'No.'

'Anyway, as you know, I sold the thirty-nine of them and got the fifteen hundred Euros from the sale.'

'Yeah, lovely, Soph told me, very nice, well done.'

'Anyway, since I've been back, without going into too much detail, I've discovered that the map seems to be leading to, potentially, a stash of wines that this ex chief of police hid during the war in an old shop in Bourg - believe it or not, an old hairdresser's salon. All this I've researched and uncovered through the walk, what was on the map, the clues, and the internet, of course.'

'A chief of police, like Dad? Interesting. And a stash of wines, eh!'

'Yes, Lou, and this is no ordinary stash of wines, believe me. This guy Bousquet stole wines from all the rich Jews in France and fabulous old restaurants during the war, and some articles I've read say the value today is something like two hundred million ruddy Euros, can you believe it?' Will gushed enthusiastically.

Lou laughed hysterically, and then calmed. 'Wow, hard to believe. All sounds a bit far-fetched to me, though. Come on,

Will, are you sure you aren't wishful thinking all this?'

'No, not anymore. I thought I could have been but now, what with the two break-ins... no, Lou, this is serious. I'm telling you the map is red-hot, it's no joke. People are onto me.' He waited a moment. 'Anyway, I've got to go now. Are we going to see you over Christmas at all?'

'I'll come down for New Year if that's okay?'

'Yes, great. We'll probably only go down to the Black Horse, though, on New Year's Eve. Is that alright?'

'Yes, fab.' She hesitated. 'I'll see you then. Obviously we'll speak before, but Will, take care; this all sounds a bit scary to me.'

'Yeah, yeah,' he replied laughing. 'Bit of fun, more like. Speak soon, bye for now.' He rushed to hang up. His sister's mixture of negativity and amusement over their inheritance, and her doubts about the implications he was alluding to, had irked him. Where was her sense of adventure?

Deflated and with nothing particular to do he flopped down in his armchair, frustrated and anxious, twisted and torn, excited yet concerned. He sat for a few minutes and then suddenly jumped up.

A shivering realisation ignited him. *Whoever's stolen my computer will be in the process of discovering that the last things I did on it was to study the photo of the shop in Bourg. And importantly they'll find on the hard-drive,* (which is what really made him leap), *that I've done the searches on the French websites. Looking up Madame Estournel and the old shop means that the people in possession of the computer will quickly and easily put two and two together and come to the same conclusions as I have. They'll find the old shop on the Bourg market square.* He pictured a computer boffin, at that very moment, relaying in French that information to whoever was searching for him and the wines.

Will's mind lunged to the final conclusion that his pursuers, whoever they were, upon discovering the information they were looking for, wouldn't bother him again. He relaxed. He calmed. He sat down again. *They won't be needing me again; I've given them all the information they require.* He sat back, feet out. *Phew! That's a relief. This is all over.*

However his calmness soon mutated to annoyance. *I haven't simply given the information to these people, they've stolen it from me. They have stolen my discovery, my legacy. Through me, and Dad, these scumbags now have the answers to the riddle they've been after. The Marshall family have served our purpose. There is no way these sorts of folk will just pop a cheque through the letter-box in due course for twenty million Euros, attaching a little thank you note saying, that's ten percent of the value of the wines for you, we really appreciate it.*

He would never know or hear of this matter again, probably. Whoever *they* were, the people who'd followed him and broken into his home and car were definitely not officials, a legitimate body, that was for sure. Or, he mused, *I may read in the papers or see a programme on TV, at some point soon, that these wines have resurfaced.*

Like stolen Second World War art discoveries that keep cropping up, the public don't comprehend that these art and wine thefts were a concerted element of Germany's policy to control the culture of each country it invaded. The Third Reich wanted to own the conquered France's soul. To rob and possess its very essence. And in France's case, which is rarely fully appreciated, the significance of wine to the nation is unquantifiable. Wine is very much a major element of France's cultural heritage; it was as if Bousquet had stolen part of France's heart.

Conversely Bousquet, Will thought, could be seen now as a visionary, a French national hero. By stealing the wines himself, and then hiding them, he'd actually preserved them for France rather than the Third Reich. His meticulous thieving made sure foreigners never got their hands on the precious wines and took them away. Therefore a missing segment of Bousquet's nation's spirit might still be intact, hidden, awaiting rediscovery – who knew? *Maybe, just me.*

As Will daydreamed on, although deflated, his mood lifted slightly at the thought that perhaps in some odd way what he had done had helped France's soul towards a rebirth with the discovery of these wines. Thinking laterally he thought that if a criminal element got them, then what? The people following him were obviously not straight down the line. It could be a disaster for France. All this liquid power in the wrong hands.

And then he went on with his mental play that if only he could get five or six cases of this wine or brandy that would be worth (he had read) £ 30,000 per bottle. Just four cases, forty-eight bottles, would be worth nearly one and a half million pound - kerching, very nice! *I'd be highly delighted with that. I could tuck that away in the boot of my car easily, no problem. I deserve it, surely? I'm the one who has solved the riddle, haven't I?*

'Fuck, fuck, fuck,' Will finally exclaimed out loud, rapping his palms on his forehead. This outburst made Nelson look up from his bed sheepishly, as if he had done something wrong.

Will was now in the throes of a full-on dilemma: it was either forget the adventure and excitement now, right now and just wait and see what happened - at some point in the future perhaps he could declare his and his father's role in the discovery - or he could go right back there immediately and see with his own eyes whether he was correct, and that there was something of value hidden in the old building in Bourg. Get there before the thieves did. There was no two ways about it. It was now or never, otherwise the computer-thieving-dog killers would pip him to the post.

If there's nothing in the shop then, who cares, I will have had one of the biggest thrills of my life, and I can write about it, dramatise it. He was talking to himself again. *I've got to go on this journey to the end. I've got over a thousand Euros left from the sale of the maps tucked away so, in effect, the two trips won't have cost me a penny. Why the hell not?* He got up again, and stopped, staring at the rain drumming on the roof of his car outside. *I've got no work commitments, Sophie's in a full-on huff with me and the car's mended and running sweetly. I can get on the night ferry tonight, get down there tomorrow afternoon, have a poke around on Saturday, too, if I want, and then get the ferry back on Sunday, easy. That'll only be the eighteenth of December, so plenty of time for Christmas, and I'll know by then for sure. Sophie will have calmed down by then, hopefully. If I don't do it, this is going to do my head in, perhaps for the rest of my life. If I don't try, it may well be one of those vital regrets, one of life's major opportunities not taken that'll give me Alzheimer's when I'm older.*

He turned back into the room and walked across to his laptop. He flipped it open, went online, fetched his credit card and booked himself and his car onto the night ferry back to St Malo in a few hours' time. He'd go it alone this time. *No Nelson. Just me.*

CHAPTER 20
IT'S ONLY BUSINESS

The next morning, with vapour rising from the tarmac, Will gunned his Audi down the empty French motorway. The crossing had been smooth, he'd had a solid night's sleep, and he felt fully refreshed, wide awake and alert.

He'd switched off his phone as soon as he'd left home and hadn't switched it on again once. He hadn't even called Sophie before he left either. He'd left a note for her instead. He'd explained that through his recent revelations, and because of all that had gone on, he just had to go back down to France and investigate his findings. A building he'd discovered might hold the secret of the old map he'd inherited. He just had to see this through to the end. He trusted she'd understand that he simply had to finish what he'd started. He had a duty to do this for himself; it was now nothing to do with his father. This was the last link in the puzzle he'd uncovered. If there was nothing there, fine, he promised he'd draw a line under it. But if he didn't go down and see for himself he would never know and he couldn't live with that: feeling weak and scared off. Will even said in the letter that he knew she'd understand. He told her not to worry as the burglars had got all the information they wanted through the laptop they had stolen in the break-in. He would be back on Sunday evening.

During the long tedious hours on the road Will thought that in his father's eyes he had never been as much of a man as James believed himself to be. He'd even said as much, a bit drunk. It was one of the last words his father had uttered to Will in person.

'You're weak,' James had declared, shaking hands, as they said goodnight on the last night of his last visit to South Africa.

Will gripped the steering wheel tighter. He knew that if he didn't complete this search he would genuinely feel pathetic and half-hearted. He couldn't allow himself to prove his father correct. If he gave up this journey of discovery before the end he would always feel a failure and would forever feebly daydream about the *what if's*, and believe his father was right. But now that he was seeing this through to the conclusion, even if there was nothing to the map, Will could look back on his father as being a wind-up merchant, a bull-shitter, and feel good about that rather than bad about himself. He had nothing to lose and everything to gain.

So on he hammered, past Rennes and La Rochelle. It was exactly the same route, at pretty well exactly the same time, as he had done precisely one week previously. Will couldn't compute that it was only seven days ago that he'd come down on his supposedly relaxed walk. This time the atmosphere had changed dramatically; there was no adrenalin involved on the last trip. No danger like there was now.

'Sir, sir,' the French lieutenant called out. 'Le lapin has arrived back in France!' Maurice had blurted across the bare, day-room-type office to his immediate superior as he peered at his computer screen.

'What?' Reynard said, turning slowly. His voice turned venomous. 'When? Where?' he hissed. Shocked, he rushed over to look at the map on the screen.

'Now, sir, see,' Maurice said, pointing at Will's car blinking past La Rochelle. 'The tracker alerted me he was back in France, but I missed it because we were loading.'

Reynard gave the seated lackey a clip across the back of his head. 'You fool. Merde!'

It was just past midday when Reynard received the bombshell. They'd all just finished clearing out the last of their stores and had loaded final deliveries of unadulterated fruit before Christmas. They were about to leave for their holidays in good spirits. The warehouse was empty. Their boss, Lafarge, had gone up to his office five minutes before, having handed out brown envelopes of cash bonuses to all his men, all of whom had now left. As soon as the lorries had departed ten minutes before the warehouse had cleared immediately, of both people and crates. It was completely empty. Reynard dashed upstairs and knocked on his boss's door.

'Entrer,' Henri Lafarge called out. His lieutenant put his head around the door. 'What is it, Renard?'

'Sir, the cowboy, Marshall, is back in France. He is driving down towards Bordeaux again, we think,' Reynard replied, breathing heavily as he entered the spacious yet spartan office.

'What!'

'That's right, sir, Maurice was alerted by our tracking programme and he is definitely on the move down through France again, I presume heading back to the Bourg, Blaye area. He landed at St Malo, and is just past La Rochelle now.'

'Sit down, Renard,' Henri Lafarge said. 'Let me think.' He pointed an excited finger to a chair and then got on the internal phone on his desk. 'Marie, two coffees.' He then turned back to Reynard. 'What do you think?'

'Well, firstly, sir, how have we got on with his computer? What more do we know?'

'They have had problems, I know that - the English hardware or something is holding them up, they say. We haven't got any information from it yet. I will phone them now.'

With that Lafarge found a phone number on the rolodex in front of him, dialled the number, had a brief conversation, barked and put the receiver down.

'Nothing, they are still working on it,' he informed Reynard coolly. 'They say they will have something for us in two or three hours.'

Reynard was not up to speed, having just got back to Marseille that morning from a pit-stop in Belgium, enforcing. He had had a hectic week and was looking forward to having a break. He was exhausted. Kissing sixty himself he felt drained from dashing between bouts of crime and extreme violence.

'Okay, sir,' he sighed. Can you get the carpenter you used in Bourg onto it immediately? He's going to get there quickest. To wait around and follow his car when he arrives, that is a start. All the men here have gone on the piss, and they won't be able to get up there for ten hours at least.'

As the two men looked at each other, panicked, there was a knock on the door. Lafarge's secretary came in with their espressos on a tray. When she saw the state of the two men the cups rattled. She put the tray down and hastily escaped the strained atmosphere without saying a word. Lafarge picked up his phone again. 'Get my plane ready, now, we are going to Bordeaux. One hour, yes, be ready.' He hung up and turned to Reynard. 'Come on, let's go. It is up to us now.'

At four o'clock that afternoon, as soft creases of daylight were receding across the flat Gironde estuary into the folds of dusk, Will swung into the outskirts of Bourg. He'd spent a brain-numbing six hours hacking down the motorway with only a few coffee breaks as fuel. But when he approached the old citadel he was greeted by an incredibly lively Christmas market in full flow. He couldn't believe it. The old town had burst into life. Will had expected to arrive in an eerily quiet Bourg, just as he'd left it on Sunday morning. He didn't expect this.

He edged into the fortified quarter and began to weave his car slowly through the bustling crowd of masked revellers and face-painted children. He crawled his way into the centre and, luckily, managed to find a parking space at the rear of the main church, high on the battlements above the vast mercurial body of water below, which, as he got out and stretched, was turning silvery by a bright winter moon appearing large above the horizon.

The streets were alive with festive decorations; strips of shimmering blue lights were the theme running across the buildings, some of which had plastic inflatable Santas climbing up them. The avenue of trees, lining the streets, had their trunks wrapped in knitted, brightly-coloured woollen eiderdowns. The sound of 'Good King Wenceslas' emanated from a barrel organ and echoed loudly through Bourg's narrow alleys and thoroughfares.

Oh shit, this all I need, Will said to himself as he pulled on his old beanie tightly, hoisted his small but heavy rucksack over his shoulders and headed into the festive crowd.

As he passed he peered, through open doors, into the warmly lit church and could see various stalls had been set up within, selling local lavender, chutneys, carved wooden toys and dreadful paintings. Outside there was someone doing donkey rides for the children. The donkeys had been dressed as reindeer and wore funny little bonnets over their ears with fake antlers attached. It was radical, the difference. Bourg, from being like a ghost town the week before, was now alive, a bustling local hub.

Following the crowd, Will slowly ambled up to the market square where many more stalls were set up around a brightly lit carousel: the fair's epicentre. Aromas of hot sugared nuts, mulled wine, candyfloss and fried onions filled the air as the smoke from barbeques plumed up into the cold still night, creating a blanket that hung in the air above the joyful scene. As Will walked around looking at the stalls his eyes darted to firmly focus on one old empty shop on the corner. He ignored the transformation the town had undergone in the past week and focussed.

He could see clearly that the old coiffeur was empty. It radiated a dense, solid coldness. It was a dark, icy lump of a space, filling only shadows. There was no sign of life whatsoever. He could just make out the outlines he'd seen of bricked-up windows on the first floor, and the large ground-floor shop window revealed nothing within. The building stood desolate with all this life going on around it, still and desperately alone. It made Will shudder.

He queued and bought himself a hotdog and continued to wander about trying to look interested and happy, inconspicuous. Then, as slyly as possible, he peeled off around to the side of the old coiffeur, and quickly walked down the narrow cobbled street that ran off the main square. A back alley then cut in left behind the old shop. He quickly glanced to check he wasn't being followed, and then walked past the rear of the old building. All was quiet; he could see an old solid wooden back door, set within the brick wall, that led into a walled courtyard. The back door looked as if it hadn't been opened for an age; dirt and leaves had collected in thick piles at its base. Will knew straight away that this was his point of entry. He carried on down past the entrance but when he reached the end of the alley he turned back and crossed over onto the opposite side of the narrow road. Keeping to the shadows now he could clearly see that this was definitely it: the back of the old hairdresser's shop. The rear, just like the front, looked so dark and cold, like a slab, a mausoleum. This fine old structure seemed to be crying out to Will, in its icy stillness, *resuscitate me, bring me back to life*. The joyful hubbub behind was wishing it on.

Will stood for a long moment gazing at the building and then, with a mere blink, his focus shifted back to reality. He began to work out his entry through the door opposite him. His eyes scanned and studied the brick walls and wooden door. And then, when a moped pulled up and stopped at the end of the road, only ten metres to Will's left, he eased back into the shadows, unnoticed. Will could just make out an older, open-face- helmeted man stare about frantically, as if looking for someone, before screaming off. The road was empty again, so Will, with a clear plan in mind, quickly headed back around the corner and into the crowds in the market square, who were now all streaming down towards the church. Will fell in and went with the flow.

Everyone was jamming in around the cars, concertinaing into one big mass at the back of the church, filling every available space around the open ramparts. Will asked a passer-by why everyone was gathering and was informed that there was going to be les feux d'artifice, a firework display. The moment he heard what was happening Will realised this was his chance, and immediately turned back. He was now moving awkwardly against the human traffic, jostling his way back up towards the market square through the crowd; then he peeled off again, into the stillness, down to the rear of the building. He knew the display's noise was going to be the perfect distraction: his perfect cover. He stood for a moment catching his breath in the cold shadows opposite the back gate where he'd stood five minutes before. Looking up he could see the stars shining brightly and he calmed himself by trying to contain the vapour-trails from his breath from jetting out too far into the heavens and giving his position away. He drew short breaths in and long, gentle ones out.

Then, quite suddenly, it started; whizzing bulbs of burning candles fired upwards, shooting heavenwards. A moment's silence and then almighty bangs commenced and explosions of red and blue incandescence splayed out, filling the night sky with coloured light. Between individual fireworks there would be a moment of darkness and then the whizzing and popping would recommence: pow, pow, pa-pow, pow. The Bousquet building in front of him for brief moments flashed to life under ominous flares.

This was Will's cue to move. He stepped forward quietly, with purpose, and strode the three metres over to the old back door. He tested its strength. Having established that the hinges were the weakest links, he stood back four feet and waited. As soon as he heard the next fizz of fireworks blasting skywards he braced himself and then, as he felt the rockets about to explode, he ran forward and butted the door as hard as he could with his shoulder, smashing into it with a thud and a creak. He gave it a hefty crack, but the door held tight. With the dead shudder of impact Will soon felt pangs of nerve pain reverberate through him. His fast over-heating mind began to throb. All sorts of notions pulsed about within, the main one being, *what the hell are you doing breaking into a property, William Marshall*? He rejected answering his voice of reason. *There's no way on fucking earth I'm backing off now*. And again he stood back; focused and determined, and put himself in the zone ready for another assault on the door. The next fizzle of a firework re-galvanised him; this time he turned sideways and when he sensed the bursts about to occur, again he charged. The impact tore away the top hinge but the lower one held firm. Will was on fire as rockets began to snap, pop and screech around him furiously. He stood back and kicked frantically on the lower half of the door as the fireworks blasted around him, ricocheting and echoing all through Bourg's warren of streets. This repeated, determined force slowly drove the lower hinge free and the door was, at last, fully loose all down one side. Without a moment's hesitation Will quickly squeezed in and around off the street, and into the courtyard behind. He pushed the door shut as fast and best as he could and then leaned back, heaving on the closed door. He felt as if the violent motions of his chest could be heard all around town and his breath visible for miles. He forced himself to calm down, crouched hands on knees, his head pumping with heat. It was as if his frantically beating heart had actually moved to lodge in his brain.

When he had calmed, and could see the back of the old shop in front of him being lit up by a rapid peppering of blue and red light from the display, like strobe lights being flickered on and off rapidly, he tried to focus on Plan B. But it was disorientating this visual sensation as it was accompanied by the disturbing noise of the firecrackers' explosions ricocheting off the buildings all around him as if it was the Bourg blitz in the war, with the little town being aerial bombed. It took a few long moments for Will to compose himself. When he had calmed sufficiently and was ready for the next move, he switched on his torch and carefully crossed the slime-ridden, rubbish-filled yard to the back door. Now back in action-man mode, he got out his crow-bar straight away and jimmied into the slightly rotten door frame. He yanked and hacked frantically as the finale of the display began to cascade around him. He worked in tune with the bangs from the illuminations, he followed the 'oohs' and 'aahs' from the crowd, and crow-barred to the cacophony of sounds ricocheting through the old town. Spots of multi-coloured lights pogo danced around him, bouncing onto and off every surface, and then… suddenly, with a tear… the door popped, and he was in: into a freezer.

Will immediately felt a sense of calm. An enveloping solitude greeted him as he gently pushed the door shut to the outside world, replaced his crowbar and fumbled for his long, heavy torch. He leant back and switched it on again. Illuminated in front of him was a dank, whitewashed, arched corridor which led straight towards the front of the building, towards the market square. He walked carefully to the opposite end of the passageway where he could hear the crowd milling around on the other side of the front door. Retracing his steps he came back to a door on the left which he opened slightly and, peering in, he could see the large, open shop space where the mirrored salon must have been and the butchers shop before it. Through chinks he could see the lights from the carousel in the square outside reflected through the dirt-darkened windows; they flickered around the empty shop. The melodious sound of 'Silent night, holy night' gently hummed out of the barrel organ. He closed the door slowly and went back up the corridor the way he'd come; the next door on the right opened easily onto a staircase, which he ignored. Five metres past this was the only other door in the passageway which was locked solid so, propping the torch on the floor, Will jimmied again. Not only was it held firm by a old heavy lock but it was hard to find an actual position to get the point of the metal crowbar into. With a great deal of effort and, having made a complete mess of the woodwork, working hard with ferocious willpower, Will had it creaking open on its hinges. As he pulled open the door fully Will felt an intense wave of solid air ooze out of the doorway like a slow-moving avalanche. The arctic blast made Will step back. It was a freezing air which met a very cold air. Yet still this intense bitter block came forward to override the already cold air within the corridor. *My God*, Will thought, as he leant down and picked up the torch, *this is frigging Siberian*. The denser air seemed to make every action feel laboured, as if he'd gone in to slow-motion or a spacewalk. He picked up the torch and shone the beam forward into the abyss. He could see that this door, which was actually quite wide, led onto a broad set of stone stairs heading downwards. Will stepped forward into the wall of chill. With trepidation he descended the icy gloom, feeling as if he were entering a cave where no one had been since the Stone Age, or like Carter entering Tutankhamen's tomb, unopened for three thousand years. It smelt so old; the air within was ancient.

The wide stone staircase curved gently around to the right and then Will was faced an expanse of vaulted white arches going into the darkness beyond the reach of his beam. It was as if he'd entered a church's under-croft. Nothing flickered or shone back at him but he could see the extensive cellar was far from empty. It was deathly cold but there was not a whiff of damp; nor was there any smell of mustiness. Will descended the last few steps and then went carefully forward, into the cavern, flashing his torch around.

As he progressed and his eyes became adjusted he could make out wooden boxes piled high all around on palettes, right up to the ceiling in some places. The crates seemed to go back into every recess and covered space. The beam of his torch flickered across the ceiling. There they were, cases piled between rusted meat hooks. *Jesus Christ*, he thought. *This must be it*. Will had recognised the hundreds of small boxes; they had Château owners' insignia burnt into their sides. They were like the coats of arms of each family. He lifted one nearest him and could feel it was full. *Fuck, fuck, fuck*, Will began saying to himself as he wandered around, giddy, shining the light on pile upon pile of boxes in every conceivable space. He stopped and looked at some of the crests and could clearly read the words Château Laffite, Château Margaux, Beychevelle and Latour. He stopped and jimmied opened a couple. The sound of dry wood tearing creaked ominously loud in the confined cellar, the noise amplified in this cavernous realm. Will read the bottles labels within the two cases, spaced nose to tail; Château Palmer 1932 and Château Ausonne 1929. *Fuck, Dad – what the hell have you led me to?* he silently implored his dead father. And then he began to laugh out loud, accompanied by occasional snorts, nervous and gigglyish. His wavering laugh bubbled out between his lips. Then he composed himself.

Okay, what the hell do I do now? he thought, and then laughed again as if he heard his father's reply. 'Just help yourself, my boy, fill your boots,' the voice said. Will began to wander around the extensive cellar again, now in a daze, like a child locked in a sweet shop; everywhere he looked was piled high with cases of rare wines.

He soon began to pick out boxes of the chateau names he knew - the most famous - and began the laborious job of carrying one case at a time up the stairs with the torch held precariously under his armpit. Each case held only twelve bottles; easy enough to carry. He even grabbed a couple of boxes of champagne; one was a Pommery 1911, one of the greatest vintages for champagne in the twentieth century. And a case of Krug 1938 which were slightly heavier to handle, but well worth it, Will thought. When he had twelve cases piled up at the top of the stairs in two neat stacks near the back door he thought, *fuck it, what the hell*, and went back down to the cellar and cranked open a case of Pol Roger champagne from 1934. He shook vigorously, released the wire cage and then eased the stopper, letting the contained fizz within detonate the cork out with an intense explosion that ricocheted around the cellar like a volley of shotguns firing. Then came the spurting sound of bubbles gushing out the bottle's neck, spilling and fizzing onto the stone floor. Will held the bottle up and slurped the fine and delicate liquid greedily. Even in this frightful atmosphere he could still appreciate a delicate fruit, the light biscuity magic that had been trapped within for over seventy-five years. His mood immediately felt loftier, as if he began to walk on air.

He left the cellar's treasure holding the bottle casually by the neck and took a last big slug at the top of the stairs before putting it, half empty, on top of one of the stacks. He picked up one case which he could carry easily under one arm and left the building closing the back door carefully behind him. He crossed the slippery courtyard and then listened; all seemed quiet on the street behind so he pulled the outer door open slightly, peered out and then quickly squeezed out onto the alleyway, tearing his jacket on a loose hinge, and finally shoved the battered doorway back into place.

He was off, moving up the empty street in the shadows. Immediately he turned into the busy carriageway he fed into the human herd again. He immediately felt relaxed, back in human company and high from the champagne. He ambled with the people in no obvious rush, enjoying the Christmas cheer. There was still a throng around the cars but Will seemed oblivious to them and they in turn ignored him. He casually put the box down, opened the car boot and then placed the case in the back. He picked up a big empty shopping bag, locked the car up and headed back to the house and then repeated the journey three times taking a huge draft of the champagne on each return visit. He'd place a single case in the shopping bag before heading back with it slung over his shoulder. He looked as if he could have been a trader. By the time he'd loaded the fourth case the crowd had thinned considerably. On each occasion he returned to the car there were fewer and fewer people on the streets.

And then, just as he placed a fifth case in his boot, the emptying scene revealed the helmeted man on the scooter whom he'd seen earlier. Will spied him facing the car, ten metres away by the rampart wall astride his moped. Will ignored him, trying to look unconcerned, and moved off back through the thinning crowd towards the house for another case. When Will peeled off onto the side road he stopped and listened. *Shit*, he said to himself. He could hear a high-pitched revving behind him. He didn't turn into the alley which led to the back of the house; instead he carried on down towards the river which he could see glistening like a great mercurial snake on the move. The vast Gironde slithered in front of him. He began to walk faster now, his head pulsating and his heart thumping, sensing the scooter stalk him, closing in. At the bottom of the hill, just ahead, he could see the road came to a dead end and opened out onto a pedestrianised cobbled area alongside the waterfront. He began to jog towards it, sensing an escape route. As soon as he reached the hard-standing Will heard the moped accelerate so he in turn picked up speed, bounding forward. The world seemed to slow again, giving Will time to clearly see what was before him and consider the threat behind. As soon as he reached a bollarded access point to the path Will stopped and turned to face his assailant who had simultaneously braked on the last bit of high ground. The biker ground to a halt immediately Will did and began to rev his tinny little engine. He was ten metres away at most. Will stood his ground and faced the rider, his face partly obscured within the shadow of his helmet. Will breathed deeply through his nostrils, inflating himself to rise up as high and proud as he could and stared unflinchingly at the man opposite. Only a few street lights softly illuminated the scene, and the massive river lapped its rhythm onto the jetty below. Will stood right behind one of the bollards, which were knee-high thick black metal posts; with one arm he reached behind himself into his rucksack, like an archer going for an arrow, and slowly removed the crowbar. The moment the rider saw a flash of steel - Will going for a weapon - he revved his scooter to maximum, released the brake and then shot forward, gunning straight towards Will. Will didn't waiver; he simply took one small step back and, just as the howling machine was about to career into him, he took an even bigger one backwards. The scooter driver smashed straight into the unseen bollard which was only now revealed to be in front of Will. It was too late. There was an almighty crunch as the motorcycle stopped dead. Fragments of wing mirrors and shards of fibreglass flew past around him. Will saw the man fly up into the air, right in front of his face; one gloved hand actually snatched at him, mid-air, as the body flew past and then thumped to the ground. Will could hear bones, probably a collarbone, crunch and an aching groan emanated from the winded biker as his helmet thrashed onto the cobbles. And then silence, apart from the scooter's back wheel spinning freely. Will couldn't believe it. He had done nothing; all the debris had just flown around him as if he were in a vortex zone of safety. He came back to reality hearing the night rider begin to moan behind him and as Will turned, he could see the man begin to rise up on one elbow. Under light from the street lamp Will could see his assailant looked enraged. His weather-beaten eyes bulged in fury at what had just happened, and his open face seemed as if it were desperately trying to burst out of his helmet; he simply hadn't seen the black metal bollard which Will had stepped behind. Momentarily Will didn't know what to do so he just stared as the man growled and tried to get up. Then anger surged through Will and misted his reason. He casually walked forward and kicked his attacker as hard as he could in the face. The man's head exploded backwards on to the pavement. Will felt a nose crunching on his toes through his walking boots and in an instant he was standing over an unconscious body. Will peered down and could see two unblinking eyes staring blindly through him towards the stars. As they began to glaze Will could make out two tiny moons reflected in each of the fast misting pupils. He furtively looked around and all was still; not a soul in sight. The French provincial market town had reverted to hibernation mode again. So he casually picked up his crowbar that was lying by the wrecked bike, put it back in his rucksack like the archer casually returning an un-required arrow into its quiver, and jogged quietly up the road, back to the house to finish what he'd come for, thinking to all intents and purposes, to the law, that the goon just had an unfortunate accident.

CHAPTER 21
SHOWTIME

'Allo, allo, Louis? Answer your bloody phone, call me back straight away, it's just gone 6:30,' the old Corsican hissed into his mobile for the third time in fifteen minutes as the hired executive Mercedes he was driving sped dangerously fast through the darkened Bordelaise vineyards. His boss sat serenely in the passenger seat beside him, seemingly oblivious to any urgency. Reynard had never seen Henri Lafarge quite as relaxed as he had been since they had boarded his private jet in Marseille three hours previously. They had had delays both with the fuelling of the plane in Marseille and then when the hire car he'd ordered wasn't at Bordeaux airport after they'd touched down two hours ago. But Lafarge, uncharacteristically, had behaved with complete ease and had remained completely tranquil throughout; whereas normally he would be swearing and cursing and threatening to tear throats out.

They had had spoken to Louis the carpenter once in Marseille to engage him and twice since they had touched down in Bordeaux's Merignac airport. Over an hour ago he'd reported that he had found Will's Audi behind the church, and then just as they'd set off on the forty-five minute drive to Bourg he had called again to say that he'd located Will and was pursuing him.

'Well, at least we know where the cowboy's car is, sir. I hope the little *connard* is still there.'

'Eh?' Henri Lafarge replied dreamily. 'Ah oui, oui, no problem,' he mumbled.

Reynard cast an anxious glance across to see if his boss was okay and saw quite clearly, for the first time, a childlike, innocent demeanour glowing about this hard, cold-blooded individual he had spent the past thirty-five years working for. Reynard swerved in surprise; he thought Henri even looked retarded, glazed over. Drugged. As if he wasn't really there.

Reynard completely missed the magic of this moment, for his employer was communing with his dead father. He was linking up with him; fulfilling his promise. This was old family business. This was his father's legacy to him; the Lafarge dynasty was being reborn. It was becoming a reality, Henri could feel it in his bones. He was certain the Lafarge name would be spoken of with reverence for ever in France. This was his destiny; he had been dreaming and waiting for this moment all his life and the only thing he could see before him was a golden, sunlit future of ease and refinement. He gazed out on the hoary, ethereal scenery from his car window with a fabulous firework display finale cascading into a crescendo across the far horizon. *His* gold lay at the end of *his* rainbow.

Reynard sped on through the moonlit night across the bare silent hectares of vines, occasionally glimpsing the silver-coloured Gironde weaving its imperceptibly powerful route to its mouth. It was all quiet, hardly a car on the road, and not a wisp of wind or cloud in the clear, brilliant sky.

They entered the ancient castellated town with the departing crowd jostling around their oversized car as they nudged their way forward. At one moment Reynard opened the window and asked for directions to the church, letting the happy atmosphere momentarily pour into their hermetically sealed vehicle.

'It's fiesta time, my friend,' Lafarge giggled, in a juvenile voice Reynard had never heard before, making the lieutenant's spine tingle.

They wove around and pulled into the now completely de-populated car-park which was still half full of vehicles. Reynard swung around, backed up and parked, professionally facing the exit; he tried to phone Louis one last time, with no luck.

'That's the cowboy's car there, sir, the Audi,' Reynard informed his boss, pointing at Will's vehicle ten metres away.

'Well, go and look, man, see what's in it,' Lafarge ordered snappily, somewhat more alertly now that they had arrived at the business end of their trip.

Without saying a word Reynard obeyed and stepped out into the chilled night air. He shivered; he was in clothes fit only for the Mediterranean. As he strolled across to Will's car he didn't notice the young Englishman sitting on the rampart wall nearby, high above the Gironde river.

Will had done two more journeys to and from the old house and, having finished the champagne, he kept himself boosted up by opening a bottle of 1934 Otard cognac, taking measured sips on each visit back to his rapidly reducing pile of cases. Although the fiery spirit was surging through his system and opening his veins, he had decided to rest for a moment. He'd only just sat down on a cold low wall when the blacked-out Mercedes pulled up in front of him. The moment before Will had stared down at the massive body of water far below and felt he had a close affinity with this river, gliding its gently eternal way up towards Bec d'Ambes, beyond to Blaye and on to the Atlantic; it was a magical setting. Will could still appreciate that.

'Oi! Qu'est-ce que tu fais? What are you doing?' Will suddenly found himself barking out loud to the dark-haired man peering into the back of his car across the way. His voice echoed around the empty church car-park, making Reynard freeze and rise up from his stoop slowly. He never did anything fast. Reynard wasn't sure where the voice had come from, so for a moment he stood very still, craning around. Will revealed himself. He had taken off his rucksack when he sat down and now that he saw Reynard he took his crowbar out and stood up, holding it out of view at his side. Neither man said another word.

There was no going back for Will; that was over the edge. Reynard weighed his odds instinctively. They were in his favour. As a result he made the first move, coming forward stealthily. About five metres apart the two men's features became evident to each other. Reynard now recognised Will clearly. In turn all Will could see was a tall, ominous creature, with black greased-back hair and the look of the grim reaper about him, crouch down. All the while his pitted black eyes were pinned on Will. The crouching Reynard slid a flashing weapon from his left ankle. All Corsican criminals carry small strong six-inch traditional hunting knives and Reynard never felt safe without his tucked in firmly under his left sock, supporting his ankle. He felt impotent without it. Will, unwaveringly, stood his ground; the ancient brandy set his eyes ablaze. He placed his stronger right foot back on the low wall ready to assist propelling him forward as fast as he could when his moment came. As Reynard rose up to full height again Will arched slightly, angling to spring. Reynard came forward confidently now, as he had done so many times in his life, arms outstretched slightly, leaning forward. His weapon glistened in the moonlight and then, four metres away, he rushed. As suddenly as Reynard made his lunge Will responded immediately and rather than come forward to meet his attacker head-on, Will twisted his posed foot slightly to the side, catching it on the edge of a stone slab and darted quickly to his right, away from Reynard's knife hand. At the same time he swung around, violently releasing a charge upwards from the hook end of the crowbar, in an upper- cut motion that ripped clean in to Reynard's chin from below, literally hooking the man like a fish; the barbed metal end tore through Reynard's palate, and forked out through his open mouth. On impact Will had to release the metal rod and he fell to the ground. He spun quickly around to see Reynard standing facing him with his back to the river, in the same spot where Will had stood moments before. The crowbar hung down unaided. It had torn his tongue out and was now hanging loose like a meat hook. Blood arrived as rapidly as the pain; a shockwave made Reynard release his grip and his beloved weapon dropped onto the cobbles with a solitary clang. He didn't fall or moan or make any noise whatsoever but stood stone still. Will could see Reynard's pitiful eyes momentarily look down to assess the pronged crowbar wedged out of his mouth, blood pouring down the metal rod like a drain in flood. Reynard put a hand feebly on the long arm of the cold steel, weighing up when he would twist it out, but the pain must have been too much.

Will, from being crouched like a sprinter, began to rise up in a fluid feline motion and now stood poised before Reynard. Will made the next move. It was his turn. He took a purposefully slow step, leaning back as he came forward and then, with all his might, sprung forward, both arms outstretched at Reynard. He shoved the numbed Corsican bandit with all his might, both hands onto his shoulders. Reynard just buckled backwards. He tripped on Will's rucksack onto the low wall behind and collapsed into a sitting position but the reverse momentum of Will's forceful shove continued and Reynard simply recoiled, his feet went up and his body went over the edge, and was gone.

Not a sound came out him, not a gurgle, not a moan, not a scream; nothing. Will heard a splat as Reynard's body hit the muddy riverbank far below five seconds later. He was vaguely aware of the corpse being welcomed by the mud. He imagined the body slipping easily into the slime-like-quicksand and the monster of a river absorb him.

Will now collapsed himself and half sat, half crouched over the low battlement wall, heaving into the darkness below, steam blasting far out of his mouth; he couldn't see or hear a thing below. It was black and it was silent. The whole town, in fact, was silent - Bourg was sound asleep.

Henri Lafarge was in poll position to view the brief encounter. He'd craned his neck around anxiously in his seat and witnessed the epic moment of his top lieutenant's final demise. It had happened so fast under lamp light that Lafarge wasn't really sure what had gone on but he had seen the final collapse, the topple and flip into oblivion. It was like a live boxing match before television and slow-motion were invented, where the knock-out punch comes out of the blue so suddenly and fast that hardly anyone in the audience can accurately recall exactly what happened. All that the crowd would remember accurately was the loser collapsing onto the canvas. Henri had blinked and it was all over.

Lafarge turned and sank back into his seat, stunned. Will gasped for air staring down at the unchanged Gironde. Wave upon wave of anxiety gushed over the two men; they were now fully aware of the grim reality of their inheritances. Both men united in the lonely implications of their dead fathers' differing yet converging legacies. These inheritances were no walks in the park. Both men were on their own.

Lafarge was not used to being alone in any sort of situation, let alone one like this. He had done his fair share of dealing with the rough end of his business when he was younger but had not got his hands dirty for many years. Bark and issue violent orders, yes, and indeed witness pain and even murder being administered - but he hadn't sunk his knife into anyone for decades and didn't even carry one anymore; he used Reynard and the others for that. Within their world guns were for weak people; it was hands that were real men's weapons.

As Henri Lafarge sat glumly absorbing his situation Will hurried past the Mercedes and glanced briefly at him but he couldn't actually see through the tinting to the interior so the two men unknowingly caught each other's eye, Will blind to Lafarge through the mirrored glass but the seventy-year-old Frenchman was able to see Will clearly. *He's fresh faced, young, scared and... easily conquered*, he thought. Lafarge immediately knew he could squeeze the life out of this upstart as easily as squishing a prawn.

Will was determined to get the last four cases before leaving, which would mean twelve cases of twelve bottles: *a good round number*. He didn't know what they were worth but now that he was here, as his father said, he was going to fill his boots. *Crazy not to*, he rationalised as he quietly and, in the shadows, headed back across the car-park and up to the house.

Lafarge's vulnerability had evaporated the moment he saw Will. He quietly stepped out of the car into the bracing night and stealthily began to follow the young Englishman from a safe distance. He saw Will turn right a hundred and fifty metres ahead just before the square, so he sped up and, upon reaching the junction, just glanced a leg turn left into a narrow lane opposite. When Lafarge in turn reached that junction he stopped and peered down and all was empty; his quarry had disappeared. Lafarge prowled even more slowly now and suddenly felt young again, stalking his prey as he had done with his family's enemies in the back streets of Marseille as a youth. He went to the end and then stood back in a dark doorway and waited, listening. Soon he heard a creak to his left in the direction from where he'd come and he could see Will wriggle out awkwardly on the other side of the lane and head back up, carrying another case. When he had turned towards the square Lafarge emerged from his shadow and approached the rear of the property; he could see where Will had emerged from. He pushed the door ajar and squeezed around the hinges and was into the abandoned courtyard. He pushed it closed behind him and, like a predatory carnivore, found a far-wall recess, a corner, to crouch in and assess the situation. It was always a case of slow but steady, one step at a time as you close in for a kill. He calmed himself and took stock. He could just make out a further door pulled to which accessed the actual building but all was quiet. It was only a matter of minutes, from behind the wall, that he could faintly hear footsteps on the street behind. The exterior door creaked again and he could just make out a solitary figure slip in and switch on a torch. Will was back.

Lafarge saw Will enter the building. He followed silently. He could see Will lean down to pick up one of the last cases so Henri, sensing his moment, rushed at Will from behind. Will felt a shocking whack to the back of his neck and, as he crumpled onto the floor, his torch fell from under his arm and rolled across the slabs, creating a flickering effect that synchronised with the flashing white lights sparkling in his head. As he'd collapsed Will had just managed to turn so he was lying on his side, fully conscious but badly dazed. Lafarge's fist had hit the side of his head, grazing him. Now he could make out a stocky older man looking down at him. Will could see an impassive blank look of complete detachment in front of him and, in Lafarge's moment of hesitation, Will managed to reach out his left hand and snatch the empty bottle of champagne he had finished and put by the wall earlier. And then, as Will saw Lafarge react and step forward, raising one foot high, ready to come down and stamp him, Will struck the empty bottle around with all the force he could muster, hitting into Lafarge's supporting lower shin just above the ankle and the contact not only unbalanced him but toppled him right over. Henri's Gucci loafers had made him slip, flipping him backwards into the darkness where he collapsed onto the stone floor awkwardly. By the thudding sound Will could tell he had hit the ground hard on his backside. Lafarge let out a single groan. He was winded. Will managed to galvanise himself; getting up on all fours and releasing the unbroken bottle, he grabbed the torch and then forced himself upright as Lafarge was doing the same. Lafarge was blocking the exit so Will instinctively stumbled down the stairs into the ancient wine cellar. Lafarge got to his feet, growled, and came down after him. The moment they reached the bottom Will staggered forward but he had only got five metres into the cavernous expanse when he felt a hand grabbing his collar, stopping him and then yanking him back. As he was being pulled backwards by his coat Will recoiled right around with the lit torch making a solid impact with the tough old man's head. Lafarge did nothing; the heavy torch cracked into his head with a decent impact but he didn't budge or release his now twisted grip. He was stunned but hardly fazed and Will could see into his eyes as the torch fell to the ground again, the beam stretching across the Bousquet family's old abattoir slate flooring to halt at a neat stack of wine cases behind. Will could see these small eyes slightly too near each other peering at him coldly above the punch-flattened nose. Lafarge wasn't breathing through pursed lips; he was virtually hissing. *He looks as if he isn't even here at all*, Will thought: *he's totally fucking vacant.* As time suspends in these intense situations the mind has time to absorb the strangest of details. The next thing Will was aware of was Lafarge's stubby and ringed powerful right hand around his throat; he was being throttled. As he gurgled, being strangled like a hapless chicken, and as oxygen was being denied him, Will went into a dream state. The cellar was now a brightly illuminated church crypt. He knew, at that moment, this was going to be his morgue, his final resting place. He was perfectly at peace as the life force in him ebbed away. Memories flashed before him; he could see Sophie and Nelson walking together in the green fields of home, his mother and father waving goodbye to him as if he were going back to school, and even an image of the jolly bar at the Black Horse flashed before him as he felt life rapidly die like the final fast-rushing grains of sand disappearing in an egg timer's cycle. And then release.

Will buckled. He crumpled down onto the floor, settling into a kneeling position, as if praying, while life began to gasp back into him. He gawped and spluttered feebly looking up at Lafarge, still completely stunned, who was standing over him like a priest about to administer Holy Communion but Will could see his head had dropped forward and now warm blood, infused with brandy, dripped freely down over Will's head, waking him up, like a perverse christening. Will could see Lafarge then raise his lolling head back up after the shock, turn around like a drunk and rush blindly towards his assailant behind. Will had regained enough consciousness to see, in the shaft of light, Louise, his sister, standing holding a broken bottle by the neck with a straight outstretched arm and Lafarge running straight into it. The bottle rammed into his neck and must have sliced clean through some main arterial veins as he stopped and then turned back towards Will clutching his throat with blood pulsing out between his fingers. He looked ghastly and haunted as he stood between the young English couple in the near total darkness of the place he had been searching for all his life. He collapsed onto his knees, face-to-face with Will, looking in crazed amazement at the cases surrounding him, as his face began to contort and then sink in every conceivable place. The two men looked into each other's eyes one final time in knowing incredulity at the result of their encounter with destiny, and then his head drooped, fatally, and he was gone. He didn't fall over but remained dead in that kneeling position. Lafarge's head finally froze to the sound of the bottle that killed him crashing to the ground behind, released from Louise's hand. Will rose to see her standing, shaking in disbelief. Will stood up as quickly as he could manage and went to his sister and saviour and took her in his arms, and then turning, without saying a word, led her slowly towards the stairs, away from this dreadful scene.

'Christ, Lou, how the hell did you get here?' he whispered gently, as they walked shakily up the stairs. 'I don't believe it.'

'I flew down from Southampton this afternoon. I had a chat with Sophie; I was worried. I just knew you needed me,' Louise said calmly and quietly.

'My God, it's incredible, I thought I'd died,' Will exclaimed in utter disbelief, still holding his sister close, an arm linked in hers for support. They passed the last three cases on the corridor floor.

'I followed you from the car.'

'Hold on a mo, Lou, I'm going to grab one last case.'

'No, you are not!' his sister snapped.

'But it's probably worth fifty grand or more.'

'Go on then, I'll carry another.'

'We'll leave one here.'

Within minutes they were in the car driving slowly out of town, clinking over the cobbles, Will at the wheel and Louise sitting impassively in the passenger seat. Being in an automatic car they were free to hold hands, which they did in silence, staring forward. Once out of the fortress town and onto main roads Will began to speed up and cruise rapidly through the moonlit vineyards.

Just before they reached the ticket barrier to access the motorway Will pulled over beside a shimmering silver phone box.

'I'll only be a moment, sis,' he mumbled. He limped across, picked up the receiver and dialled. 'Allo, police...'

THE END.

'When weapons flash, feel no pious sentiments,
Though you confront your fathers, you must feel.
No, slash their venerable faces with steel.'

                                    Montaigne.

Acknowledgments

Practically, I would like to thank Cornerstones and Sarah Quigley in particular for the thorough editing assistance on the manuscript, Victoria Stroud for illustrating my vision for the cover and James and the team at Spiffing Covers for, again, interpreting that image into another terrific book-cover for me.

Inspirationally I cannot deny the stimulus and joy I have received from reading Robert MacFarlane. His ability to transform the wonder of nature into prose is simply spellbinding. The novels I read, amongst others, during the writing process were Treasure Island by Robert Louis Stevenson, Caravan to Vaccares by Alistair MacLean, Rogue Male by Geoffrey Household, The Singing Sands by Josephine Tey, Erskine Childers's The Riddle of the Sands and Quentin Rees's book about the bravely ambitious Cockleshell Heroes.

Thanks to Bonney at Wildmind Creative for her marketing assistance and Robert Franks and Leon for creating and patiently maintaining my web presence.

To finally acknowledge a faithful companion, Mr B, my Patterdale terrier, who has never left my side once during the long walks, the note-taking, the writing process and subsequent journey to publication… and beyond.

Lightning Source UK Ltd.
Milton Keynes UK
UKHW041036030320
359622UK00017B/308